RAW DESIRE

Books by Kate Pearce

The House of Pleasure Series

SIMPLY SEXUAL

SIMPLY SINFUL

SIMPLY SHAMELESS

SIMPLY WICKED

SIMPLY INSATIABLE

SIMPLY FORBIDDEN

Single Titles

RAW DESIRE

Anthologies

SOME LIKE IT ROUGH

LORDS OF PASSION

Published by Kensington Publishing Corporation

RAW DESIRE

KATE PEARCE

APHRODISIA

KENSINGTON PUBLISHING CORP.

www.kensingtonbooks.com

APHRODISIA BOOKS are published by

Kensington Publishing Corp.
119 West 40th Street
New York, NY 10018

All Kensington titles, imprints, and distributed lines are available at special quantity discounts for bulk purchases for sales promotion, premiums, fund-raising, and educational, or institutional use.

Special book excerpts or customized printings can also be created to fit specific needs. For details, write or phone the office of the Kensington Special Sales Manager: Kensington Publishing Corp., 119 West 40th Street, New York, NY 10018. Attn. Special Sales Department.. Phone: 1-800-221-2647.

Aphrodisia and the A logo Reg. U.S. Pat & TM Off.

ISBN-13: 978-0-7582-4140-5
ISBN-10: 0-7582-4140-2

First Kensington Trade Paperback Printing: September 2011

10 9 8 7 6 5 4 3 2 1

Printed in the United States of America

This book needed a lot of help. Special mention goes to Robin Rotham, Jennifer Leeland, Loribelle Hunt, and Susan Pierce for contributing their unique points of view. Thanks also go to the Romance Divas Forum for various answers about the worst jobs in small diners, and how to deal with someone wielding a knife. You really can learn anything on there. ☺

1

"I'm going to kill him!"

Ally Kendal ripped the slim plastic bag from under her windshield wiper and stuffed it into her pocket. She got into her battered truck, backed out of her driveway with a screech of tires, and drove the five minutes into the center of Spring Falls. She was barely aware of anything except the red mist before her eyes and the urge to wrap her fingers around Rob Ward's neck and finish him off once and for all.

There was only one parking space left outside the small historic building that doubled as the courthouse and the sheriff's department. She slammed out of the truck, into the reception area, and straight through the metal detector, which thankfully didn't go off.

"Hey, miss, hold up."

Too intent on her prey, Ally ignored the uniformed officer and headed down the narrow hallway to the door marked SHERIFF'S OFFICE.

She entered without knocking, saw the source of her troubles sitting at his desk, and marched right on up to him. He flicked a glance at her.

"Hey, Rich, can I call you back? Something's come up."

He put the phone down with a decisive click and looked beyond her to the officer who had just caught up to her at the door.

"I've got this, Jeff. You can go back out front."

His pale blue eyes contained no hint of his feelings as he turned to study her from head to toe.

"What can I do for you, Ms. Kendal?"

His polite, lazy drawl made her clench her jaw so hard her teeth hurt. She yanked the plastic bag out of her pocket and held it out.

"You can stop giving me frickin' tickets!"

His frown was so genuine that if she hadn't known him better, she might have doubted herself.

"I haven't given you a ticket since the day you arrived back in town."

"Yeah, when I had to park on the street for a pathetic *half hour* while I cleared a space on the driveway." She waved the bag. "So what's this? A mirage?"

He held out his hand, and she tossed the package onto his desk and waited, her foot tapping as he unfolded the single sheet of paper.

"Did you actually read this? It isn't from the Spring Falls Sheriff's Department."

Ally leaned across and snatched the paper from his unresisting fingers. His smile was so condescending she wanted to scream.

"It's from your local homeowners association. They want you to water your lawn every night and put your trash cans away after the garbage collection."

She bent her head to read the note, allowing her long dark hair to shield her blush. After reluctantly paying the first ticket, she'd chucked the rest of the letters unopened in the garbage without reading them. *Shit, now what was she going to do?*

"Can these people actually enforce this?"

He regarded her steadily, then leaned back and put his hands behind his head. Damn, he looked good. He was thirty: Why couldn't he have developed a paunch and thinning hair like most guys his age while she'd been gone? It was typical of him to try and undermine her by still looking hot.

"It depends. Was your mom's place part of a homeowners association?"

She put her hands on her hips. "How would I know?"

"If you're getting mail from them, I'd assume it was. You'll need to check."

"But I don't intend to live in the house, just clear it out, sell, and leave."

Rob raised his eyebrows. "You're gonna leave again? Who'd have thought it?"

Ally sighed. "Don't try and be sarcastic, Rob. What did you expect me to do? Settle down?"

"Why not? Even though my parents have retired to Florida, Spring Falls is a great place to live. That's why I'm still here."

God, he was so arrogant. "Why is that? I thought you were planning to go away to college with me and never come back."

He shrugged. "Things changed after you dumped me. I didn't want you to think you'd run me out of my own hometown as well. After college, I decided I'd rather come back and live in the place I loved."

"After *I* left, I never thought about you at all."

His blue gaze sharpened. "Yeah, I should imagine guilt does that to a person. Much easier to pretend you never slept with my best friend and dumped me right before our engagement party."

Ally took a deep, calming breath and wished she'd kept her mouth shut. "All I want to know is if this stupid homeowners association can actually bring charges against me for not watering my lawn. Can you at least do your civic duty and tell me that?"

"What does *she* want?"

Rob didn't relax his grip on Ally's arm. "Miss Kendal says she has attempted to contact me here on more than one occasion. Why haven't I seen a message or a report?"

Jenny folded her hands in her lap. "I didn't want to bother you with such minor issues, Boss. We all know how busy you are."

Ally glared at the older woman. Yeah, she bet that was it. It had nothing to do with the fact that Jenny had always disliked Ruth, Ally's mom, and was obviously itching to get back at Ruth's equally faithless daughter.

Rob didn't look pleased, and that made Ally want to smile. He'd always been a big believer in telling the truth and doing the right thing, and he hated being in the wrong.

"I like to see every report and every message that comes through here, Jenny. Please remember that in the future."

Jenny pursed her thin lips. "I make sure Deputy Smith gets all that information. I thought he would've passed it on to you, but maybe he didn't think it was important either?"

"He's been out of town for the last three weeks, so nothing's been getting through him. That's why it's important that you copy me."

Ally frowned. Smith was a common name, but somehow from the way Jenny was smirking at her, she guessed it wasn't just any old Deputy Smith being talked about. Rob put a hand in the small of her back and maneuvered her out into the hallway. She turned to face him, aware of his height and breadth, and inhaled a hint of the citrus aftershave he'd always worn.

"Don't tell me—Deputy Smith is Jackson. Right?"

"Yeah."

"*Right.*"

He raised his eyebrows. "It's a small town, Ally. Everyone comes back eventually."

"And I bet you were a lot more pleased to see Jackson than you were me."

She started to walk away from him, but he followed her, pushing open the door to allow them both out into the parking lot.

"Yeah, I was pleased to see him—eventually. So what?"

"So how come you welcome him back with open arms and can't wait for me to leave? There were two of us in that bed, you know."

A muscle flicked in his cheek as he stared at her, his arms crossed over his chest.

"I didn't exactly welcome him back. We worked it out eventually. Jackson and I have been friends for years."

Ally swallowed hard. "And we weren't? God, Rob, you have such double standards."

"And you don't? Hell, you're the one who fucked him, not me."

Ally bit down hard on her lip. There was so much she yearned to say to him, but was there any point? She'd been judged and condemned years ago, and he had a right to be angry. She glanced around at all the open doors. This definitely wasn't the place to have a heart-to-heart. She'd have to wait until they were in a far more neutral place to broach that idea. There was no way she was giving him the satisfaction of using his power over her as sheriff. She pulled her keys out of her pocket and headed for her ancient Toyota truck.

"Ally, I'm sorry that I didn't get your messages. You're right. We do need to talk."

His voice stopped her. She stared at his reflection in the dirty window of her truck and tried to imagine he was really only eight inches tall. He still looked too big and intimidating. This time she wasn't going to turn around and make him think she wanted to listen to him.

"Okay." She opened the door and stepped up into the cab. "You take my complaints seriously and I'll talk to you."

She started the engine and backed carefully out of the parking space. Rob tapped on her window, and she reluctantly opened it.

"Don't park there again, honey. That's Jackson's spot."

"Don't call me honey." She glared at him as she gunned the engine. "What are you going to do, give me another ticket?"

"Sure I will. That's my job, and I'm not letting you get any ideas about taking up any of Jackson's space again."

This time his smile didn't reach his husky-dog-blue eyes, and it transformed his face into a man she hardly recognized. She swallowed hard.

"Jackson's a big boy. I'm sure he can take care of himself."

Rob's expression didn't change. "He's not the same, Ally. The army nearly destroyed him."

"Jackson enlisted?"

He shrugged. "Yeah, right after you left. He was honorably discharged about three years ago. After he got his shit together, I was able to offer him a job as a deputy."

Ally fought an impulse to cry and bit the inside of her cheek instead.

"I suppose you blame me for that as well, don't you?"

Rob sighed. "You asked. I'm just telling you what happened."

"Well, thanks, I'll see you around."

She pressed her foot on the gas and roared out of the parking lot. A stupid thing to do in front of the sheriff, but she had to get away. As she drove, she wondered about Jackson. Had he left because of her? He'd known where she was headed, but he hadn't bothered to keep in touch. Was that why? Had he been too busy getting shot at?

Tears stung at her eyes as the familiar tree-lined streets unrolled around her until she found herself parked in her mother's driveway. She stared at the single-story ranch house and groaned. It needed painting both inside and out, the floors required refinishing, and the plumbing was a disaster. Her plans to run in, sell the house, and get out had taken a big hit. In the current market, there was no way the house would ever sell.

Ally got out of the truck and headed for the peeling front door. An all-too-familiar burning sensation gripped her stomach, and she struggled to force it down. There was no way she'd allow her mother's unwelcome legacy to defeat her. And, if she was honest, she hadn't come back for the house or for her mom. She'd come back to face the people she'd hurt, which was way more frightening than she could ever have imagined.

Rob Ward watched Ally's dented green truck screech out of the parking lot and head out of town. In her pink T-shirt and cutoff jeans, she'd looked way too thin and pale for his liking. His memories of her were warmer, her skin tanned all over from the California sun, her cheeks sunburned and her dark hair held back in a long braid.

He smiled slowly as he headed back into his office. Whether they realized it or not, the homeowners association had done him a favor. Rob had wanted Ally's attention and now he'd gotten it. Her expression when she realized she'd come after him and he hadn't been hounding her after all had been priceless. Rob's grin faded as he shut the door to his office and sat down.

Why the hell had she contacted him? He'd half hoped she would and yet had half dreaded it. Okay, so she'd looked tired, but he still wanted her. Wanted those long legs wrapped around his hips while he fucked her stupid. His cock stirred at the image, and he smoothed his palm over his impatient shaft.

He still had no idea why she'd come back to sell her deceased mother's house. It wasn't as if they'd ever been close. He frowned as he remembered the scandal of her departure, Susan Evans's death that had followed, and Ally's mother's defiant disregard for everyone in the town. Was there something at her mother's house Ally wanted? Surely she didn't need the money. From what he read in the tabloids, she earned more in a year modeling than he would probably make in a lifetime.

And why the hell was she driving that ancient truck? Something wasn't right. He glanced down at his brown uniform pants, which were now tented. He thought she'd ripped his heart out when she'd run out on him, but time had shown him that wasn't true. He'd moved on, hadn't he? Fucked other women, eventually made things right with Jackson, created a new life and career for himself . . .

So why did he care whether Ally was back or not? Because she was unfinished business and she knew how he felt about that. She'd probably say it was because he'd never gotten over being dumped, and maybe she had a point.

But it was a lot more complicated than that. He'd missed her, and not just for the sex. She was right. She'd been a part of him for too long for it just to be about that.

He turned on his computer. Yeah, it was definitely time to seek closure with Ally. He'd been semihard ever since he heard she was back, and that wasn't good for a man. Sure, there were plenty of women who'd be glad to help him out with his problem, but now his dreams were all of Ally, of her on her knees begging his forgiveness before he gave in and fucked her.

And there was Jackson to consider. How the hell would he feel about Ally's return? Her scathing comment about his forgiving Jackson and not her stung. Why was it so much more difficult to forgive Ally than his oldest friend? Jackson had betrayed him as well.

Rob pretended to check his e-mail, but he wasn't really in the mood. It had taken him a long time to even consider trusting Jackson again. Would he be able to start afresh with Ally? The idea was tantalizing and too damned attractive to ignore. Whatever happened, the next few weeks were sure going to be interesting.

2

Rob pressed the yellowing plastic bell on Ally's battered front door and waited. As a kid, he'd simply jumped over the rickety fence, run through the backyard and into the kitchen—until he'd figured out that Ally didn't like him being anywhere near her mom. It wasn't until they were teenagers that he realized Ruth Kendal was an addict who had no compunction about stealing and lying to get her drugs of choice. But by then, he'd been glad to stay outside.

There was no sound inside the house, so he knocked instead. Eventually, the door opened to reveal Ally, with a paintbrush in her hand and an aggrieved expression.

"What?"

"You have paint on your cheek." Before she could reply, he stepped inside and shut the door behind him. "It's in your hair too."

"Thanks."

She balanced the paintbrush carefully on the windowsill and crossed her arms over her chest.

"What do you want?"

He ignored her, his attention having drifted to the stacks of boxes that filled the hallway, dining room, and as far as he could see. Last evening, on a whim, he'd pulled the old files for the Susan Evans case. Unconfirmed reports had placed Susan, the dead girl, in this house on the night of her death.

After the judge decided there wasn't enough evidence to obtain a search warrant, Ruth Kendal had refused to let anyone on her property even for an unofficial search. A quick verdict of suicide on the teenager had shut the case right down. The investigator in him yearned to take a closer look at the boxes. He'd always wondered whether his gut instinct about that night had been right, and now he was finally in a position to find out.

"What's with all the boxes?"

Ally shrugged and the spaghetti strap of her worn black top fell down. Rob's fingers twitched as he resisted the urge to fix it for her.

"All my mom's work."

"Why?"

"How should I know? You saw her more than I did in the last ten years."

"Yeah, but . . ."

Rob turned around, noticing the dirt and the smell of neglect, the torn drapes and netting, the filthy carpet.

"I didn't realize she'd let things get this bad."

"Neither did I."

Ally picked up the paintbrush and went down the hallway toward the kitchen. Rob followed her, inhaling the scent of fresh paint. To his relief, the kitchen looked a lot better than the other rooms. He nodded at the gleaming sink and scrubbed linoleum.

"Did you do this?"

"Yeah, after the bathroom it was the first room I cleaned." She shuddered. "It's not great, but at least it's sanitary." She swung around to look at him and leaned back against the sink. "So, what do you want?"

She wore frayed denim shorts that showed off the endless length of her legs, and her feet were bare. Drips of white paint splattered her from head to toe.

"I came to update you on your nuisance reports."

"Really?" She stared pointedly at his khaki shorts and black T-shirt. "You don't exactly look official."

"I'm just on my way in to work. I thought I'd drop by and give you the news firsthand." He shifted his gaze to the door. "If I'm bothering you, I can come back later."

"And disturb me all over again? Did you find out who was responsible?"

"No, but we're going to increase our patrols in this area, and I've asked the local Neighborhood Watch organization to put you on their at-risk list."

She clasped her hands to her chest. "Oh, wow, I feel so much safer now. You know that most of the people who live here hate me, right? Do you really think they're going to waste their precious time worrying about graffiti on my walls or broken glass?"

"If I ask them to, yeah."

"Oh, right, because if the town's star quarterback, homecoming king, sheriff, and jilted wonder guy forgives me, everyone else will too? Get real."

Anger churned in his gut, but he tamped it down and took two steps closer to her.

"I haven't forgiven you."

"Exactly, and they'll understand that. In fact, they probably think that scaring me away is good for the town and good for you."

Determined not to let her rile him, Rob took a deep breath. "Now it's your turn."

"To what?"

"To talk to me."

"You haven't caught anyone yet."

He closed the gap between them and stared down into her defiant face. "That's not what our agreement was."

She smiled. "Are you sure? Did you write it down?"

He cupped her chin. "No, did you?"

Her breathing was as fast as his, and the tips of her breasts grazed the front of his T-shirt. He inhaled her familiar butterscotch scent and let it flow through him. It reminded him of the past. She licked her lips, and he was instantly hard.

"Rob, I really do want to sit down with you and clear the air."

"Clear the air? Sure. Then let's fuck."

Her eyes widened but she didn't look away. "I'm covered in paint, you hate me, and yet you still want to fuck me."

"Yeah, I'm a man. That about sums it up."

He bent his head and took her mouth in a hard, unforgiving kiss, then winced as she bit his lip and pulled away.

"I didn't say you could kiss me."

"I didn't ask."

She retreated to the sink, her nipples now showing through the thin fabric of her top. He waited while she looked him over; doing nothing to hide his erection, he let her see it and think about it thrusting between her legs.

"I don't hate you, Ally. But I don't understand why you did what you did. You fucked up four lives. Was it really worth it?"

She rinsed out her mug in the sink. "I had to leave. I was too young and too stupid to know how to do it any other way."

"Hell, you could've just talked to me, told me how you felt."

"And would you've listened? You weren't real good at that back when we dated."

"At least you could've tried."

She moved restlessly to the newly painted window, presenting him with her back.

"What do you want, Rob? An apology? Because I'm quite happy to give you one." She hesitated. "In fact, it's one of the reasons I came back."

He smiled, even though he knew she couldn't see his face. "I told you what I want."

She turned slowly to face him. "To fuck me. Why on earth would you want to do that? Is that your perverted idea of revenge?"

He shrugged. "Maybe."

"You know that makes no sense, right?"

He kept on staring at her. Hell, he knew that, but until he got rid of this itch to have her, he couldn't move on, couldn't let go.

"And why, exactly, would I let a man who hates me make love to me?"

Rob leaned back against the wall. "You fucked me over big-time."

"So you're going to fuck me right back?"

"Works for me. And I know you, Ally. I know what you want in a man." Rob caught something on his radio, which he always carried with him, and glanced down at it. "I've got to go. I'm on duty in ten minutes. I'll keep you informed about the troublemakers, and you let me know about the sex."

She looked away from him, her arms folded over her breasts. "Go away, Rob. I have a lot to do."

"I can see that." He glanced around the room again. "How come you don't get someone in to do it for you?"

"I can't afford it. In fact, I might have to get myself a job to cover the costs. I didn't realize how much my mom had let it go."

Her blunt statement made him pause.

"You're a supermodel—of course you can afford it."

"Not anymore. I haven't walked a runway or shot a fashion spread for years."

"But you had savings, right? And a manager and a modeling agency to protect your ass?"

"*Had,* yeah. Not anymore. They all dropped me."

He continued to stare at her. "Why?"

She walked away from him, back toward the front door, her posture rigid and her chin in the air. "That's none of your business."

"I suppose it isn't, but I'm still asking."

Ally flung open the door, flooding the dirty hallway with sunlight.

"Good-bye, Sheriff. Come back when you have something useful to say."

He stopped next to her, his shoes lined up with her bare feet so that she had to look up at him to see his face.

"I'll come back when you decide about the sex."

She sighed. "I don't need to decide anything. I just want to talk things through with you properly, not have sex."

He slid his hand in her hair and kissed her, ravaging her mouth until her whole body pressed against his.

"You still want me."

She licked her now-swollen lips. "I don't."

"Liar." He kissed her again, pulling her tight against his erection and rocking into her. "You still taste the same, you know. You still turn me on."

She turned her face away from him. "So what? It doesn't mean I have to do anything about it."

"That's true, but I'm not giving up. I'll even help you out with the house, if you want."

"Why?"

"I told you why."

"Rob, there are probably hundreds of women in this town

who would jump at the chance to fuck you. Why are you so fixated on having me?"

He drew back a little, propped his hand on the door frame above her head, and considered her. She was tall for a woman, just under six foot in her bare feet, only three inches shorter than him.

"Because you'll be gone soon?" He thought he saw a flash of disappointment in her eyes, but she quickly masked it. "What, you thought I was going to make you a big speech about still being in love with you and wanting you back? I haven't been pining for you for ten years."

"Then why do you still want me?"

"Because we used to burn up the sheets, and I can give you what you really need."

She angled her head to one side. "What's wrong, Rob? Are you trying to recapture your youth because you can't get it up anymore?"

He took her hand and placed it over the swell of his cock. "Does that feel like I have a problem to you?"

She wrenched her hand away and tried to turn toward the door.

"As I said, I have a lot to do, so can you go now?"

"Run out of insults for the day, have you?" He blew her a kiss. "It's okay. I know you'll come around."

He stepped back as the door slammed in his face and strolled back to his truck. All things considered, that had gone well. Was it wrong that her anger simply turned him on more? And, dammit, he was turned on and so was she. Had their relationship always been like that?

He stopped walking. No, she'd adored him, would've done anything he asked until he'd scared her into running. He'd been so sure he knew her, but had he ever really bothered to listen to her opinions? And now she wanted to clear the air, whatever the hell that meant.

He frowned as he started the engine. The idea of asking her to fuck him to make amends had come out of nowhere. It wasn't really about the fucking anyway; surely she knew that? He'd expected her to turn him down flat, but there had been a hint of interest behind her denial that had turned him on and kept him insisting that was what he wanted.

Rob wanted to bang his head on the steering wheel. Ten minutes with Ally and he was already behaving like a teenager. And he didn't need that right now. He had to meet Jackson, who was due back from a training course today, and tell him about the return of the town's infamous black sheep.

Through a crack in the dirt-encrusted net curtain, Ally watched Rob leave. His arrogance continued to take her breath away. He thought she'd be good for a quick fuck while she was in town, did he? The trouble was, her hormones agreed with him. She hadn't had sex with a real person for over a year, and she was slowly dying of frustration.

Rob, of course, had always been able to turn her on, and nothing had changed there. He'd ruled her world when she was a senior in high school and he was a college sophomore. She wanted him big-time, and somehow her body still trusted him to make it good for her. She picked up her paintbrush and retreated to the kitchen. He kissed like a god—that slight hint of power, of menace, of compulsion she always craved was still there. It made her want to do what he said, when he said it, and not regret a single thing.

"He's dangerous, Ally."

She glanced around the empty kitchen, aware she was talking to herself again. If she stayed, she should definitely get a cat. With a sigh, she washed the paintbrush out in the sink. But she wasn't staying, was she? And a cat would only be something that depended on her, and she couldn't handle that responsibility yet.

She really shouldn't argue with Rob, either, but it was so hard to resist. It had been so long since she'd reacted so fiercely to anyone, cared enough to even fight. On some deep level, she knew he wasn't the kind of guy who would hurt her, even though she'd walked out on him. She couldn't decide if Jill, her good friend and AA sponsor, would be pleased or horrified with her thought process.

There was so much work to do in the house; she could do with some help. But could she be alone with Rob for five minutes without jumping him or letting him jump her? She slowly shook her head. "Uh-uh, missy."

She pretended to pet her imaginary cat and returned to sorting out the kitchen cupboards. Rob was too much of a temptation; she'd have to get a job and pay someone to do the heavy work instead.

"Ally's back."

Rob braced himself for Jackson's reaction, but his deputy kept eating his fries as if he hadn't a care in the world. Spring Falls's only sports bar was half empty this early in the afternoon. The regular patrons would turn up later to fill the place and give it some much-needed buzz.

"Did you hear what I said?"

"Yeah." Jackson stopped eating to stare at him. "Do you want to talk about it?"

Rob recoiled. "What am I, a girl? What do you want me to say?"

"I dunno, something, I guess."

"I knew she'd come back one day."

"You did?"

"Yeah." Rob drummed his fingers on the red and white checked tablecloth. Jackson wasn't known as a chatterbox, and since his aborted army career, he'd clammed up even more. But he still had this disconcerting habit of expecting Rob to tell *him* stuff, embarrassing stuff Rob really didn't want to share. "You'll probably see her around town. She's planning on fixing up her mom's old house and selling it."

"Yeah?"

Rob set his jaw as Jackson went back to eating his fries. "Is that all you have to say?"

Jackson sighed. "What are you worrying about?"

"I'm not."

"I'm okay with it." Jackson fixed Rob with a hard stare. "You're the one who seems to have a problem."

"I don't like it."

"Ally coming back?"

"Yeah, it stirs up stuff I thought I'd forgotten." Rob took a gulp of his beer and refused to look at Jackson.

"Like the fact that I fucked your girlfriend?"

"I hadn't forgotten that."

Jackson rubbed the side of his face. "Neither have I. You almost broke my fucking jaw."

"You fucking deserved it." Rob glared at Jackson for a long moment. "Sometimes I wish I could just sort it out like that with Ally. But you can't have a knockdown fight with a girl."

"That's the truth," Jackson agreed. "You'll have to think of some other way of telling her what an asshole you were."

Rob decided not to answer that. "There's other stuff that bothers me about that last night Ally was in town. Susan's death and all that."

"Why that?"

"Jesus, Jackson, don't you think about Susan too? She was your fucking girlfriend."

Jackson glared at him, his dark eyes smoldering like coals. "Susan killed herself after she found me and Ally in bed together. Of course I think about her. I'm just not sure why Susan is the first thing *you* think about."

Rob leaned closer and lowered his voice. "Don't you think

it was weird the way Susan was seen at the Kendal house that night?"

"Not really. She probably wanted to confront Ally. That's what girls do."

"But this was later, after Ally had supposedly gone."

"So?"

"There were reports that Susan left the Kendal house *with* someone that night. After the suicide verdict came in, the authorities had no legal means to search Ruth Kendal's house, and she refused point-blank to help them. What if Susan didn't throw herself off that bridge after all but was helped?"

Jackson angled his chair back from the table. "And you care about this because . . . ?"

"Because I'm a cop and no case is ever completely closed, is it?"

Jackson got to his feet and leaned over the table. "Fuck that, Rob. This is all bullshit. You want a reason to get into Ally's house, into her pants, and back into her life. Don't use Susan's death as an excuse to reexamine the past."

Rob stayed put as Jackson threw some cash on the table, grabbed his jacket, and headed out the door. He let out his breath and finished his beer. Damn, that hadn't gone as he'd wanted it to. Jackson was pissed and maybe he had a point. But Rob didn't need a way back into Ally's life. She'd already said she wanted to "talk" to him.

With a curse, Rob ordered another beer and turned his attention to the baseball game on the big-screen TV. Jackson would get over himself; he usually did. And Rob would continue to investigate Susan's death in whatever way he damn well pleased.

3

Ally held her breath as the truck's engine coughed and reluctantly turned over. For a second, she allowed herself to rest her head on the steering wheel and breathe a quick prayer of thanks. Her day was not going well. She'd been to almost half the businesses in the small town and asked for work, but no one was hiring.

Some people were openly hostile, others polite but distant. It was her own fault. She'd run off and made no attempt to keep in touch with anyone from Spring Falls. It wasn't surprising no one wanted to know her, let alone employ her. But, hell, with the way her finances were tangled up, she needed to keep her savings intact if she was going to follow her dream and go back to college in the fall.

Her stomach grumbled as she backed out of her space and headed for the gas station. Ten bucks of gas went nowhere these days. If she didn't get lucky soon, she'd be walking into town to save money. To her relief, the old guy who sometimes manned the pumps and liked to talk had disappeared. She got out of the truck and went inside the small cramped shack that smelled of oil, tobacco, and fish bait to hand over her money.

"Is that you, Ally?"

She looked up to see a vaguely familiar face smiling at her.

"Yeah, I'm Ally."

"I'm Jane Evans. Do you remember me?"

Inwardly Ally braced herself for an attack. If she remembered correctly, Jane was the younger sister of Susan Evans, the girl Jackson had been going out with when Ally had hooked up with him. Just like in some cheesy soap opera, Susan had been right there, alongside Rob, to discover her and Jackson in bed together. The tragic consequences of that god-awful moment had haunted Ally ever since.

"Hey, Jane, what's up?" Inwardly she winced. Now she sounded like some flippant teenager.

"Nothing much, thanks. I heard you'd come back."

Ally managed an awkward smile. "I'm not staying. As soon as I fix up the house and sell it, I'll be off again. You don't have to worry about bumping into me all the time or anything."

Jane looked carefully around the small space and then leaned closer to Ally.

"I don't mind if you stay. I've forgiven you, even if nobody else has."

"That's . . . very decent of you. I was really sorry about what happened to your sister."

Jane shrugged. "Susan was a fool to get so worked up over a man like Jackson. How weak can you get?"

Ally took a small careful step to one side so that she had room to get around Jane if she needed it. So much for sisterly love and solidarity.

"It was nice to see you anyway."

Jane waved and walked toward the open door. "You too."

Ally paid for her gas and went back outside. Jane's behavior was weird to say the least, but if she was willing to forgive, Ally wasn't going to stop her. One less person to worry about in a town full of haters was a start.

She pumped the gas, replaced the pump, and got back into the truck. The setting sun made the raindrops splattering her windshield gleam for an instant before they evaporated on the warm glass. Ally shivered as she started the truck. God, she was so tired of being afraid, of facing the people she'd let down, of owning up to her mistakes and moving on.

Her AA sponsor, Jill, had told her it was important to get rid of her baggage, but sometimes it felt way too heavy to lift, let alone sort out. Jill had also told her that even if she apologized, some people might not want to forgive her and that she had to accept that. An image of Rob's unsmiling face filled her mind. Of all people, she had to make things right with him.

As the sun disappeared swiftly behind the surrounding hills, the valley became a landscape of deep shadows and stark silhouettes. Ally decided to visit the twenty-four-hour convenience store, microwave herself something fattening, and go home. Maybe she'd even splurge and buy a doughnut or two to cheer herself up.

She lingered in the small store, drawn by the lights, the smell of cheese nachos, and the array of glossy magazines, until the young kid behind the counter began to look at her suspiciously. She nuked a burrito to eat on the way, grabbed two doughnuts and headed out. It was much darker outside now, but the house was only five minutes away.

"What the hell?"

Ally glanced in her rearview mirror at the flashing blue and red lights of a patrol car. Dammit, she was only two minutes from home, and she'd been right on the speed limit. What on earth was she being pulled over for?

She sat rigidly in the driver's seat and refused to turn her head as the police officer leisurely approached. She reluctantly let down the window and tried not to inhale as Rob's lemon-scented aftershave wafted over her.

"*What?*"

Rob wasn't smiling. "Driver's license and insurance, please."

Ally flipped open the glove compartment and handed over the insurance, pulled her license out of her back pocket, and gave him that too.

"Ma'am, this is a New York state license. California law states that if you intend to reside in California, you must get a California driver's license within ten days."

"I'm not residing here."

"Ma'am, to my knowledge, you've been residing here for at least three weeks and you are a property owner."

Ally set her teeth. "I didn't know that was the law. I'll fix it tomorrow, okay? Now, is there anything else?"

"Get out of the vehicle, please, ma'am."

"It's Ms., and why do I need to get out? I said I'd sort out my license."

Rob leaned in the window to stare at her.

"Get. Out."

Ally glared right back at him. "You have no right to bully me. I hope you're taping this because I'm going to sue you for every pathetic penny you earn."

Rob stepped back, and she flung open the door of the truck and got out, instantly regretting the loss of her height advantage in the cab.

"What are you going to do now, Sheriff? Beat the crap out of me?"

He still didn't smile, just walked toward the rear of her truck and pointed. She followed him, her temper rising, and then stopped.

"Oh my God. What happened to my lights?"

Her left taillight was shattered, and the light illuminating her license plate had also gone out.

"That's why I stopped you, ma'am."

Ally stared at the damage, and a sick feeling built in her stomach. "It was okay when I left Main Street. I saw the reflection in the shop windows when I backed out of my parking space."

"Did you stop anywhere else?"

"The gas station, the 7-Eleven... Who the hell would do that to me?"

"I don't know, but you'll have to fix it."

Ally put her hands on her hips and swung around to look at Rob. "Thanks for the advice. And how much is that going to cost me?"

He shrugged, and the movement outlined his broad shoulders in the glare from his headlights.

"Your insurance should cover it."

"Not the kind I have. By the time they take off my deductible, I'll be paying them. I'll have to get it fixed myself."

"I'm going to run your documents. I'll be back in a minute." Rob turned on his heel and headed back toward his car, leaving Ally stranded in the road.

She continued to stare at her damaged taillight. She didn't have the money to fix the house up, let alone her truck. She glared at Rob's retreating form. And how dare he act like he didn't know her?

She blinked as he turned off the flashing lights on his car and came back to her. His radio chirped and muttered away at his belt but he ignored it. He handed her back her documents, and she stuffed them into her pocket.

"Can I go now?"

He stared down at her. "Aren't you going to thank me for alerting you to the fact that your vehicle was damaged?"

"Thank you? You're a cop. It's your job to harass people, isn't it?"

His expression cooled. "It's my job to keep people safe, ma'am."

"*Ma'am?*" She wanted to kick his ass but instead gave him her best dismissive smile. "Well, thank you, then."

He took a dog-eared business card out of his top pocket. "This guy deals in secondhand car parts. If you give him a call and tell him I sent you, he'll probably be able to find you a new taillight real cheap."

Ally bit down hard on her lip. God, she didn't want him to be nice. It made it so much harder to ignore the heat between them.

"Thanks . . ." She met his amused gaze. "Really, I mean it."

She moved toward her truck, and he followed her. He opened the driver's door and waited as she seated herself behind the wheel.

"I'll follow you home."

"You don't have to do that."

He sighed. "Ally, are you going to fight me about everything? If I'm behind you, there's less likelihood that someone will run into you on the road. My shift is over, and I'm going back to town anyway." He paused and looked into her eyes. "And I'm ready to talk."

"And you expect me to wait up for you?"

"Yeah. I do." He touched the brim of his hat. "I'll come 'round the back, so leave the kitchen door unlocked."

She wanted to scream that she would do no such thing, but he'd already walked away. She jumped as he flashed his headlights and obediently started the truck. He followed her as far as her driveway and then peeled off back into town, leaving her to park and run inside.

She didn't bother with the lights as she walked through the quiet house to the kitchen, her whole body so alive and needy it almost hurt to breathe. How dare he be nice to her when she'd expected nothing but disdain and anger, and how dare he think that having sex was the only way she could make anything up to him? But she wanted him, wanted to be dominated, to forget about how crappy her life had been recently and just enjoy the physical.

Would that be so wrong? Somehow she still trusted him, and he knew exactly how to push her sexual buttons. After the awful day she'd just had, she wanted to be held. She moved toward the back door, touched the small glass panes, and looked out into the shadowed yard.

And Rob wouldn't expect anything from her. He already thought the worst of her, so she certainly wouldn't be letting him down. It would just be about the sex. He'd get payback and she would start a new sexual journey after her year of abstinence.

Her fingers crept toward the latch, and she slowly turned the key.

Rob parked his truck a block away from Ally's place and walked through the quiet streets until he reached the back of her mother's house. Part of him knew that by coming to see her, he was behaving like a complete bastard, using that hint of vulnerability Ally had shown by her truck and exploiting it big-time. But she wanted him. There was no question of that; her body had told him everything she hadn't wanted to say.

He paused outside the darkened lot and peered over the fence into the backyard. Nobody challenged him. He frowned. So much for the local Neighborhood Watch. The grass was at least three feet high, and the smell of rotting fruit from the unpruned trees cut through the sweet scent of the night. Had Ally unlocked the door, or had she regained her fighting spirit and gone to bed alone? He pushed open the back gate. There was only one way to find out.

To his relief, the door handle turned and he entered the dark space. Moonlight filtered through the newly washed windows, revealing Ally standing by the table, her arms crossed over her breasts. Rob let out a breath he wasn't even aware he'd been holding. She was waiting for him, and he was more than ready to give her what she needed.

He sat down at the kitchen table and nodded at the chair opposite. "Sit down, Ally."

She raised her chin at him but complied. Her hands folded together in front of her. She licked her lips. "I meant it when I said I wanted to apologize."

"And I meant it when I said I'd take that apology in sex."

She shivered. "You mean you want to try and dominate me again."

"I get that I scared you back then, but I'm not twenty anymore, and I'm no longer into that scene." He shrugged. "I tried it for a while, but it didn't suit me."

"You can't change who you are, Rob."

"Yeah, I know that, but I play by my own rules now." He held her gaze. "If you choose to 'submit' to me, and I hate even using that word, then you need to understand I'm not into safe words and all that ritual crap. You either trust me to know what you want and what you need, or you don't."

Her quick indrawn breath made his heart beat faster and his cock swell in his pants.

"You want me to decide whether I'll have sex with you, and *then* you'll tell me how it's going to be."

"Yeah, because I know what you want."

She shifted uneasily in her chair. "Don't you think I might have changed too?"

"Sure." He studied her closely. "We'll find out, won't we?"

"I'll have to think about it, Rob." Ally stood up abruptly. "I wasn't really anticipating having a sexual relationship with anyone while I was back here."

Rob stood, too, and looked down at her. "Then start thinking about it." He slid his hand around the back of her neck and kissed her mouth. "I want to fuck you right now, but I'm willing to wait until you're ready."

She pulled away from him. "Wow, that's big of you."

He caught her hand and pressed it against the front of his pants, almost groaning as his cock reacted. "Honey, you have no idea."

She eased her hand away. "Go home, Rob, and I'll think about it."

Rob checked his gun belt and radio and let himself out of the house the way he'd come in. As he walked the quiet, moonlit streets, his body hummed with sexual frustration. He'd be taking a cold shower when he got home and jerking himself off like a teenager.

He stopped and turned to look at the faint silhouette of the shabby house, his sexual high fading as other, unexpected emotions grabbed hold of him. God, he'd missed her. He wanted to hold her, comfort her, make everything right again, and he couldn't understand why. Was he some kind of masochist who enjoyed having his heart broken? Wasn't he supposed to be the one who was in control, the "dominant" one?

During his first couple of years at college, he'd gotten way too involved in the "scene." Of course, when he tried to tell Ally what she really needed and just how he was going to give it to her, he scared her into running away. It had taken him a long time to realize he wanted to be Ally's "Rob" not some nameless chick's "Dom."

And that was the truth of it. A truth he'd struggled to acknowledge over the years and had finally had the balls to admit. He was Ally's. And if this was the only way she would let him get close to her, he'd go for it with everything he had. With a soft, heartfelt curse, he got into his truck and turned the key. Dammit, he was already committed. Whatever he'd started, he was determined to see it through to the end.

4

Ally straightened up and rubbed her aching back. Between painting the house and not sleeping well, her whole body was complaining. At least the kitchen walls were a gleaming white now, the blue tiles scrubbed, and the gray bleached out of the grout. There was still a lot to do, but it kept her busy. She pushed her hair out of her face. Busy was good. It gave her less time to brood.

A knock at the back door made her turn, and she frowned at the big brown shape through the frosted glass. Was it Rob again? He'd said he wouldn't be back until she asked him, but he was so full of shit. She walked across to the door and then hesitated. Years of living in New York had sharpened her sense of self-preservation.

"Who's there?"

"It's me, Jackson Smith."

Ally brought her hand to her mouth. She hadn't seen Jackson since that night when she'd sought comfort in his arms and all hell had broken loose. She took a deep breath. He was just another obstacle she had to overcome. She'd faced Rob; surely Jackson would be easier? He certainly was sweeter.

Ally turned the key and opened the door. Jackson took off his sunglasses, but he didn't smile as he looked down at her. His skin was the color of burnished copper, courtesy of his Lakota father, and, as usual, his almost-black eyes concealed his thoughts.

"Hi."

"Hi, would you like to come in?" Ally gestured awkwardly into the house.

"Sure." He followed her inside and waited by the table, his gaze roaming the kitchen as if he expected an ambush.

Ally folded her arms over her chest and leaned against the countertop. "You look well."

"Thanks." His gaze briefly connected with hers. "You look thin."

"Models are supposed to be thin. Don't you know that?"

He studied the faded linoleum. "But you haven't been modeling for quite a while now, have you?"

Ally tensed. "Did Rob tell you that?"

A brief smile flickered over his stern face. "No. I can read."

"All that shit on the Internet?"

"Not just that."

"Then what?"

"Police reports, that kind of stuff. I worked as an NYC cop for a while before I moved back to California."

"Oh." Ally felt like he'd shoved his fist in her gut. "Then you know why I'm here."

Again he considered her. "Not really."

She sighed. "To make things right for one thing, to apologize to the people I hurt, and that definitely includes you."

His head came up. "Are you sure about that?"

"Jackson, I put you in an appalling position. I almost destroyed your friendship with Rob—and what about Susan? I sure did ruin her life, didn't I?"

He shrugged. "You had your reasons."

"What the hell does that mean?"

His smile was gentle. "It means you should forgive yourself."

"Easy for you to say."

"I've had plenty of time to think it through, and the blame wasn't all yours. I was equally to blame; you know that."

Ally studied him for a long moment. How come it was so much easier to be honest with Jackson than it was with Rob? "I know that now, but I'm still sorry, Jackson."

"Apology accepted." He dug his hand into his pocket and pulled out his keys. "Now, give me your car keys."

Ally's tentative smile faded. "What?"

He looked at her as if she'd gone nuts. "I'm taking your truck to Vic's shop."

"Says who?"

"Rob said it needed fixing, so seeing as I'm on duty and not using my truck this week, I thought we'd swap until yours was repaired."

"No."

He paused. "You're getting it done somewhere else?"

"I haven't even called the guy yet!"

"So, what's the problem?"

"The *problem* is that it's nothing to do with either of you what I do with my truck."

"You have to get it fixed, right?"

Ally gritted her teeth. "I know that, but I am not accepting help from you, or Rob, for anything."

"Why not?"

"Because everyone would assume I was taking over my mother's position as the town slut."

Jackson put his keys back into his pocket. "How about I get you the parts, and I help you fix it right here?"

"How about you go home?"

He held her gaze, and she looked desperately for some sense of what he was feeling and found nothing. Had he always been so guarded?

He shoved a hand through his short black hair. "Ally, just accept my help, won't you? I'll come around after dark if it makes you feel better."

Ally slumped back against the cupboard. Why was he being so nice? It made her feel like a bitch all over again. "I can't afford to have the truck fixed at a shop, and I won't let you or anyone else pay for it. Do you understand?"

"I hear you loud and clear." Jackson put his sunglasses back on and headed for the door. "Have a good morning, Ally. I'll see you around."

When he shut the door, Ally closed her eyes tight. She didn't want his charity. She wanted—she *needed*—to fix things for herself. How hard could it be to replace a light? She'd get a book from the library and take it from there. If she could just get a job to help her through the worst of this financial mess, she'd be able to pay for anything she damn well wanted.

She picked up her coffee mug and washed it out in the sink. Jackson had accepted her apology and seemed disinclined to discuss the past with her at all. She wasn't sure if that was a good or a bad thing. Behind his calm façade, she'd sensed something different in him, something far harder and darker than he wanted the world to see.

The alarm on her cheap plastic watch beeped and Ally opened the fridge. She didn't feel like eating, but she had to. That bit of wisdom was one of the hard-earned lessons from rehab about having a healthy body to go with a happy, healthy mind. She made herself a peanut butter and jelly sandwich, with "wholesome" brown bread, and opened the free local paper she'd picked up at the store the previous night.

Of course, there was nothing in the jobs section that a washed-up supermodel could do. Ally finished her sandwich and then put her head down on the table. Sometimes it felt as if she'd just climbed one mountain to be faced with another. She forced herself to be positive. She wasn't in debt anymore, and she didn't want to go back there. So she'd wait until she got a job and would fix the truck then. The walk into town would be good for her too.

With a groan, she got up and stretched out her tired muscles. Next up was stripping the ancient linoleum from the floor and checking the state of the wood beneath. With a deep breath, Ally reached for her gloves. It was time to search out the vermin that probably lurked under the linoleum. She'd spent years around vermin of the human kind, so a few bugs really shouldn't bother her.

"Ally wouldn't give me the keys to her truck." Jackson came into Rob's office and shut the door firmly behind him.

Rob looked up from the report he was completing. "She wouldn't? Why not?"

"Because apparently, she doesn't like you interfering in her life."

Rob sighed. "I was trying to help. She needs to get that light fixed."

"Yeah, I get that, but she wants to do it herself." Jackson leaned against the closed door and shoved his hands into his pockets. "You might've told me you hadn't agreed about anything with her."

"I suppose I'm so used to looking out for her that I forgot she's changed."

"Rob, she left you. You hate her guts. Why would you still be looking out for her?"

"Because I don't hate her, and I'm an idiot?"

Jackson studied him for a long moment, and a sick feeling twisted his gut. "You've already gotten into her pants again, haven't you? What are you? Fucking stupid?"

"I haven't, it's just that she—"

"Wrestled you to the ground and took advantage of you?"

"No!" Rob pushed his chair away from the desk and stood up. "It was all me and she was..." He hesitated. "She's like a drug. I can't seem to get her out of my head."

"Jeez, man!" Jackson shook his head. "You need to stay away from her until you get your brain out of your dick. Mess around with her and then try and build your stupid case against her mother. She'll have your ass in court before you can count to five."

"Give me a break. I have no intention of involving Ally in anything." Rob sat down, but Jackson didn't move from his position by the door. Eventually, Rob had to look up at him. "*What?*"

"How about you give Ally a break, Rob? Let her get on with whatever it is she has to do here and leave."

Jackson turned to go and Rob stared down at his report. "I don't know if I can let her go again."

"Then talk to her *before* you fuck her. Find out what's really going on in her head and then decide what you're going to have to do to make her want to stay."

Rob looked up at him. "Do you want her to stay?"

Jackson paused, the door half open, and addressed his answer over his shoulder to Rob's desk. "Of course I do. I like her. I always have."

"You more than like her, Jackson."

"What's that supposed to mean?"

"I've always suspected you want her as much as I do."

"And she wanted *you*, Rob. She made her choice."

"But Ally's not a scared eighteen-year-old anymore. Maybe she doesn't have to choose between us."

Jackson's gut tightened even more. "What are you trying to say?"

Rob shrugged. "Just that I wouldn't make the same mistake again. If she wanted us both, I'd be happy to go along with it."

"Are you *serious?*"

"Yeah." Rob held his gaze. "I am."

Jackson struggled to think of a reply as his cock thickened in his pants. The thought of sharing a bed with Ally and Rob was something he'd consigned to his deepest, darkest fantasies. His fingers tightened on the door handle.

"You're doing it again, buddy. Making decisions for Ally that aren't yours to make."

"Jeez, Jackson, give me a chance here. I'm just asking how you feel. It's not like I'm going to spring the decision on Ally and just assume she'll go along with it."

Desperately, Jackson tried to change the subject. "If you want Ally to stick around, finding her a job might help. Have you asked Lauren?"

"Lauren hates her guts."

"Everyone hates Ally in this town. Imagine how that feels and yet she's back here facing it, dealing with it."

"*All right.* I get it. I'll ask Lauren."

For the first time, Jackson managed to smile. "Thanks."

Rob waved him away. "Don't thank me yet. My little sister is a hard nut to crack."

"Don't I know it. Appeal to her mercenary side. Tell her that everyone in town will be by to take a look at Ally, and that will increase her business."

"Yeah, that might just do it."

Jackson retreated, leaving Rob staring at the wall. He deserved Jackson's wrath. He was behaving like an asshole. But he'd never been able to be cool around Ally; the fire between them, the closeness, the sense that they were meant to be together made that impossible. And it seemed that heat was still there.

And Jackson's reaction to his admission that he wouldn't object if they both got to fuck Ally hadn't been quite as enthusiastic as he'd hoped either. But then Jackson always kept his emotions to himself, and he hadn't exactly said no.

If Rob wanted to clear up the mysteries of the past, he had to stop leading with his dick and start using his supposedly first-class brain. The least he could do was try and help Ally get a job. Then she might stick around until they sorted everything out.

He put on his jacket and checked to make sure his radio was on. Midmorning, before the lunch rush, was a good time to call on Lauren at the diner. He shied away from the thought of what Lauren would make of his asking for a favor—for Ally of all people.

When Rob came into the hallway, Jackson's door was closed and he went past without knocking. He'd tell the front desk where he was going on his way out. It occurred to him that Jackson had spoken more this morning than he had in the last six months, and all on Ally's behalf. *Shit.* Had Jackson realized that Ally was the woman he wanted? Was that why he'd been less than enthusiastic about Rob's confession?

Rob paused to consider. After he'd punched Jackson in the face, they'd ended up apologizing to each other and eventually had resumed their old relationship. But what if Jackson now wanted Ally all for himself?

Rob found himself retracing his steps and knocking on Jackson's door.

"Yeah?"

He went in and shut the door. Jackson looked up from the report he was reading.

"What's up?"

"When I talked about us both having Ally"—Rob paused and Jackson groaned—"I should've asked you if you wanted her just for yourself."

"Jeez, Rob. You're making it sound like a done deal. She's her own person. You're not fucking God. Don't you have to talk to Ally about this first?"

Rob set his jaw. "I'm just trying to make sure we're clear with each other." He hesitated. "Do you want me to butt out?"

"Like Ally would agree to that?"

"Hell, you're the person she turned to when I let her down." God, it was hard to say that, and impossible to look at Jackson.

"Rob." Jackson sounded incredibly gentle. "If Ally wants us both, I'm more than okay with it. After the way I fucked up, it's more than I ever imagined having a shot at. But it's her decision, buddy, and let's get real here—she's unlikely to want to shack up with anyone in this town, especially you and me."

Rob nodded and turned to leave. For some reason, speaking at that point was not an option. With a sense that his life was getting way too complicated, Rob walked the short distance across town to Lauren's diner and went in the back to the kitchen.

Lauren was leaning against a countertop, eating an egg sandwich, her face flushed, her blond hair escaping the confines of her regulation hat. She was about a foot shorter than Rob and a lot curvier than Ally. He loved her to bits and she knew it.

Her gorgeous smile flashed out. "Rob? What's up?"

He removed his sunglasses. "Can't I just stop in to see my lovely sister without a reason?"

She finished off her sandwich and washed it down with a gulp of soda. "Now I'm really worried. What do you want?"

"A favor." He took up a position opposite her, trying to keep his expression relaxed and friendly. "For an old friend."

Her smile disappeared. "What old friend?"

"Someone you used to be best buddies with."

"Ally Kendal?"

"So you know she's back?"

"Everyone knows she's back." Lauren pursed her lips. "What I want to know is what it has to do with you."

Rob glanced around, but everyone else in the small kitchen appeared to be occupied. "She needs a job."

"So?"

"I was hoping you had an opening."

"Even if I did, why would I give it to her?"

"As a favor to me?"

Lauren's brown eyes flashed fire. "Ally dumped you. Why the hell would I want to help her?"

He met her furious gaze. "Because I need her to stay around for a while."

"So you can what? Make things right with her?"

Rob thought quickly. "No, so that I can clear up something that's been bothering me about Susan's death."

"Susan Evans?" Lauren studied him for a long moment. "Like I believe that."

"It's part of the reason. Ally was there that night, and no one got to talk to her. She might have evidence that will help me solve the case."

"The case was solved, Rob. Susan committed suicide." Lauren turned on her heel and headed into the tiny cramped back office. Rob followed her and waited until she swung around to face him. "I still don't believe you."

"I can't help that. But Ally really does need a job." He met her gaze. "Hell, I never ask you for anything, sis. Will you do this for me?"

She folded her arms over her chest. "That bitch hurt you, Rob. She almost destroyed you."

He shrugged. "It was a long time ago. I've gotten over her."

"Don't lie to me. Sure, you date lots of women, but you've never allowed any of them to get close. I know because they come and complain to me about it all the time."

"*Okay.* Part of me wants to have it out with her, make her tell me why the fuck she did what she did."

She nodded slowly. "I'd like to hear Ally try and explain herself as well. I'll give her a job. I need a new busboy since Joe left."

Rob frowned and stood up. "If you're going to treat her like shit, I'll go and find someone else to ask."

"I'll treat her the same as any other new employee. I swear."

Rob considered her carefully. "You promise?"

Lauren smiled way too brightly. "Sure."

He wasn't convinced, but what else could he do? If Ally hated the job, she'd quit soon enough. "Now, how am I going to get Ally to find out about the job without telling her?"

"Easy, put a flyer in her mailbox. She'll assume everyone got one with their junk mail and she'll come over."

"You are a genius."

Lauren sat down at her desk and typed away on her computer. "I already had something drafted for the ad, so here you go." The printer rumbled into action, and she leaned across to retrieve the single sheet from the mouth of the printer and handed it to Rob.

The paper smelled like fried chicken, but Rob was okay with that. He'd gotten used to his sister smelling the same way since she'd taken over the diner three years earlier. "Thanks, doll."

She grimaced at him. "I'm not going out of my way to be nice to her, and if she gives me any trouble, she's out, just like anyone else."

"Totally." Rob hesitated. "But give her a chance, Lauren, won't you?"

"God, Rob, what does that woman have to do to you to make you stop caring about her?"

"I don't—"

"Yeah, right, don't even try that crap with me." Lauren got

up and headed back to the kitchen. "I'll let you know if she takes the job, okay?"

"And you won't tell her it was my idea?"

"Of course not! I don't want her getting ideas about you again, do I? Although that's probably why she's back here anyway."

Rob smiled down at her and resisted the impulse to smooth a hand over her obviously raised hackles. "That's not the impression I got. She came back to sort out her mother's stuff."

Lauren grabbed a clean apron and tied it around her waist. "That place is a dump. I wonder why she just didn't send some of her 'people' down to sort it all out for her."

"I guess she doesn't have 'people' anymore." And that was another mystery. What had happened to make her return?

"Good. She deserves to have to come and face us and sort out all that crap."

"As I said, I'm quite looking forward to hearing her side of the story."

Lauren wagged a finger under his nose. "You keep away from her. She's trouble."

Rob could only nod, knowing he'd already gone too far along that particular road to ever find the courage to turn back. All he could do was go forward, sort out his personal shit, and hope Ally did the same.

"I'll see you tomorrow, Lauren."

"Sure. Now let me start on lunch." She paused and brandished an onion at him. "Do you want a sandwich?"

He declined and headed back to the station. Ever since their parents had retired to Florida, she'd tried to feed him and take care of him, and she was younger than him. Did everyone think he needed to be babied because of what had happened between him and Ally? It was an interesting thought and one of many Ally's return had stirred in his brain.

Rob took out the flyer Lauren had given him and approached Jeff Stevens, who was manning the desk. "On your way home, can you do me a favor and stick this in the Kendals' mailbox near your street?"

Jeff didn't bother to look up but held out his hand. "Sure."

Luckily Jeff was new to the area and had no idea of the past scandal, which suited Rob just fine. "Thanks."

Rob returned to his office and shut the door. He sighed as he viewed the pile of paperwork cluttering up his inbox. So much for the computer age; he was still stuck in paper world. He considered the problem with Ally's truck and wondered exactly how Jackson had left it.

Tomorrow evening, he'd take a trip by Ally's house and see how things were. His body stirred at the thought of seeing her again, even as he tried to suppress it. She had already reeled him in without even trying, and he was determined not to be caught out. But this time he'd be trying damned hard not to direct their relationship. It was way past time for some honest conversation.

5

Ally dumped the load of trash from her mailbox on the kitchen table and sorted through it. At least the newspapers would come in handy for the floors and for packing up her mom's stuff. The coupons she would also keep—a habit she'd gotten into when she'd first had to learn to live within a miniscule budget. She sat down and sorted through the rest of the stuff. There was nothing from her bank, which was good, but there was a redirected postcard from her old rehab buddy Dave, who'd ended up backpacking across the country.

She smiled as she read his two-line comment. He seemed fine and so free. So unlike the zombified cokehead she'd first met at the Caring Heart Rehab Center.

She found a pair of scissors and carefully cut coupons, pausing to read the local news and scan the meager job section as she worked. A flyer caught her attention, and she pulled it from the pile and smoothed it out. The local diner was looking for help. Ally's heart gave a little jump. Who owned the diner now? Hopefully someone who'd moved into town after she'd left and had no idea who she was. She'd present herself there early tomorrow morning and hope for the best. It wouldn't be the first time she'd washed dishes or put out the trash to earn a few bucks.

A tap on the back door made her turn around and peer at the all-too-familiar shape of Rob outlined in the glass. She tidied up the coupons and folded the job ad before putting them all away in the nearest drawer. It was only then that she crossed to the door and opened it a crack.

"Rob?"

"Ally. Can I come in?"

"Is it police business?"

"Not really. I just wanted to see how you were doing."

She let the door swing wide and walked back to the kitchen table. "I'm doing fine."

His smile was slow to come. "I'm glad to hear it." He hesitated, one hand still on the door. "I'm off duty."

"I guessed that."

"Why?"

"Because you came around the back so that no one would see you. I bet you parked two blocks away too."

"You said you didn't want any gossip, Ally."

"And you do?" Ally squared up to him. "No one in this town wants you anywhere near me."

"I'm not responsible for what the town wants or thinks. I'm an adult."

"Who's quite happy to mess around with me on the quiet?"

He came closer. "You don't have to be quiet for me, honey. I like it when you scream."

Ally suppressed a shiver as the tone of his voice deepened. "Does everything have to be about sex?"

"Between you and me? I guess so." He took the chair opposite her. "So how about that?"

"About what?"

"The sex."

"Is that why you're here?"

"Of course."

She sighed. "I don't know, Rob. You...confuse me and I don't need that right now."

"What's confusing?"

She took a deep breath and met his intent blue gaze. "I've spent a long time trying to sort my head out. I've learned a lot about myself, and I'm a better and stronger person." She grimaced. "I'm not trying to go all Oprah on you, but I really am."

"And what does that have to do with sex?"

"Because..." She paused. "God, Rob, you *know*."

He sat back and studied her. "That's one of the reasons why you ran away, isn't it? I scared you."

She shook her head. "You were always intense about sex. What I've got to try and understand is what *I* want, and that still isn't clear."

"Now you're just confusing me."

She clasped her hands together tightly on the table. "Do you know why I quit modeling?"

"I didn't know that you'd quit it completely. I kind of assumed you'd been working overseas or something."

"No, I had to quit."

He studied her face. "Because you were getting too old?"

"Very funny. Thanks for the confidence boost, but I quit before I was pushed." She forced herself to meet his skeptical gaze. "I had a severe addiction to alcohol and drugs, and I checked myself into rehab."

His blue eyes widened. "I don't remember reading about that in the tabloids."

"That's because I got out before I totally disgraced myself. There were a couple of close calls that my agency and publicist managed to keep out of the press. Jackson probably knows the details from when he worked in New York." She bit down on her lip. "I lived with an addict, Rob. I knew the signs, and I really didn't want to become my mother."

"That was a pretty brave thing to do," he said softly.

"It didn't seem so at the time. It was the death knell of my career, because it meant I defaulted on a lot of long-term contracts and modeling assignments. I kept trying to put it off, but eventually I knew if I didn't take care of myself, I'd end up dead."

"So you did the smart thing." He reached across the table to squeeze her hand. "Not that I'm surprised. You've always been braver than you realized."

"Running away wasn't very brave." She looked down at his hand holding hers. "That was stupid and I hurt you."

He nodded, his expression stark.

She took a deep breath. "I still don't think having sex is the best way to make it up to you, though." God that was a lie. The thought of having sex with him again made her squirm.

He frowned. "But shouldn't it be up to me to decide the best way you can make amends?"

She regarded him warily. "I suppose that's one way of looking at it."

"Do you like having sex with me?"

"I'm not sure." Another lie. Would he see through it? A quiver of anticipation ran through her.

"So why can't we just have sex?"

"Because nothing is ever that simple, is it?"

"It can be."

"But that's the whole point, Rob. I can't just 'let' you take over my sex life."

"Yeah, you can." He let go of her hands and stood up, suddenly filling the small kitchen. She waited as he pushed back his chair and came around the table to her. His fingers slid under her chin, and he raised her head until he could fit his mouth over hers. His kiss was dark, needy, and totally possessive, and she loved it, felt her whole body turn liquid with longing.

His other hand slid around her waist, and he drew her to her feet. She moaned as he continued to devour her mouth, nipping

at her lips, his tongue thrusting deep. When he drew back, she
was panting and couldn't look away.

"Don't overcomplicate everything. You want it, and you
want me. That's it, honey. You can definitely make amends and
I'll definitely let you."

His hand slid under her thin T-shirt, and his palm flattened
on her back, pushing her even closer into his embrace. She
could feel the beat of his heart, his harsh breathing, and the hot
press of his erection.

"Suck my cock, Ally."

"Rob..."

He just looked at her, and she found herself sinking to her
knees. He shoved down his pants and presented her with the
sight of his thick, heavy shaft, already wet and straining toward
her. "Suck me, Ally."

The note of command did it, and she leaned forward obediently to swallow his cock down. He groaned his appreciation, his
hips rocking into her, adding to the friction, to the need, making
her take all of him and at his pace and direction. No one else had
ever taken control of her like this. No one had ever dared.

After Rob, she'd picked her boyfriends very carefully and ul-
timately found them deeply unsatisfying. Was that why this was
so deeply rewarding? To be on her knees, her head held in Rob's
firm grasp, her mouth full of his thrusting, demanding cock.

He gasped her name and thrust even harder, holding her
chained to his rhythm until his final push emptied his come
way down her throat in long, pulsing waves. She shivered as he
slowly released his grip on her and helped her to her feet.

"Are you wet for me now?"

She could only nod and lick her lips, tasting him all over
again. He backed her up against the nearest chair and guided
her down onto it. She didn't stop him from stripping off her
shorts and panties and spreading her thighs wide. With a soft
sound, he went down on his knees and licked her sex, his

tongue lingering and gliding through her already-wet and swollen folds, his fingers following the path of his tongue to create their own magic.

She gasped as he pushed three fingers deep, his thumb flicking at her clit as she writhed under him. His radio crackled to life, and she felt him curse against her flesh. While he fumbled for the radio, he kept his fingers embedded inside her.

"Yeah." He sounded remarkably calm. "Ally's."

He put the radio on the table and returned his attention to her, used his mouth and fingers on her until she had to climax.

When she eventually opened her eyes, she saw he'd taken the chair opposite her again, his skin flushed, his lazy blue gaze full of sensual satisfaction. Ally struggled to match his composure. "Who were you talking to?"

"Jackson."

"He was checking up on you?"

His smile was brief. "He's like that."

"I know, but..."

"He wants me to keep away from you."

Ally stared at Rob. "Because he doesn't want you to get hurt, right?"

"No, because he wants me to give you a chance to sort out your shit and get out of here without my input."

"It's a bit late for that, isn't it?"

"Yeah." Rob looked down at his unzipped pants. "I'd better go or he'll turn up here."

Ally imagined Jackson busting in on her and Rob having sex. "I wonder what he'd do if he did?"

His smile died to be replaced by something far more intimate. "You'd probably like it if he joined in, wouldn't you? I seem to remember that was always one of your favorite fantasies."

Ally felt her skin heating. "The reality wasn't quite as exciting as I'd always pictured it."

"You mean when I found you and Jackson in bed?" Rob

sighed. "Hell, if Susan hadn't been there screaming abuse at you both, I'm not sure what I would've done."

"I think you expressed yourself quite adequately when you told me to get out of your life."

Pain and something that looked like regret flickered in his direct blue gaze. "I was a complete fucking idiot."

Ally raised her eyebrows. "I thought I was supposed to be the one apologizing."

His heated gaze slid over her flushed face and her thin T-shirt. "Honey, I'm not stopping you from 'apologizing.'"

Sometimes it was both a blessing and a curse that Rob knew her so well. She raised her chin and gave him back his stare. "After what happened last time, Jackson would probably be scared to come near me anyway."

Rob smiled. "You'd be surprised what Jackson wants. Can't you picture it? You bent over this table right now, me fucking you and Jackson's cock filling your mouth. You'd love that, honey, wouldn't you?"

Ally could only stare at him as he kissed her again, his taste her taste, his breath mingling with her own. He whispered against her lips, "Shall I call him, Ally? I'll do it if you want me to."

Ally pushed him away and retreated to the other side of the table. "Do you remember that bit about 'complicated,' Rob? Don't you think adding Jackson to the mix would make it even worse?"

He straightened up his clothing, retrieved his belt, and buckled it low around his hips like a gunslinger. "It sure would make it interesting. But if it got some animation into Jackson's face, I'd be happy to go along with it."

Ally picked up her sweater and wrapped it over her shoulders. "He does seem different somehow. He was always kind of quiet, but now ..."

"He's closed off completely."

"Yeah." For a moment their eyes met, and Ally was thrust back into the past when they'd all worried about each other and tried to deal with all the stresses of being teenagers.

Rob took a key out of his pocket and laid it on the table. "This is for the back door of my house. When you're ready, come and see me." He retrieved his cap and headed for the back door. "We're not finished here, and it's not complicated at all. We both want sex. What could be simpler than that?"

Ally bit her lip. "But the kind of sex you want, Rob, isn't simple at all."

"Sure it is." He nodded at her. "Now you're old enough to decide if that's what you want too. You've been so brave about dealing with all the other stuff in your life. How about dealing with me too? I'll be waiting, Ally, so make up your mind."

"What happens if I say no?"

He considered her for a long moment. "I won't form a posse to drive you out of town, if that's what you're worried about."

"You'll just let me go?"

All the animation left his face. "I can't force you to stay, Ally."

She watched him leave and locked the door after him, her emotions in turmoil, her body berating her for not inviting him into her bed and having the best sex she'd ever had. But it *wasn't* that simple. She had to understand what she was getting into, and despite what Rob said, they had a history that would surely interfere with his notion of a clean slate of remorse-free sex.

Ally wrapped her arms around herself. What would submitting to Rob reveal about her, and did she really want to take the risk of finding out? Since Rob, she'd steered clear of any man who'd wanted to boss her around in bed.

She washed her hands and stared out the window. But she'd be doing it for Rob, not for herself. It was only sex after all. She'd fought so hard not to be a doormat in all the other areas of her life that it felt like giving in to Rob was a betrayal. But was it? She eyed the key he'd left on the table. Didn't making that choice for *herself* reaffirm her own independence?

And he was giving her a choice. That at least, she believed. This time she'd be going in with her eyes open, not feeling like some frightened eighteen-year-old who'd had no idea how to deal with Rob's demands. And she wanted him, wanted him to make love to her so badly her whole body shook with it.

Rob walked slowly back to his patrol car, aware that his cock was hard again and that he wanted to turn around and beg Ally to let him into her bed. But he was done with begging and done with the past. He needed her to make a choice. Why couldn't they simply start fresh, pretend they were strangers just interested in a quick fuck with no strings attached?

A dog barked as he came close to someone's back fence, and he almost jumped. His admiration for Ally grew. The thought of her struggling to deal with drugs and alcohol without much support made him wish he'd been there for her. But he knew from talking to Jackson that choosing to get clean was something that had to come from within.

Had his behavior contributed to her issues? Perhaps he'd been too intent on making her into what he wanted her to be. He'd thrived on her adoration and her desire for him. Hell, any teenage guy would've been the same.

"Rob!"

Rob looked up from his contemplation of the fence to find Jane Evans smiling at him. He'd forgotten she lived in this neighborhood. "Hey, Jane, how are you doing?"

"I'm just fine, Rob. What are you doing out and about this fine evening?"

"Just checking up on the development. We've had some reports of graffiti and broken glass."

Jane patted his arm. "That would be at the Kendal house. Poor Ally has such a lot to put up with."

Rob looked her over. "You're okay with Ally being back?"

She squeezed his bicep. "Of course."

"You don't bear a grudge for what happened to Susan?"

"Oh, Susan." Jane shrugged. "I've already told you I think she was stupid. I would never have allowed myself to get into such a state over a guy, especially over Jackson." Her smile was inviting. "I'm glad Ally left town and left you behind."

Rob gently disengaged her hand from his arm. He'd been out with Jane a couple of times and found her good company, but he hadn't taken her to bed. Sunny do-gooders were never really his type, and she was supersunny today.

"Well, good to see you, Jane." He nodded and started walking toward his patrol car. She followed him, which he noted was back the way she'd come.

"There's a new movie opening in Grandstown tonight. Do you want to go?"

He fitted his key in the lock and opened the car door. "I can't tonight. I'm working, but thanks for the offer."

She smiled. "No worries, I'll catch you another day. See you around."

He started the engine and watched her walk away, her soft floral skirt swinging over her nicely rounded ass, her long dark hair blowing in the breeze. There was no doubt she was easy on the eyes and she never took offense when he said he had to work, which, in his profession, was a good thing. He never felt pressured by her either; they had a good time, they both went home, and that was the end of it.

Rob sighed and looked over his shoulder before pulling away from the curb and heading back to town. Pity he couldn't fall in love with Jane, when she'd make it so easy for him. Ally really had a lot to answer for. He smiled. She'd obviously made prickly and defensive his thing.

6

Ally wiped her hands on the back of her jeans and walked through the open door at the rear of the diner. She coughed as the stench of cooking oil competed with the smell of cleaning products and caught at the back of her throat. Everyone in the small space appeared to be busy, so she waited for someone, anyone, to acknowledge her.

After a while, one of the two guys looked up, and she smiled at him. "Is the boss here?"

He nodded and pointed to the rear of the space. "She's back there in the office."

"Thanks." Ally squeezed past him and headed toward the rear of the kitchen where a tiny office had been created out of one corner of the rectangular space. The door was half open, but she knocked on it anyway.

"Yes?"

Ally froze as an all-too-familiar figure swung around to stare at her. "Hey . . . Lauren. How are you?"

Lauren sniffed. "What do you want?"

Ally wanted to turn around and run for the hills, but that

wasn't possible, and besides, she was tired of running. Time to face up to another of the people she'd hurt. "I came about the job."

Lauren raised her eyebrows, her expression very reminiscent of Rob's. "You want *me* to give you a job? Why the hell should I give you anything?"

Ally let out a long, slow breath. "You shouldn't and I'm sure you won't, but seeing as I'm desperate, I'm still asking."

"You're desperate for a job? Why don't you go and 'model' or something?"

"Because I'm too old?"

"That's hardly my problem, is it?"

Ally leaned against the door frame and jammed her shaking hands into her pockets. "You asked why I needed a job, and I just told you."

"I want someone to bus tables. I'm sure you wouldn't want to soil your beautiful hands with that."

"I've done it before. It's hard work, but I promise I'll be reliable."

Lauren stood up, her brown eyes fixed on Ally. "I bet you wouldn't last a week."

Ally held her gaze. "How about you give me a try? If I don't make it, you get to keep all my wages."

Lauren stared at her for a long while. "Okay, then."

Ally straightened up. "When do you want me to start, and how many hours will you need me?"

"Don't get ahead of yourself. I'll give you your ongoing schedule tomorrow when you start, but expect to be getting here early and leaving late."

"I wouldn't expect anything else," Ally murmured, and Lauren's head came up.

"I don't need any attitude from you, Ally Kendal. I'm only doing this so I can enjoy watching you fail." Lauren rummaged in her desk. "Fill out this paperwork, and bring it back with you tomorrow before you start your first shift."

"No problem. What time do you want me here?"

"Five-thirty a.m. sharp. Don't be late."

Ally folded the papers in her hand and turned to leave. "Thanks, Lauren. I really appreciate it."

"Don't try and be nice to me now, Ally. You've done too much damage in this town to ever change my opinion of you."

The venom in Lauren's voice made Ally feel sad, but she forced herself to turn around. "You have every right to hate me, Lauren. I know 'sorry' isn't going to cut it, but it's all I can offer you. I behaved appallingly and hurt a lot of people—you included."

Lauren sat back down and swiveled her chair around to face her computer screen. "I'm not interested in your attempts to make me feel sorry for you. Just turn up, do your job, and leave. Okay?"

Ally went then, fighting an urge to defend herself. She and Lauren had once been so close that even Rob had been jealous. And that was all gone now, destroyed by her desertion and inability to face her own demons. She'd do what Lauren wanted, though. Keep to herself, do her work, save her money, and get out of town.

The guy who'd shown her where the office was looked up as she went by him. She was at least six inches taller than him. "Did you find her okay?"

"Well I *found* her." Ally forced a smile. "Thanks for the help."

"Sure." He wiped his hands on his apron and regarded her speculatively. "I'm Mike, one of the grill cooks, but everyone calls me Fig."

"It's nice to meet you, Fig."

He followed her to the door, his bright smile undimmed. "Have you just moved here? You look familiar somehow."

"I have to go. I'm sorry I can't stay and chat." Ally kept moving. She got that a lot, especially from men who seemed to have the image of her writhing around in her underwear from the billboard ads seared on their collective consciousness. "I'll be working here, bussing tables, so you'll get to talk to me again, I promise."

His smile blossomed into a grin. "For real? That's cool. I'll see you tomorrow, then."

Ally escaped down the street and headed for the library only to realize it was far too early for it to be open. She slowed her walk and gazed at the upcoming façade of the Easy Breezy Coffee Shop. Did she have enough for a cup of coffee? She sure needed one, and it would make the wait for the library to open go quicker. She fingered the coins in her pocket and guessed she had at least two dollars.

She pushed open the door and was enveloped in a welcoming cloud of smoky roasting coffee with just a hint of burned chocolate. The smell was so heavenly she breathed it in and smiled. A quick check of the board and a more detailed inspection of her coins indicated she had just enough for a regular coffee plus tax.

The shop was crowded, and she joined the back of the line, her height making it easy to count the six people in front of her. While she waited, she scanned the odd collection of notices pinned to the crooked board, which advertised everything from organic produce to lost puppies to poetry recitals. She even spied something about AA meetings that she'd have to check back on. Spring Falls had always had a great sense of community spirit, and it seemed nothing had changed.

As Ally's gaze drifted back along the cluster of tables, she realized that she'd become the focus of some attention. She caught her name being whispered, and several pairs of eyes swung in her direction. With all the grace she could muster, she willed herself to look forward and ignore her growing sense of unease.

Why did it take so long to order coffee these days? Why did

everyone have to have these crazy-ass complicated specials? At last she hit the front of the line and smiled at the woman behind the counter, who thankfully she'd never met. The woman had the name NADIA embroidered on the top of her blue apron and appeared to be in her late forties.

"Hi, I'd like a small coffee, please."

"Just coffee?"

"Yes, please."

Ally dug out her small pile of coins, handed them over, and waited for the woman to get her coffee. "Thanks."

"You're welcome."

Ally turned and headed for the station where the milk and sugar were provided. She was just about to reach for the milk when someone collided with her, spilling the hot coffee all over her hand and down her leg.

With a hiss of pain, Ally dropped the half-empty cup on the table and grabbed a handful of napkins to blot the worst of it away. She thanked God she was wearing jeans.

"Oh, sorry, I didn't see you there."

Ally looked up into the sneering face of Pauline Jones, one of her old classmates. "Yeah, right."

"Are you suggesting it was deliberate? What are you going to do? Call the cops on me?"

Ally tipped cold water out of a jug onto a bunch of paper napkins and placed them on the heated flesh of her hand.

Pauline tittered. "Oh, no, you won't do that, will you, because Rob Ward's not exactly going to help you out, is he?"

Ally ignored Pauline and concentrated on soothing the raging pain in her hand. Somehow it was easier to deal with that rather than facing yet another confrontation. She was still shaking from her encounter with Lauren. Vaguely, Ally wondered if the woman behind the counter had some ice and whether she'd let her have any.

She jumped when a familiar voice behind her said, "Here

you go, Ms. Kendal." A jiffy bag full of ice appeared over her shoulder, and she pressed it against her throbbing skin.

Rob kept his hand on her arm as he spoke to Pauline. "Now, what were you saying, Ms. Jones? Are you admitting that you deliberately dumped coffee on Ms. Kendal, because whatever you think of me, if you've committed a crime, I'll do my duty whoever the victim is."

Ally swallowed hard. "It's all right, Sheriff. I'm sure it was an accident."

Pauline made a rude noise and turned on her heel. She left the coffee shop, followed by two other women who looked vaguely familiar. Rob took Ally's elbow and maneuvered her into the chair Pauline had vacated.

"Are you all right, Ms. Kendal? Do you want me to call an ambulance for you?"

"Please don't. I don't have health insurance, but thanks for the thought." She resettled the bag of ice over her hand. "I'm sure I'll be fine in a moment."

Rob hesitated beside her and then turned back into the crowd. Ally didn't watch him go; she just concentrated on mastering the pain in her hand and the sickness Pauline's openly confrontational attitude had started. She'd been a fool to come back here. A fool.

"Ms. Kendal?"

She looked up to find the woman who'd served her the coffee offering her a fresh bag of ice. "Thanks," Ally said. "I'm sorry about the mess."

"That's not a problem." Nadia indicated Ally's hand. "Are you all right?"

"I'm sure I'll be fine. It just caught the back of my hand, so not much damage done."

Nadia reached forward and patted her shoulder. "Now you just sit there and make sure you feel all better. I'll get you another cup of coffee."

Ally didn't argue. She was quite happy to wait for the shop to return to normal and for everyone to stop staring at her like she had risen from the dead or something. Rob took the seat opposite and pushed a paper bag over to her.

"Here. Eat something."

Ally peered inside the bag and saw a chunky blueberry muffin topped with sugar crystals. Her mouth watered at the sight, and she ripped open the bag and slowly peeled back the paper case.

"Let me help." Rob reached across and broke the muffin in half, right through the middle, and handed her the bottom part. "I know how you like it."

"I always eat the boring part first."

He smiled. "And save the best until last."

"Unless you got to it first."

"I never did get that 'saving it' thing."

His voice had a soothing quality that helped Ally relax a little. "I'd forgotten about Pauline. I can't believe she's still hanging around with the same two losers from high school."

"I guess some folks find it hard to grow up."

"Obviously." Ally lifted her chin at him. "I guess you think I should leave before it gets nasty, right?"

"I don't want to see you get hurt."

She met his gaze and found it impossible to guess what he was thinking. Had she done that to him? Had she stripped the sweetness away and left him too emotionally detached to risk another relationship? Or was it just a cop thing? Jill would tell her not to exaggerate her importance in his life, but then Jill had never known Rob.

"But I can't leave, Rob. I created most of my own problems, and I'm just going to have to deal with them."

"Even if you get treated like that?"

"Yeah, even then. Sometimes you just have to suck it up and

move on. I *chose* to come back here, and I knew it would be hard."

"I know all about getting on with life, Ally."

She bit her lip. "I suppose you do."

He shifted in his seat. "What are you going to do when you sell the house? Go back to New York and model?"

"Nope." She ventured a tentative smile. "I'm planning on going to college."

"Yeah?" He looked genuinely interested. "To do what?"

She shrugged. "To train to be a teacher. I've been helping out with the kids at the YMCA for the last couple of years, and I think that's what I want to do."

"You always wanted to be a teacher."

"You remembered." She met his gaze. "And you always wanted to be a cop."

His smile made her smile in return, and she couldn't look away from his approving gaze. Remembering her plans for the future always made her feel better about herself. Hell, having plans that didn't involve finding her next fix were amazing. She suddenly felt a lot more hopeful.

Nadia returned with two large coffees and put them in front of Ally and Rob.

"She okay, Rob?"

Rob looked across at Ally for confirmation, and she nodded. "She's fine, Nadia. Thanks for not making a fuss."

Nadia snorted. "I saw what happened. That Pauline deliberately knocked your lady's elbow."

Ally was too shaken to refute the notion that she was Rob's lady and was way too grateful for the other woman's kindness. "Thanks for the fresh coffee."

"Well, I could hardly expect you to lick it off the floor, now, could I?" Nadia winked at her and returned behind the counter.

"She's nice," Ally said as she took another bite of the sweet, tart muffin.

"Yeah, she and her husband, Chen Li, bought the place about a year ago. He roasts all his own coffee beans, and she makes all the baked goods."

"Mmm..." Ally murmured, and licked the crumbs from her lips. Rob's gaze fastened on her mouth, and she went still. He got to his feet and picked up his coffee.

"Well, I'd better be getting back. Jackson will be expecting me."

"Don't you take him coffee too?"

"Nope, I usually take him a muffin, but I'm sure he won't begrudge it to you."

"Oh." Ally felt her cheeks burn. "I'd give you the money for it, but..."

"It's okay." He smiled at her, and she felt it like a punch in the heart. "He's getting fat anyway. I'll see you around."

Ally watched him leave, realizing he'd probably done more for her reputation in the five minutes he'd sat with her than she'd accomplished in a month. She continued to sip at her coffee, mainly to dispel the gathering lump in her throat. She didn't want Rob being nice to her. She wanted him cold and distant so that she could keep *her* distance and just fuck him. But it seemed he wasn't going to allow her that luxury. She knew him well enough to know he'd just keep bugging her until she gave in.

Ally finished her coffee, waved good-bye to Nadia, and walked across to the library, which was now open. Another familiar face greeted her at the main desk.

"Well, well, well, who do we have here?"

"Hi, Mrs. Orchard. How are you doing?"

The white-haired old lady who'd managed the library since before Ally was born smiled. "Much better for seeing you, my dear. Did you want to renew your library card? Everything's on computer now and much more accessible."

Ally breathed in the familiar scent of paper and wax polish and immediately felt at home. She'd spent a lot of time hiding out from her mother at the library. As long as she kept quiet and was working on something, Mrs. Orchard had always let her stay.

"That would be great."

Mrs. Orchard beckoned her over to an unoccupied computer screen and keyboard. "You can fill in the application online, and I'll confirm it right now. You can pick up to fifteen items now, including audio books, magazines, interlibrary loans—"

Ally smiled. "That all sounds wonderful. Actually, I'm looking for a general guide to car maintenance and a handyman repair book."

"I'll go take a look while you fill in that form." Mrs. Orchard frowned. "Your mother let that house get into a terrible state."

"I know." Ally concentrated on the screen and hoped the librarian wouldn't say anything else. She heard Mrs. Orchard sigh and then the clack of her heels on the polished parquet floor. Truth to tell, the noisiest thing in the library had always been Mrs. Orchard's heels, but no one had ever had the guts to tell her.

By the time Mrs. Orchard returned with a stack of books, Ally was almost a fully authenticated library patron. She spent a few moments looking through the books and settled on the two that seemed the simplest.

Mrs. Orchard was behind the desk again, helping a young guy who wanted to know if they had manga books. Apparently they did, and she sent him off to a dark corner already inhabited by two other guys dressed in black whom he seemed to know. Ally placed the books on the counter.

"I'll take these two, please."

"When your proper card comes through, you can check out yourself these days."

"That's cool."

Mrs. Orchard sniffed. "I'm not sure about that. I always enjoyed seeing what folks were reading. You'd be surprised." She readjusted her wire-framed glasses. "Your mother, for example, liked to take out self-help books and romance novels."

"That's an interesting combination." Ally took the books and put them in her backpack. "Two things my mom never managed to master in her life." Wow, she sounded bitter.

Mrs. Orchard frowned at her. "Your mother had her problems, Ally, but she was trying to sort them out. She'd kicked the drugs, you know, and she volunteered at the charity shop every week."

Ally struggled to pick up the backpack and keep her face blank. She didn't want to talk about Ruth. She really didn't. There was nothing to say—nothing of any use anyway. She'd run out of excuses and sympathy for the woman years ago.

"Well, it was nice to see you again, Mrs. Orchard," Ally said brightly. "I'll probably be back in a few days."

"I'm sure you will, but remember, you can renew your books online now. That's what your mother used to do."

With a parting wave, Ally left the library and headed for home. Her steps slowed as she considered what Mrs. Orchard had said. Did her mom really have a computer buried under all that crap in the house? She supposed it was possible. It was more likely that her mom had pawned it for drugs or something, but she really should go and look.

As she walked, she thought about Rob and how he'd stood up for her in the coffee shop. A wave of longing coalesced in the pit of her stomach. She wanted him so badly, wanted to let him take care of her, and she knew that he'd get it right too. But it would be on her terms this time. She wasn't weak. She had plans. She was *making* the choice.

Her battered truck came into view in her driveway, and she fished her key out of her jeans pocket. Tomorrow was the start of her new job, so tonight was hers and she intended to grab the moment.

7

Ally fitted the key to the back door of Rob's ranch house and stepped inside. The range hood light was on, and the scent of pizza and coffee lingered in the air. She half expected to see Rob's mom cooking or Lauren sitting at the table watching TV and arguing with Rob. His parents had retired to Florida, but did Lauren still live there? Ally paused for a horrified moment. Surely Rob wouldn't have invited her over if that was true.

The hum of the TV and a faint glow of light illuminated the hallway that led to the family room and the three bedrooms beyond. Ally slid the key back into her pocket and bit her lip as she contemplated her next move. Rob's truck was in the driveway, so she was pretty sure he was home. It was time to make a choice and live how she wanted to, even if only for a short while.

She took off her flip-flops and walked barefoot on the warm cherrywood floorboards. She saw the back of Rob's head first. He was lying on the couch watching some baseball game. He didn't turn around as she approached, but she sensed he knew she was there. She came around the edge of the couch and deliberately dropped her gaze to the floor. With shaking fingers, she unbuttoned her thin pink blouse and took it off, then shimmied out of her jeans.

"Leave your bra and panties on."

She still didn't look at him as she sank to her knees and locked her hands in the small of her back.

He reached out and caressed her cheek. "Yeah. That's better. Move closer."

She shuffled awkwardly toward him until she knelt between his spread jean-covered knees. She held her breath as he cupped her breasts in his hands, his thumbs unerringly locating her nipples. She kept her gaze on his big hands as he plucked at her nipples with fingers and thumbs, drawing them into hard, aching points. He kept it up until the pleasure became edged with an intense throbbing, and she leaned into his touch.

"Take your bra off."

She fumbled with the catch and caught her breath as the thin lace brushed against her hard nipples. He stared at her small breasts for so long that she almost wished to cover herself up again. His thumb circled her areola, and she fought back a whimper as he lowered his head.

Her breast was small enough that he could draw almost all of it into his mouth. He sucked hard, forcing her already-tender nipple up to the roof of his mouth before concentrating all his attention on it. She wanted to moan, wanted him to stop, and wanted him to keep adding to the sensations that were surrounding her until she came apart in his arms.

The ache deepened until it felt like a red-hot wire connected her nipple to her sex. His teeth closed over her flesh, and she gasped his name. He immediately released her nipple and sat back, not touching her, leaving her shaking with need and already missing the hot suction of his mouth.

"Are you wet for me, Ally?"

She nodded but kept her gaze fixed on his hands, which now lay on his lap, framing the impressive bulge of his cock. She stiffened as he unbuckled his belt and drew it out of its loops. He folded it in his hand and rubbed the leather against her breasts. She couldn't help the hitch in her breathing and he noticed it too.

"You took your time making up your mind, Ally."

"Yes."

"Yes, what?" She dared to look up at him, and his gaze was cool. "You can call me sir, or Officer, or master—I'll let you choose."

"I thought you weren't into those kinds of power games."

"It's not a game. I just want to hear you say it."

She studied him for a long minute as she frantically considered her options.

"Ally..."

"Yes, *sir.*" She dropped her gaze and fixed her attention on the leather belt.

"I don't like being kept waiting."

Ally said nothing, and he let the belt hang free; then he slapped it gently against the side of his thigh and let it flick out over her, catching her hip bone, her thigh, the front of her panties. The soft slap of the supple leather made her feel centered inside. She closed her eyes to savor it, only to open them again when the belt flicked more aggressively against her skin.

"Turn around and lean over the coffee table."

"What are you going to do to me?"

"I'm going to paddle your ass. What do you think?" He gently cupped her chin and made her look at him. "I thought by coming here you'd accepted the rules."

"What rules?"

"My rules. Now do it."

Ally swallowed convulsively and did what he said, using her arms to pillow her head against the coldness of the glass tabletop. She shivered as she felt him pull down her panties.

"I'm not telling you how many strokes you're going to get,

because I don't want you thinking there's an end to what I choose to do to you."

Ally didn't say anything. Her body was already anticipating the first real touch of the leather on her skin. They'd played this game before, and he knew it turned her on. It had been so long since she'd allowed anyone to touch her like this, far too long. His first stroke was more of a caress than a slap, and she found herself arching her back into the blow.

Rob muttered something that sounded like a curse and kept going. After the sixth stroke, she forgot to count, her mind too taken up with finding that perfect peace inside her, the place where the pain and the pleasure melded together to make her feel safe. She sighed and let go, left it up to Rob to judge when he should stop.

She shuddered when his hands grabbed her hips, lifted her up, and swung her around, pressing her against the front of his jeans, her panties soaking now as she tried to impale herself on the throbbing bulge of his covered cock. His mouth descended over hers, and he kissed her voraciously, his tongue going deep, his hands deliberately fondling her sensitive ass, forcing new sensations through her and adding to the pleasure.

"Do you want me to fuck you now?"

Ally moaned into his mouth. He wrapped his hand in her hair and tilted her head back until he could see her face. "Yes, oh God, yes."

He kissed her again, his hands cupping her ass and rubbing her against the rough fabric of his jeans. "I want to give you more than just a good fuck. Would you like more?"

Ally tried to steady her breathing. "What?"

"I want you to have both of us. Me and Jackson."

"He's here?" Ally whispered.

"Yeah, we share the house." He bent his head and nuzzled her nipple, making her even wetter. "See, while you're busy making amends to me, I'm going to be busy making amends to you and Jackson."

Ally licked her lips. "I've never had two men at the same time. I'm not sure..." She gasped as Rob lifted her off him and set her on the couch. He folded his arms across his chest and simply looked at her.

"Your choice, Ally."

"But your rules."

"Yeah."

"And what if I just want you and not Jackson?"

Rob tensed as he sensed another presence behind him and heard Jackson's soft voice.

"Am I interrupting?"

Rob wrenched his gaze from Ally to find Jackson leaning against the door frame, his interested gaze fixed on the couch.

"I was wondering where you were." Rob nodded toward Ally. "She's thinking about it."

"Thinking about what?"

"Whether she wants to fuck us both."

"What?"

Rob stared at his best friend. "I was just explaining that it seemed like the perfect way for me to make amends."

"For *you* to make amends? From what I just heard, Ally doesn't want to fuck me." Jackson held up his hands. "And that's okay. It's *her* choice, so why don't you just go ahead and enjoy yourselves, and I'll go to bed."

"Jackson," Ally said.

Jackson turned slowly to stare at Ally. "It's okay—you don't have to explain. I know what an idiot Rob is."

Ally held out her hand. "I don't want you to go."

He came closer to the couch, and Rob saw him swallow hard as he gazed at Ally's naked body. "You're okay with this?"

Rob held his breath as Ally looked up.

She met his gaze first. "Yeah."

Rob wanted to punch his fist in the air and yell in triumph. He hid his relief behind his cocky manner. "See? Ally's fine with it. You're the one causing problems here."

Jackson ignored him and knelt down on the rug beside Ally. "Are you sure?"

She smiled at Jackson and touched his cheek. "I am, but only if you want it too."

Jackson kissed her bare toes. "Ally, I want to fuck you more than I want to breathe."

As he watched Jackson with Ally, something eased in Rob's chest. This was the right thing for all of them. He knew it in his very soul. He reached over, picked Ally up, and deposited her on his lap again. She moaned as her ass met his thighs, and grabbed on to his shoulders. He waited until she met his gaze.

"I want you to suck Jackson's cock."

There was still a hint of uncertainty in her eyes, and Rob kept on looking at her. Did she want him to order her to do it? Some part of him wanted to do just that, but it was never that simple. She had to make the choice, and this was definitely not the time to start barking orders. He had to make sure she wanted it by applying just enough pressure to allow her to back off if she wanted to. He asked her again.

"Do you want to suck him?"

She nodded, and Rob was aware of Jackson letting out his breath behind him. He motioned Jackson closer.

"Fuck her mouth."

Jackson unbuttoned his fly and shoved down his black jeans. Rob slid his hand into Ally's hair and angled her head around. "Do it." She didn't argue with him anymore as he guided her toward Jackson. "Take him deep, honey. Make him come down your throat."

Rob watched Ally take Jackson's shaft into her mouth and nearly groaned at the erotic image. Somehow it felt right to see Jackson there, the three of them together, fucking. His own cock throbbed so hard he thought he might come in his jeans. He had to be inside her, had to have her right now. He fumbled in his pocket for a condom and made some space on his lap to unbutton his fly.

"I'm going to fuck you, too, Ally, so don't bite him while I get inside you."

With a savage sound, Rob grabbed her hips and brought her down over him, groaning as he was encased in her tight, wet sheath. Still holding her hips, he guided her into the rhythm Jackson was setting with his cock and tried not to close his eyes. Slick heat enveloped his thrusting shaft. He could see Jackson, his expression focused, his dark eyes narrowed as he fucked Ally's mouth like a sledgehammer.

Rob's come gathered in his balls and he grabbed Jackson's arm. "Come with me."

Jackson groaned and shoved his hips forward one more time. Rob did the same and climaxed deep inside Ally, his vision turning red as his come pumped out of him in thick, long waves. She came, too, and he wanted to groan as the pressure on his sensitive cock increased like a tightening fist.

Jackson moved away first, his hand lingering on Ally's hair in a slow caress. He collapsed onto the coach next to Rob, who took the opportunity to kiss Ally. He tasted Jackson on her and didn't care anymore.

Ally was breathing hard, her long legs wrapped around him, her breasts resting against his chest. God it felt so right to have her like this, naked, her nipples hard from his sucking. His cock stirred inside her, and he slid a hand into her hair.

"This is what I should've done the last time. Joined you two in that bed and not cared about what anyone thought."

"What?" Ally struggled to sit up and stared at him.

Rob shrugged. "I'm just saying."

Jackson chuckled. "He does have a point, Ally."

"As if he would've done that," Ally muttered.

"Hell. Part of me wanted to, even then, but I'd already scared you enough without adding Jackson to the mix." Rob lifted her off his cock. "And maybe we all needed to grow up a bit to realize what we really wanted."

Ally tried to move away from him, but Rob caught her hand. "You needed to get out there and do your thing, and Jackson and I needed to do ours."

"You make it sound so easy."

"I'm sure it wasn't." Rob studied both their faces. "But maybe that was because you were both after the wrong things."

Jackson's smile died. "Meaning we should both have been after you? Like who made you Dr. Phil tonight?"

"I've been thinking about this a lot, that's all." Ally tried to pull out of his grasp again, and he held her still. "You already made your choice, honey. Now quit fighting me."

"I made a choice about the kind of sex I want, not to be psychoanalyzed by a cop!"

He held her gaze. "The kind of sex you *need*, honey." She dropped her eyes, and he squeezed her hand. "The kind of sex where I tell you what to do, and you do it."

Jackson shifted uneasily. "Rob..."

Rob glanced at Ally. "Shall I tell Jackson what I think? Then you can tell him if I'm right. Ally thought she wanted every guy in the world to want her—that's why she chose modeling and that's why it nearly destroyed her."

Jackson touched Ally's shoulder. "Models get hit on all the time. It doesn't have to destroy them."

Rob kept talking. "But what she realized was that those guys wanted her image, not her. They wanted to project their sexual fantasies onto her and not allow her to have her own needs and desires."

"Stop talking about me as if I'm not here!" Ally climbed off Rob's lap and started to gather up her clothes. "You have no idea what my life was like, and you have no business trying to tell me how I thought or what I wanted from a man."

"You're only mad because I'm right," Rob replied.

"I'm mad because this is just typical of you!" She glared at him. "There's a reason why I never dated another man like you."

"Because you knew deep down that no one else could ever live up to the original?"

Her eyes flashed fire, and he braced himself for an attack.

"I dated men who were considerate of my feelings both in and out of bed."

"And yet here you are, back making amends with me."

She exhaled slowly and he tensed. "I liked modeling because I was *told* how to pose, how to do my hair and makeup, how to smile, and, most importantly, how to keep my mouth shut." She looked at him. "Who does that remind you of, Rob?"

"That's not fair, I never—"

She held up her hand. "If I'd stayed, you would've controlled me like that eventually. Maybe I just preferred to earn good money while I did what I was told."

Ally struggled into her clothes and headed for the door. Rob didn't stop her. He'd never tried to control her life like that, had he?

Rob glanced at Jackson, who had already risen from the couch and started after Ally. "You'll see her home, right?"

"Yeah, you bastard."

Rob shrugged. "She needed to hear it, and so did you."

"Your interpretation of the truth?" Jackson grabbed his keys. "Easy for you to say, Rob, when you sat here and did nothing while Ally and I made *choices.*"

The sarcasm in Jackson's voice made Rob wince, but he kept his expression bland until Jackson left the room. Rob disposed of the condom, slowly tucked his cock back into his jeans, and eased his zipper up. Some things had to be said whether Ally and Jackson liked it or not.

Ally's point about her modeling career had made him think, though. Had he really been that inflexible? He hated that Ally believed that of him. Guilt stirred in his gut. Despite what Jackson implied, he hadn't spent ten years doing nothing. He'd been working things through, admitting his responsibility for what had happened, and now he had a chance to set things right, and by God he was going to do it.

As she ran toward the back door, Ally pulled up her jeans and buttoned her blouse. She'd been a fool to come here. Even more of a fool to let both men fuck her. Even as she thought that, her body betrayed her with a shiver of delight. She felt better than she had in years, her mouth full of Jackson and her body holding Rob deep inside. . . .

With a quick glance into the deserted street, she started back home, glad for once that they lived quite close and that she knew the way blindfolded.

Would Rob now understand what modeling had meant to her and why it had eventually destroyed her? He'd looked shocked when she'd told him the truth.

Jackson caught up with her as she unlocked her back door.

"Are you okay?"

She let him into the house and dropped her keys on the table, not bothering to turn on the lights. His hands came down to rest on her shoulders, and he turned her into his embrace.

"Did I hurt you, Ally?"

She leaned into him, inhaling his familiar sandalwood scent. "No."

He kissed the top of her head. "I should've said no. I shouldn't have let Rob push you into sucking me off like that."

Ally brought her fingers up to cover his mouth. "No apologies necessary." She sighed. "Rob's right. I wanted you both. I think I always have."

Under her fingers, he smiled and his tongue flicked over her flesh. "Good to know, because, damn, I wanted your mouth on me. I think I always have too."

She took her hand away, and he bent his head to kiss her, his mouth warm and comforting. Ally clung to him, felt her nipples harden against his chest and his quick physical response.

"Ally..."

She slid her hand down between them and cupped his balls, heard him groan as she ran her thumb up the hard ridge of his already-erect cock. His hips rocked, pushing him harder against her palm.

"I want..."

She opened his jeans and slid her hand inside to grip his hard, wet shaft, felt her own body soften with welcome. "He's right, damn him, Jackson. No one else did it for me. I came back because I missed you both so much."

Jackson picked her up and backed her against the wall, shoved down her jeans, and impaled her on his hard length. She gasped as he began to pump into her, her heels digging into his ass. He kept up the fast tempo even as she climaxed, didn't stop until he'd driven her through two more orgasms, each one more intense. Ally clung to him as he continued to fuck her. One of his hands worked its way between them, and he fingered her already swollen clit.

"Come for me, Ally."

She screamed into his mouth as he pinched her clit, and he finally emptied himself inside her in big shuddering waves. When she finally got her breath back, he was on the move again, carrying her down the hallway and laying her on the bed.

He knelt beside the bed and kissed her clit, licking at the wetness pouring out of her. "Good night, Ally."

Ally tried to sit up. "Jackson, you don't hate me, do you?"

His smile was slow and beautiful. "How the hell could I hate you? We'll work it out. You, me, and Rob. Don't you worry yourself."

Ally sank back down into her pillows and watched him leave. Would he tell Rob they'd had sex? And what would Rob do about that? She glanced at her clock and groaned. It was already midnight, and she had to get up for work at five. With the ease of long practice, she shoved all her worries about Rob to the back of her mind and willed herself to sleep.

* * *

Jackson took his time walking back to Rob's house, his body still dealing with the mind-blowing aftereffects of fucking Ally, his mind even less willing to deal with anything at all. God, the feel of her in his arms, the way he'd pushed her over the edge, taken her so hard against the wall that she should've been complaining. But she hadn't, had she? She'd taken it all and come for him several times.

His cock stirred at the thought of it, and he smoothed a hand over his groin. What a way to break his self-imposed celibacy. He let himself in the back door and walked through to the family room where Rob still sat on the couch.

"Ally's home safe."

Rob looked over the back of the couch at him, his blue eyes narrowed. "You took your time."

Jackson managed a shrug. "What do you want me to say?"

"How about you tell me that you fucked her?"

"Yeah, I did."

Rob's answer was slow to come. "Good for you."

"Really?"

"Look, we've had all this out before." He hesitated. "It fucking hurt when I found you and Ally together, but I thought we'd talked it through and gotten over it."

"You sure about that?"

"Yeah." Rob held his gaze, and then he nodded. "Yeah, I'm sure. It's what I said. This is a way for me to make it up to both of you for being such a dickhead back then."

Jackson leaned against the door frame. "What exactly made Ally come 'round here tonight?"

"To the idea of fucking us both?"

"No, just 'round here."

"She wanted to make amends for what happened back then."

"And, what, you insisted she had to pay you back with sex?"

"Something like that." Rob must have seen the skepticism on Jackson's face. "It's only sex, Jackson. That's all she offered."

Jackson shook his head. "For such a smart guy, you can be such a dumbass sometimes."

Rob started to get off the couch. "What the hell is that supposed to mean?"

"Don't blow it this time, buddy. Ally is way too special to lose."

Rob shoved a hand through his hair. "I know that." He hesitated. "It was the only way I could think of to get close to her again. The only way she'd let me."

Jackson eyed his best friend and silently agreed with him. "I'm going to bed. I start at six."

"Ally's starting a new job tomorrow as well."

"Doing what?"

"Working at the diner."

"For *Lauren?*"

"It was the best I could do. It was your idea!"

"That's like throwing a Christian to the lions."

"Ally will cope."

"I sure hope so."

Rob stretched his arms over his head. "I had to find a way to keep Ally in town."

"Because of the case or because of the sex?"

Rob's hard gaze met his. "Quit hounding me, okay?"

"Sure. Night, Rob." Jackson pulled off his T-shirt and went into his bedroom. He could do with a shower, but he was reluctant to lose Ally's scent from his skin. With a groan, he pulled off his jeans and stroked his growing shaft. The scent of sex curled around him, and he decided on the shower.

It wasn't until he was standing under the hot water that it occurred to him that he hadn't worn a condom. . . .

8

Damn, she was tired. Ally wiped her forehead and concentrated on stacking the pile of dirty glasses on the tray. It was quieter in the diner now, the breakfast rush over and the lunch crowd not yet in sight. With a sigh, Ally hefted the tray and headed back to the kitchen, using her shoulder to push through the swinging door.

She took the glasses and plates off the tray and started to load them into the middle of the three sinks. Mal, the dishwasher, wasn't at his post, so she contemplated washing the dishes herself.

"Ally? There are five tables to clean out here!" Lauren yelled.

Fig, the fry cook, gave her a sympathetic grin as she gathered up a clean wet cloth and her cleaning stuff and went back out. "You're doing good, Ally. Boss is just in one of her snits."

Ally nodded and kept going. Lauren waited on the other side of the door, her expression impatient, her foot tapping. "Can't you go any faster? We need them all cleaned and reset before lunch."

Ally didn't bother to try and defend herself. She probably

was slow compared to Leon, the other busboy. She headed for the first of the tables and started loading things onto her tray.

Lauren followed her and Ally tensed. "Make sure you clean properly, and don't leave that there!"

Ally bit her lip and kept moving as fast as she could. Her feet hurt and her back was already killing her. She didn't dare glance up at the clock in case Lauren saw her.

"Boss?"

Lauren turned back to the kitchen door where Fig was waving at her. "What?"

"Someone on the phone for you."

Ally watched Lauren's retreat with a grateful sigh. Was Lauren going to be like this every day, literally on her back critiquing everything she did? It seemed likely. With a soft groan, Ally kept clearing up, wiping tables and stacking dirty plates. One thing she'd learned was that hard work never killed anyone. She had to think about all the money she was saving for college. And at least it stopped her thinking about other stuff she didn't want to deal with right now.

She took the full tray back to the kitchen and sorted out the stuff. Mal was back at his post cleaning dishes and putting the glassware in the small machine by the side of the end sink. Ally's phone beeped, and she surreptitiously drew it out of her pocket to check it.

"I hope you're not using your phone at work, Ally."

She looked up to see Lauren frowning at her. "Actually, my shift finished five minutes ago."

Lauren carried on as if she hadn't heard her. "I don't allow cell phones."

"I get that." Ally eased the cheap phone back into her pocket. "As I said, I've already finished for the morning. I'll be back at nine tonight to clean up, okay?"

Lauren stepped out of the way, her expression still sour, as if she was almost disappointed that Ally had lasted this long. "Don't be late."

"I won't be." Ally manufactured a smile and headed for the back door. Fig met her coming the other way. He handed her a small wrapped parcel. "Here's your lunch."

Ally glanced back at Lauren, but she was deep in conversation with one of the waitresses. "I don't think I get lunch."

Fig shrugged. "Take it with you. It's an egg muffin sandwich."

"Thanks, Fig." Ally clutched the paper bag in her hand. "That's really nice of you."

"No problem. See you tomorrow."

Ally nodded and walked out, the heat from the wrapped sandwich warming her hand, much as Fig's thoughtfulness warmed her heart. The waitresses hadn't been too friendly with her either. But then she hadn't expected them to be. Her name was mud in this town and that was that.

She opened the paper bag and bit into the soft egg, fighting a moan of pure greed. By this time she was almost home, so she slowed down to finish the sandwich and then tucked the paper into her pocket. She heard her name being called and looked up to see Jane waving at her and managed a smile. "Hey."

Jane strolled over, a small white dog peeking out of her big plaid purse. She wore a blue denim dress that reached midcalf and matched her eyes. "How are you doing, Ally?"

"Okay, I guess. How about you?"

"I'm fine." Jane fell into step beside Ally. "What were you doing in the diner?"

"I'm working there, just temporarily."

"Doing what?"

"Clearing tables, taking out the trash, the usual stuff." Though Ally tried to keep her voice light, she knew from Jane's shocked expression that she wasn't buying it. "Where are you working now?"

"I teach fourth grade at the elementary school. That's why I'm not exactly busy right now." Jane shuddered. "The thought of teaching summer school this year was too awful to contemplate."

"Actually, I'm going back to college in the fall to train to be a teacher. That's one of the reasons I'm working through the summer, so I can save up some money."

"You're going to be a teacher?" Jane smiled politely. "Well, good luck with that. I'm just about ready to retire, but the benefits are too good to lose."

"I'm sure it's very hard work," Ally said diplomatically. Jane wasn't the first teacher who had warned her off the career. Ally turned the corner onto her street and paused.

"Well, I have to get home now. I'm sure I'll see you again."

But Jane was already looking past her to the sight of Jackson's big black truck parked in Ally's driveway. "Is that Jackson in your drive?"

Ally pretended to squint. "I'm not sure. Is that his truck?"

"It sure is." Jane started walking again. "I wonder what he wants."

It seemed from Jane's fierce expression that although she had forgiven Rob, and even Ally, for what had happened to her sister Susan, she didn't feel the same way about Jackson.

Jackson straightened up as Jane and Ally approached him and wiped his hands on an old rag. His black hair glinted with blue lights in the fierce sun. "Hey."

"What are you doing here?" Jane demanded. "Don't you think Ally has enough to put up with without you bugging her?"

Over the top of Jane's head, Jackson met Ally's gaze. "I just came by to fix her truck light. I clipped it at the gas station the other evening."

Ally frowned. "I already said you didn't have to do that, Jackson."

Jackson shrugged, his muscles shifting under his black T-shirt. "It's no bother. Much cheaper than going through my insurance."

Jane swung around to stare at Ally. "Do you want me to call Rob and have him get rid of Jackson?"

"No, it's okay. I'm fine with it." Jane opened her mouth as if to argue and Ally continued. "But thanks for asking."

Jane patted her dog's head. "Someone has to look out for you." She directed a final glare at Jackson. "Now, you just finish up and leave Ally in peace, okay?"

Jackson nodded, his expression unmoved. "Yes, ma'am. It's already done anyway."

"Then you can leave," Jane stated.

A corner of Jackson's mouth kicked up. "I sure can. Later, Ally."

He got into his truck and backed out of the driveway, waved to Ally, and disappeared down the street. Jane watched him go.

"Well that's the end of that."

Ally shaded her eyes as the truck turned the corner. "I suppose he was only trying to be nice."

"Nice? That man isn't nice. He broke Susan's heart—probably killed her as well."

Startled, Ally stared at Jane. "You think Jackson killed Susan?"

Jane waved away the suggestion. "He might as well have. He messed up everything for you, Susan, *and* Rob, didn't he?"

"I hadn't really thought of it like that," Ally said carefully, uneasy at the underlying venom in Jane's tone. "As far as I remember, I was the one who caused all the problems."

"Huh, I always reckoned Jackson had a lot more to do with it than anyone thought. Who told Susan where to find you and him? That's what I've always wanted to know."

Ally took out her door key and edged past Jane. "Thanks again, Jane. I really have to get going."

With a shake of her head, Jane started smiling again. "No worries, Ally. See you 'round."

Ally closed and locked the front door and watched until Jane took herself down the street. It was common for someone who suffered a violent bereavement to fixate on the causes and place blame everywhere, even when it obviously wasn't due, and it seemed that poor Jackson was Jane's chosen target. From what she'd seen, Jackson had no more forgiven himself for what happened that night than Ally had.

Ally paused to open the door into what was supposed to be the dining room of the house. She'd wondered, too, how Susan and Rob had known exactly where to find her and Jackson on that fateful night.

She snapped on the light and blinked at the closely packed boxes. What on earth had been going through her mother's head the last few years of her life? Had she ever thrown anything away? If there *was* a computer in here, it would take a while to find it. Ally rubbed her cheek and felt the accumulated grime and grease from the diner kitchen.

With a shudder, she retreated down the hall to her bedroom and then to the shower. A wash, a short nap, and she might be able to face the dining room again. It would have to be cleared out at some point.

Jackson knocked on Rob's door and went in. "Hey, I fixed Ally's truck."

"She let you?"

Rob looked up from the report he was typing into the computer. Well, *typing* was perhaps too technical a word for the hunt-and-peck method he apparently favored.

Jackson straddled the chair in front of Rob's desk. "I didn't tell her I was going to do it, although she caught me just as I was finishing up."

Rob grinned. "And how did that go?"

"She had Jane Evans with her, so she couldn't really lose it, and Jane was pissed off with me anyway."

"She's always pissed off with you."

"I know. She flat out tells everyone who'll listen that I killed Susan."

Rob frowned. "She's never said that to me."

"Well she wouldn't, would she? Number one, she doesn't want to make it official because it's not true, and two, she's infatuated with you and she knows we're good friends."

"She's not infatuated. We share a good time occasionally, but there's no pressure."

"Jeez, Rob, are you really that clueless? In her mind, she's already got you measured up for your wedding tux."

Rob chose to ignore that. "Jane's always struck me as a level-headed woman. Maybe she really has forgiven Ally."

"Yeah, maybe because she's decided that it's all my fault."

"Do you want me to talk to her about it?"

"And say what? 'Jackson doesn't like it when you are mean to him'? That's gonna work."

"Then what do you want?"

Jackson studied Rob for a long moment. "I don't know. I'm not sure why Jane was hanging around Ally either."

"Why shouldn't she?"

"Because most people blame Ally and me for Susan's death, and you'd think Jane would be the first on that list."

"I don't blame you or Ally. I'm way more interested in what Ally's mom was up to."

"Really? I can't wait to hear you try and explain that to Ally. She might think you're looking up this old case to bring her down."

Rob snorted. "As if I'd do that."

"It sure would be a great revenge on us both, wouldn't it?"

Rob gave Jackson his full attention. "Just drop it, okay?"

"I'm not sure I can. I've just got this weird feeling that Ally coming back has changed everything."

"Because we're both fucking her?"

"Maybe that's it. Maybe I'm waiting for it all to go wrong again."

"That's because you've gotten used to not having anything good in your life. Why not just enjoy it?"

"Easy for you to say when you're just trying to get her on your side so that you can solve a forgotten case."

"That's bullshit." Rob's lazy smile disappeared. "Don't tell me what I'm doing."

Jackson opened the door. "I wouldn't dare. Trust me. It will all come back and bite you in the ass anyway."

Ally's cell phone beeped, and she checked the time. She couldn't believe she'd spent three hours trying to sort out the junk in the dining room. The place looked as packed as ever, and she was coughing and sneezing up dust like a coal miner. With a groan, she studied the space she had managed to clear. There was definitely a dining table under there and what she thought were six chairs. After that was anyone's guess.

The doorbell rang, and welcoming any excuse to move, she went to answer it. Jackson stood there, dressed in his tan uniform, his black hair tamed and still wet from the shower.

"Can I come in?"

"Sure." Ally stepped back to let him in and kept going toward the kitchen. "What can I do for you?"

Jackson paused at the open door of the dining room. "Jeez, you're cleaning in here now?"

"There's a rumor that my mother had a computer. I'm trying to find it."

Jackson edged into the small space she'd created. "Have you

checked the wall sockets for power cables? You might be able to work your way back to the computer."

Ally groaned. "Why didn't I think of that?"

He produced his heavy flashlight and turned it on. "This might help."

Ally gave a cry of triumph as she noticed the twin black cables arching away from the wall and up toward the table. "It must be here! Help me pile this stuff up onto the other end of the table."

With Jackson's help, Ally uncovered an old screen, a keyboard, and a square box. "I wonder if it still works?"

Jackson touched her shoulder. "I have to get to work." He hesitated as she turned toward him. "There's something I wanted to ask you."

"About what?" Ally's smile faded as she studied him.

"Last night. I didn't use a condom."

"And you're wondering if you've caught anything from me? It's a good point, seeing as I'm an ex-drug user."

"Ally . . . it's not that. I was wondering if you could get pregnant."

She swallowed hard. "It's okay. I'm on the pill."

He let out his breath. "That's good. I wouldn't want—"

"To start a family with someone like me."

He put his hand over her mouth. "Stop finishing my sentences and don't put yourself down. I just wanted to make sure you were okay and tell you that health-wise I'm clean." He bent to kiss her nose. "Now I really have to go."

Jackson retreated down the hallway and let himself out, leaving Ally leaning against the wall. He was so quiet and gentle with her—apart from when they had sex, where he seemed to want to dominate her. In many ways he was the opposite of Rob, but at the core they were more similar than people would believe.

Ally glanced at the old clock above the fireplace and calculated how long she had before she had to go back to work. Lauren had made sure to give her the most awkward shifts. No surprise there. Ally remembered the relieved expressions on the three waitresses' faces when Lauren had declared they wouldn't have to share their tips with Ally. Not that she'd expected to get tipped. Most front-of-house servers hated pooling tips let alone sharing them with the kitchen staff.

It was just that minimum wage wasn't going to take her very far in her efforts to clean up the house and save for college. But there was nothing she could do about that, and she'd definitely learned that patience was a virtue. A reluctant smile curved her lips. Sometimes it paid to look on the positive side. If she made enough money to get by *and* she got to have sex with Rob and Jackson for a little while longer, how could a girl complain?

9

"Hey, Ally."

Ally turned from her contemplation of the library shelves to find Rob blocking the light at the end of the passageway. He came forward, his wide shoulders taking up almost all the narrow space between the stacks of books.

"Hey, Sheriff."

He came even closer, and she felt his warm breath on her neck. "You're not at work?"

"I just finished. I've got to go back at nine tonight and clear up for an hour or so."

"Lauren said she'd hired you." He paused. "How's that working out for you?"

Ally sighed. "As well as you might expect." She wasn't stupid enough to complain to Rob about his own sister. "Lots of folks come in to gawk at me, so I suppose I'm providing some entertainment for the town."

"And we in law enforcement appreciate that. Keeps the criminals off the streets."

Ally found herself smiling, and Rob nuzzled her hair. "You smell nice."

"I can't imagine why."

"French fries and coffee, the way to a man's heart."

"You should mention it to Lauren—maybe she could sell it as a fragrance."

His chuckle made her feel warm for the first time in days. "My shift's over at eleven tonight. I'll be coming around to your place."

"I don't remember inviting you, and by then I'll be asleep."

"No, you won't." His teeth settled on her earlobe, and he bit down until she felt it. "You'll be too busy being fucked."

"Rob..."

His hand slid around her waist and eased up to her breast. "You've forgotten your decision already?"

"No, I'm just—"

He squeezed her nipple hard between his finger and thumb, and she started to tremble. "You're mine until you leave this town. Mine and Jackson's if you want to be precise." He licked her ear, his voice little more than a seductive whisper. "Here's what I'd like you to do for me. After you shower, stay naked and go lie on your bed. I want to see you touching yourself when I get there. I want to watch you make yourself come before I fuck you so hard you'll be screaming my name."

Ally licked her lips as his right hand cupped her sex.

"I bet you're wet now, aren't you? I'd like to stick my hand down your panties and find out, but I know that once I touched you, I'd want to be inside you." He kissed her again. "Will you do that for me tonight, honey? Touch yourself and think about me?"

Before she could answer him, his fingers slid into her pocket and his voice became all business. "I need your back door key. I'll get a couple of copies made for me and Jackson and bring it back with me tonight."

He stepped away from her, leaving her shaking with need. He calmly slid the key off the ring and handed her back the others. "I'll see you later, then, Ally."

She nodded as he left, aware she'd probably be doing exactly what he'd asked her to and that she wasn't even ashamed of the fact. She knew that for a lot of people who didn't share her particular sexual tastes, that meant she was allowing him to tell her what to do, but for her there was a world of difference. Choosing to submit had its own power. Even she understood that now.

Ally gritted her teeth and used the knife to try and lever the gum off the underside of the table. Lauren had left her all the most unpleasant jobs, including the bathrooms and the final indignity, gum cleanup. Ally sat back and flexed her fingers. Half an hour of sitting on her ass on the tiled floor was not the best way to end a night.

"Are you done?"

Ally looked up to find Lauren standing over her. She had her coat over her arm and looked as fresh as if she was just starting her day. "Almost."

Lauren sat down on the red leatherette booth seat opposite Ally. "I still don't get why you're doing this. Is it to make Rob feel sorry for you? Because it isn't going to work. He's over you. He's seeing Jane Evans."

"So I hear." Ally continued scraping and kept her back to Lauren.

"So why are you here?"

"I thought you didn't want to know anything about me, Lauren. You said I should do my job and shut up."

"Well, perhaps I do want to know." Lauren's voice was sharp.

"I'm here because I need the money."

"But you must've earned a fortune."

Ally smiled and briefly rested her forehead against the banded metal edge of the table. She was so tired of being noble, and maybe it would do Lauren good to hear the unvarnished truth. "Earned it and lost most of it."

"How?"

"Well, put it this way. After a while, I had no idea *where* my money was going, because I relied on other people to handle it for me. And then, if I hadn't started taking every drug known to man, I might not have had to turn myself in to a rehab program and break all my contracts."

"There's nothing left?"

"There's some, but I'm trying not to touch it because I'm saving to go back to college. The rest is tied up in litigation. And in the meantime, I have to eat."

"You're going to college?"

"Yeah. I'm going to be a teacher."

"You always wanted to do that."

"Yeah, I did."

There was silence as Ally carefully levered the last piece of gum free and let it drop into the bucket. She stood up and heard her knees crack. "Anything else you want to know?"

"Not really." Lauren stood, too, her gaze fully on Ally for the first time. "I still don't feel sorry for you." She gestured at the kitchen. "I need to lock up. Get your things."

Ally took the bucket through to the now-silent and pristine kitchen and emptied it in the trash. She took her time washing her hands and then went back to Lauren, who had remained standing by the booth.

"I'm ready."

Lauren walked to the front door and held it open for Ally, the bell jangling softly into the warm night air. Lauren set the alarm and then locked the door. Ally felt in her pocket for her keys and started toward the sidewalk. "Night, Lauren."

"Where's your truck?"

"I'm not using it right now."

"Why not?"

"I have to change my license or your brother's going to book me."

Lauren half smiled. "That's so typical of Rob. He even tried to give *me* a ticket once."

Ally started to smile back, but Lauren had already turned away. Her smile died and with it the warmth inside her. How long had it been since she'd had a girlfriend? During her modeling days, no one had really wanted to be "friends," and she'd gotten out of the habit of sharing stuff. Her only real friend was Jill, who had worked part-time at the modeling agency while she completed her degree and then offered to become Ally's AA sponsor.

Ally waited a moment to see that Lauren was safely in her car and then hurried toward the corner of the street. It was so mild she didn't need her sweater and she wasn't afraid of walking. Luckily, Spring Falls wasn't exactly a hotbed of debauchery, even after ten.

She was startled when Lauren pulled up alongside her and opened the window. "Get in, Ally."

"I'm fine to walk, Lauren. It's a beautiful night."

"Ally, get in."

Ally knew from long experience that there was no point arguing with Lauren when she used that tone, so she crossed behind the car and opened the passenger door.

After a minute, Lauren glanced her way. "Rob can be a real pain in the ass when he gets going."

"He sure can."

"I can see that might be a problem if you were dating him, but it still doesn't excuse what you did to him."

"You're right; it doesn't excuse what I did."

Lauren sniffed. "Just so long as we're clear on that."

In the three minutes it took to drive Ally home, Lauren didn't speak again. When she pulled up, Ally murmured her thanks and got out without Lauren even acknowledging her.

After a cautious look around, Ally took out her keys. At least there was no sign of Rob or his silver truck for Lauren to object to. She let herself into the house and took a long, slow breath. Time for a shower and then ... then Rob would be here. Her body quickened at the thought of him touching her, and she started to hurry.

Rob let himself in with the new key and laid Ally's old one on the kitchen table. The house was quiet, but he caught the steamy fragrance of the shower drifting in the air. He'd always liked lavender and so had Ally. He followed the faint light to Ally's bedroom, his cock already hard, his mouth dry.

She lay on the bed, one hand between her long legs, the other on her breast. Her dark hair was still wet and slicked back away from her angular face. As a kid, her nickname had been "Giraffe Girl" and she'd hated it. She wasn't classically beautiful, he knew that, but it didn't make any difference. She photographed like every guy's favorite wet dream. He licked his lips as her gaze turned toward him, and his cock jerked in response to the sleepy sexuality in her eyes.

He went and stood next to the bed so that he could watch her more closely. Her index finger was circling her swollen clit, 'round and 'round, up and down to the slick red wetness of her folds. He wanted to lean down and nuzzle her clit, use his teeth and tongue to make her even wetter, drive her even higher.

"What are you thinking about, Ally?"

She raised her eyes to his. "About you and Jackson, about how you make me feel."

"Yeah?" He sank down onto the side of the bed and listened to the sound of her moving fingers. "And what are we doing to you in your dreams?"

She pinched her nipple and a shudder ran through her body. "Fucking me, both of you."

He leaned forward and buried his face between her thighs,

took her fingers and her clit into his mouth, sucked around them, and then drew her deep until she squirmed. When he moved away, she was panting, her pupils wide, her gaze fixed on him. "And how many times have we fucked you?"

She briefly closed her eyes as if picturing the scene. "Many times. I'm sore but you won't let me stop until you are both satisfied."

"Until we run out of come because it's all over you?"

"Yes, God, yes."

Rob unzipped his jeans, climbed between her legs, and shoved himself deep. Her hand was trapped between their bodies over her clit. "Touch yourself while I fuck you. Do it," he ordered as he started to move. He felt her legs wrap around him, her hand grab on to his shoulder to anchor herself. And then he forgot about anything but pounding into her warmth, about the tightening of her sheath around his cock and the fierce need to come. Too quick too fast but she'd take him again; she'd have to. He climaxed and brought her with him, held himself deep as her body shuddered around his, and he released his come.

Rob rolled off her and knelt up to remove his clothes. Ally lay still as if waiting for him to tell her what to do next. He liked that. Liked it enough to make him want to give her what she needed. He slid a hand into his pocket and showed her what he'd brought with him. Her eyes widened and she licked her lips.

He shook his head. "You'll have to wait until I'm ready." He heard the faint slam of the back door. "Jackson needs to be here as well."

Jackson appeared in the doorway, his quick gaze moving between Rob and Ally and returning to linger on Ally's flushed skin.

"Did you bring the stuff, Jackson?"

"Sure." Jackson wore cargo shorts and a khaki T-shirt and

carried a duffel bag over his shoulder, which he placed on the bed. "Let me just wash up."

"And get naked," Rob called after him.

Jackson didn't reply, but when he returned to the bedroom, he was naked, his darkly muscled skin gleaming, his cock already riding high.

"So how do you want to do this?" Jackson asked Rob as he leaned in to kiss Ally's cheek. "Hey, Ally."

"I want us to fuck her together first, and then when she's all nice and wet, we can play with her for a while."

"Yeah." Jackson kissed Ally again, this time on the mouth, his wet cock grazing her hip as he leaned over her. "I want her ass."

Rob handed him some lube. "Then you'd better get her ready. I haven't had her that way yet." He turned to Ally, who was listening intently. "Do you like it up the ass, Ally?"

She bit her lip. "I've never really enjoyed it."

"Why's that, honey?" Rob asked her.

"I've never understood why any woman would want..." Her voice trailed off as she studied Jackson's thick, wet cock.

"Then whoever it was didn't get you ready properly," Jackson said. "I won't hurt you, Ally. I swear it."

Rob studied Ally's flushed face. "Do you think that nice girls don't like taking it in the ass, Ally? Is that why you didn't like it?"

"That's not fair, Rob." Ally glared at him, but he wasn't buying it.

"How about you let Jackson try and then if you still hate it, we'll let it go?" He kissed her mouth. "Don't you like the thought of the two of us fucking you at the same time, filling you up, making you come and come until you think you can't take any more?"

He felt her heart rate kick up against his bare chest and the little shivers of excitement that coursed through her skin. Whatever she said, she was certainly interested enough to try.

He held out his hand and Ally took it, her fingers trembling in his grasp. "Turn around and face the headboard. Put your hands on the top." He took two of the silk scarves Jackson had brought and tied her wrists to the brass rail of the bed. Then he reached around and fingered her nipples, heard her breath hiss out as he pulled hard on them.

On her other side, Jackson uncapped the lube and was coating two of his fingers. His expression was serious, his gaze fixed on the luscious curve of Ally's ass. Rob sighed as Jackson eased his index finger deep inside Ally and moved it back and forth. "Do you like that, Ally?"

She moaned and arched her back, and Jackson added another finger, moving closer to her, the crown of his wet cock gleaming in the lamplight. Rob inspected the nipple clamps he'd shown Ally earlier and cupped her right breast. "You ready for this, honey?"

He captured her nipple and slid the clamp around it, gradually tightening it until she made a small mewling sound. He caught her chin and made her look at him. "That's not even halfway yet. Breathe through it, and give in to it." He screwed it even tighter, and she bit down on her lip. "Let it go, Ally, breathe it out."

She kept her gaze on him, and he felt her relax, her breath easing, her body swaying toward him as if he wasn't the one causing her pain. He wanted to kiss her, wanted to catch those moans in his mouth, feel her take what he gave her and own it. He took a moment to glance over at Jackson's absorbed face, saw that four of his fingers were now easing in and out of Ally's ass.

"Now the second one."

Ally shivered as he tightened the clamp, but he could see from her eyes that she was already halfway to that good place, where pain and pleasure became one and where she just wanted him to keep giving it to her.

He kissed her long and slow until she was moaning into his

mouth and then drew back. Jackson looked over at him, his fingers still moving in and out of Ally.

"Do you like what Jackson's doing to you, Ally?"

She didn't reply, and he flicked one of her nipples and her eyes widened and focused on him.

"I...don't know."

"Is he hurting you?"

"No."

Rob nodded at Jackson to keep going and fingered Ally's clit in time to Jackson's gentle finger thrusts. Ally's frantic gaze fixed on his face.

"Do you want him to stop?"

She bit down on her lip. "No, please, I..."

Rob smiled. "We're going to make you come just like this, with Jackson's fingers in your ass and my finger on your clit. Do you think we can?"

"I..." Ally moaned and pushed her hips back toward Jackson. "Please."

"But nice girls can't come like that, can they?" He pinched her clit and she climaxed, making his cock jerk in anticipation. "Oh, yeah, look—they can."

He caught her chin and made her look at him. "So do you want Jackson's cock up your ass?" She met his gaze and swallowed hard. He could see the conflict in her eyes and he pushed a little harder. "Tell him what you want. Say the words."

She licked her full lips, and he wanted his cock right there, right between them. "I want...Jackson's cock in my ass."

Rob kissed her. "That's good, honey, and it's just going to get better."

"I'm so ready," Jackson said as he moved into position behind Ally. "Aren't you gonna fuck her too?"

Rob sat back and eased a hand over his throbbing shaft. "Not until I've watched you take her ass."

Jackson's faint smile disappeared as he rolled on a condom

and fitted the thick bulbous head of his cock to the tight bud of Ally's ass. He eased in that first inch, through the tight ring of muscle, and wanted to howl with the pleasure of it, with the constriction, with the way she took him in. Rob was watching, too, and somehow, even though it wasn't the first time they'd had the same woman, it made it even better. Rob continued to stroke Ally's clit as Jackson took his time, gently rocking his hips back and forth until his entire shaft was embedded deep in Ally's ass.

Rob touched his shoulder and Jackson shivered. "She feels fucking awesome."

"And tight, I bet."

"Yeah." Jackson breathed hard through his teeth against a sudden need to come. "Fuck her pussy, Rob. I want to see that too."

Rob crawled around and sat against the headboard, Ally's bound wrists on either side of his head. Rob's smile was more of a grimace as he wrapped his hand around the base of his shaft. "You'll have to lift her over me."

Jackson groaned. "Jeez, Rob, you'll make me come."

Rob met his gaze. "No, you won't. You want to feel me right there next to you, don't you? Feel Ally all around us?"

Jackson had nothing to say to that as he gripped Ally's hips, and moving with her, he brought her down over Rob's big, thick cock. All three of them gasped, and Jackson's grip shifted upward to Ally's breasts, where he palmed the clamps. The heat from Rob's cock seemed to sear a line down Jackson's shaft, making him feel like they were both in the same place and not separated by anything.

With a hoarse groan, Jackson began to move, and Rob took up the counterrhythm as if they'd discussed it. Why hadn't he realized before that he'd feel both Ally and Rob? Was that what he'd wanted, though? What he'd craved all along—this connection between the three of them?

* * *

Ally moaned as Rob lifted his face to hers, grabbed a handful of her hair, and kissed her hard. She'd never felt like this before, caught between the grinding, pulsing domination of two big men, her hands literally tied. She wanted to touch them both, feel the flex of their straining muscles as they both drove into her, but she was constrained, her movements controlled, her body at their mercy.

Harder, she wanted it harder, and as if he knew it, Jackson increased his pace, slamming into her ass, shoving her down onto Rob's cock. His fingers settled back over the clamps, and he tugged on her nipples. Sensation sent her reeling even closer to a climax as Rob reached between their bodies and rubbed her clit.

It was too much; it was all too much. Ally climaxed with a scream and tried to pull her mouth away from Rob's but he wouldn't allow it. His hand tightened in her hair and kept her chained to him while he continued to pump into her. She tried to keep her eyes open and watched his face tense as he climaxed, felt Jackson's breath on her neck, his teeth settling against her throat and biting down.

"I'm coming, Ally." Jackson's hoarse shout shoved her closer to Rob, and she felt the kick of his climax as he shuddered and collapsed over her back. Rob was quieter, if no less fierce, his come filling her in long, hot spurts.

When she was able to open her eyes again, Jackson had disappeared into the bathroom and Rob had untied her hands and now lay alongside her, removing the nipple clamps.

"I'm going to get some of these for your pussy. Have you tried these before?"

His voice sounded husky, and his lemon scent was all over her. She winced as he released the clamp and let out her breath, tried to stop herself from tensing when he did the other one. His mouth descended and lapped a wet bath over her distended nipple. "It's okay, honey."

His hand settled between her legs, and she sighed as he touched her there, his fingers swirling in the wetness. "You'll be nice and wet for Jackson now."

Ally shivered at the assurance in his tone, that she was ready for more sex and that she didn't have a choice about it. Jackson emerged from the bathroom smelling of her lavender soap and knelt on the bed beside her. His body was nicely muscled, his stomach flat with a hint of defined abs. His cock was already hard again. He touched her wet nipple with his fingertip.

"That was awesome, Ally." She smiled at him and he bent to kiss her. "I want more."

"So I gathered," Ally murmured.

Rob touched her hip and then spread her legs wide. "Lick her with me, Jackson."

Ally could only sigh as they both bent to the task. She was already swollen and wet down there, so every sensation was magnified. The rasp of stubble on her inner thighs, each flick or penetration of the tip of a tongue almost unbearable. As her hands were no longer tied, she was able to reach down and touch their heads, their shoulders, any part of them she could grab.

They both changed position, allowing Jackson to settle between her thighs and Rob to move up the bed, his cock gripped in his hand. Ally gasped as Jackson slid inside her, his hands under her ass lifting her into each short, hard stroke.

Rob touched her face. "Suck my cock, Ally."

She gladly opened her mouth and took him in, tried to suck him in rhythm with Jackson's fast, unforgiving pace.

Rob groaned and cradled her head in his hand. "Yeah, just like that. Give it to me hard. Let me fuck your mouth like Jackson is fucking your pussy."

Ally forgot about anything else than the pleasure of the two of them taking her. They were both so demanding that she had little choice but to pay attention to them and only to them. She climaxed so many times that she stopped counting, only aware that they kept pushing her on to heights she'd never managed to scale.

Her world narrowed to the sensations of flesh and touch and the glorious sound of skin slapping against skin. At some point, the men changed places again, Rob now between her legs and Jackson's stiff cock thrusting into her mouth. She climaxed again and closed her eyes only to blink when Jackson tugged on her hair.

"Don't stop looking, Ally. I want you to see it all."

Rob's mouth latched on to her already-sensitive nipple, and she moaned around Jackson's cock, screamed as Rob sent her over again, and she finally felt him come, too, his wet, pumping heat searing her inside.

Jackson pulled out of her mouth and reached for her, his dark eyes black with lust, his face set in lines of pure pleasure. "Like this, Ally, here, between your tits." He cupped her breasts and shoved his cock between them. He groaned as he tightened his grip, making her nipples ache, and climaxed all over her breasts, his come dripping down over her stomach.

He fell forward over her, his face planted in the pillow beside hers, his big body shuddering through each kick and twitch of his shaft. Ally touched his dark head, her fingers shaking, her body throbbing in time with his.

Rob shoved at Jackson, and he rolled over onto his back beside Ally. His satiated expression made Rob want to smile, as he reckoned he looked just the same. He stared down at Ally's sprawled figure. Her skin was pink and rosy and marked not only with the graze of their teeth, but also their come. Damn, he wished she could stay like this forever. In this bed, just waiting for them to come and fuck her. He wanted to lick her between the legs and suck her breasts clean, then kiss her until she tasted only of them.

His cock stirred painfully and he winced. But even he had his limits, and that last bout had just about worn him out. Ally caught his gaze and held it, her eyes steady, and no sense of shame in them. He was glad about that at least. She'd made her choice, and she obviously wasn't regretting it. He leaned down and kissed her belly, tasting Jackson and Ally's own lavender scent. She shivered but she didn't push him away, just watched him breathe her in.

Something close to anger twisted his gut. Why the hell hadn't he made her stay with him all those years ago and work it out? Why had he pushed her away? They'd wasted so many years together.

"What's up, Rob?"

Jackson's calm voice intruded on his tangled thoughts and made him sit back. He had no right to feel angry anymore. He wasn't one of those sad, fucked-up guys who never got over being dumped. He'd moved on, hadn't he? Made a good life for himself. And he had to remember this sexual playtime was just until Ally left him again.

Rob swung his legs over the edge of the bed. "I've got to shower. I'm on the early shift tomorrow."

He didn't wait to see their reaction to his sudden decision to leave. And he did have an early shift, so he wasn't making shit up. He showered fast and got back into his clothes, all the while wishing he could just go back to bed and hold Ally again. He banged his head gently against the outside of the glass shower door. Stupid, stupid, that's what he was. Why the hell had he pretended this was just casual? He was just asking to be fucking dropped all over again.

When he went out into the bedroom, Ally and Jackson hadn't moved. Rob inhaled the enticing smell of sex, nodded briefly, and left. It was hard to give the impression that he wasn't running away when they all knew he was.

Ally stared at Rob's departing back.

"Did I do something wrong?"

Jackson smiled. "Nope."

"So why did he go?"

"He's got an early shift."

Ally came up on one elbow and studied Jackson's bland face. "Does he?"

"Yeah."

"And that's it?"

He shrugged, his muscled shoulders gleaming in the lamplight. "Yeah."

Ally gave him a hard stare. "You need to work on your communication skills."

Jackson rolled her onto her back and reared over her. "I communicate." He kissed her hard, and she slid a hand into his black hair. His knee nudged between her thighs and she tensed. "Let's see if you understand this. I'm going to fuck you real slow now, and you're going to take it just how I want it."

She pulled out of the kiss and stared at him. Up close, his expression was cool and determined. "Are you sure about that?"

He placed his hand over her mouth. "I'm sure. I want my cock in you."

She couldn't look away from his almost-black eyes, felt her body stir even as her tired mind tried to form a coherent argument.

He took his hand away and continued to stare down at her. "Have you got anything else to say? I don't want to have to turn you over my knee and spank you."

A wave of desire flooded her and she couldn't speak. "I don't..."

He regarded her seriously. "You keep saying that, Ally. You keep denying that you want us. When you ran away, did you leave everything behind, especially anything to do with sex?"

She moved away from him and sat up, her arms wrapped around her raised knees. "So I tried a different kind of sex. What's wrong with that?"

"Nothing, if it made you happy." He watched her carefully. "And did it?"

She swallowed hard. "How do you know if it didn't?"

"Happy people don't fuck up their lives with drugs and alcohol. I learned that myself the hard way."

Ally rested her forehead on her knees. "I wanted to find other ways to get my sexual highs." She hesitated. "I didn't want to be ... different."

"Because you thought that wanting what Rob wanted was wrong?"

Ally raised her head and stared at him. Was that true? Had she tried to force herself into having the kind of sex she thought was normal? And in doing so, had she denied an essential part of herself?

"Come here." Jackson settled himself against the headboard and motioned for her to come toward him. She found herself crawling between his legs, aware of a new flood of energy coursing through her, the seductive crack of adrenaline and endorphins firing.

"Here's what we're going to do. You're going to suck my cock very gently, and I'm going to spank your ass."

"Jackson ..."

He touched her lips with his index finger. "Ally. Don't doubt yourself. Just do it, okay?"

His shaft was already half erect, and she took him deep in her mouth, bracing her hands on his muscled thighs. The first smack of his hand on her ass made her jump. Several slaps followed the first, and she forgot about complaining as she struggled to deal with the conflicting sensations.

Heat gathered in her sex, and she could feel the wetness both the men had left in her trickling down her thighs. She wondered if Jackson could see it, too, and whether he liked it as much as she did. Another slap made her want to clench her teeth against the pain, but her mouth was full of Jackson's rapidly growing cock and she couldn't bite down on him.

She focused on sucking, the only thing she could control and the only thing that kept her from writhing against the sting of Jackson's palm. The slow, gentle rhythm kept her sane, gave her the ability to let the pain sink into her system and lose herself in a red haze. Oh God, she was going to come soon without him even penetrating her. . . .

"Ally."

She forced herself to open her eyes and looked up at Jackson.

"Tell me the truth. Do you like this?"

He eased his stiff shaft out of her mouth and took his hands away from her body. She remained on all fours between his thighs, her body poised on the brink of pleasure and her mind in chaos.

Jackson tugged on her hair, his voice gentle. "If you don't like it, you can tell me to stop."

She felt the threat of tears and swallowed hard, tasting Jackson all over again. "Don't stop," she whispered. "Please don't stop."

He rolled her onto her back. "That's it, Ally, own it, enjoy it, and take it from me."

She moaned as her well-slapped ass made contact with the sheets, but then Jackson was on her, his cock poised to enter the swollen entrance of her sex.

He took his time getting inside her, each inch a battle against her flesh, each thrust a gain for him and his mastery over her. She didn't fight him; she let him sink deep, felt every throbbing, thick inch of him as though he were becoming part of her.

When he was buried deep, he caught her chin in his hand. "Look at me, Ally."

She slowly opened her eyes and let her gaze fix on his face. He looked different somehow. The quiet exterior shredded to show the cool, determined warrior underneath. A man who wanted to be in control, who demanded she submit to him. Not so very different from Rob after all.

"You think I should come now and let you sleep?"

She didn't say anything, just kept watching him through myriad intense physical sensations and mental emotions that crowded her brain. He pulled out until just the tip of his cock was inside her; the drag on her oversensitive flesh made her bite her lip.

"But what if I'm not done yet?"

He watched her carefully as he repeated his slow penetration and retreat until she was clutching at his biceps and constantly moaning. "You'll take me any way I want it."

"Yes."

She couldn't deny it, her body open to him, her mind and her pleasure totally in his hands. His palms slid from her hips to her ass, and he shoved his cock deep and squeezed her butt. She screamed into his mouth and climaxed so hard she couldn't breathe. He came with her, his come pouring out, filling her and making her as limp as a piece of water weed.

He pulled out and stayed straddling her, one hand on his cock. "If I wanted to, I could have you again. Make you suck me until I was hard, take me in your pussy or your ass, couldn't I?"

She nodded. There was nothing else she needed to say. He'd proved his point. Taken her to a dark, satisfying place where all she cared about was pleasing him and giving him what he wanted.

"Good." He kissed her mouth and moved off her.

The moment his heat deserted her, she started to shiver, and he paused. "Hold on, Ally." He drew her back into his arms and held her until she stopped shaking, until the sudden crash from the high evened out to a pleasing satiated numbness.

He stroked her hair back from her forehead and wrapped her up in her covers. "You gonna be okay?"

She wanted to turn her face into his chest and cry. This was what she craved, this sense of being sexually taken care of. That Jackson understood what she needed, gave it to her and then held her while she dealt with the aftershocks was proof that she'd made the right choice. He wrapped her in his arms and held her close, murmuring soothing nonsense to her until she stopped shaking and started to feel sleepy instead.

Jackson kissed her again and got out of bed. "Hold up, there, Ally. You can sleep after I've helped you shower."

God, her legs didn't seem able to hold her up, and she was grateful for his care as he held her upright under the water and washed her clean. He wrapped her in a big fluffy towel and carried her back to bed.

"Do you want me to stay?"

She shook her head. It was an effort to form words. "That's nice of you, but I've got to be up really early."

His smile was full of sweetness. "I don't mind."

"Really, I'll be okay. You go check on Rob."

"You're sure?"

"I'm sure."

He still hesitated. "Call me if you need me, okay?"

She waved at him to go, and he pulled on his shorts, blew her another kiss, and headed out. She wondered if he'd tell Rob what they'd done together and hoped he did. Jackson was right—she had to stop second-guessing herself and just allow the sex to happen. Ally glanced at her alarm clock and groaned. It was already one in the morning, and she needed to be up at five. She fell asleep even as she had the thought.

10

Jackson eyed Rob over his second cup of coffee. It was the end of the day, and he was preparing to leave for work while Rob had just returned. Sunlight streamed through the half-closed blinds of their kitchen, dappling the work surfaces with bands of glaring brightness.

"What was up with you last night?"

"I told you. I had to work."

"So did Ally."

"Which is why you came home straight after me, right?"

Jackson ignored the sarcasm and sipped his coffee. "I stayed to fuck her some more."

"You seem to be making a habit of that."

"And it bothers you?"

Rob looked up. "I told you already. No."

"Remember, you're the one who keeps leaving me alone with her."

"Sure." Rob got up and paced the small kitchen. "Ally makes me behave like an idiot."

"So it's all Ally's fault?"

"Shit, Jackson, whose side are you on?"

Jackson shrugged. "I didn't realize we were picking sides. I thought we were all in this together."

"Ally . . ." Rob shoved a hand through his hair. "Ally makes me mad—with myself, all right? Mad for letting her walk away."

"You couldn't have stopped her."

"I could. You don't know what happened."

Jackson eyed his oldest friend. "Neither do you."

Rob held his gaze. "I tried to push her into admitting she was a sub. I tried to tell her that I knew what she wanted, tried to show her." He sighed. "And that's not how it works, right? She has to give me her trust. I can't just take it from her."

"So her leaving was a good thing, then, wasn't it? Because she's come back and now she's old enough to know what she wants and who she wants it with." Jackson finished up his coffee and rinsed out the cup. "You didn't lose anything. You got a second chance."

Rob studied him, his expression thoughtful. "Yeah, I suppose that's one way of looking at it. I'm just worried about fucking it up again."

Jackson picked up his hat and belt. "It's the only way. Stop worrying about the past and concentrate on the future."

"But Ally's not going to stay, is she?" Rob's expression hardened. "It's a temporary truce so we can all fuck this out of our systems. She'll be out of here the moment her mom's place is sold."

Jackson paused at the door. "If that's what she wants to do, she'll do it. But I'm not so sure. If we handle it right, maybe she'll want to stay, but you've got to give up all that crap about finding out what happened to Susan, okay?"

Rob's face set into the obstinate lines Jackson knew so well. "Ally won't care whether I find out anything that implicates her mom. She never liked her."

"If it's that simple, why not just ask her straight out?"

Rob shrugged. "Because this is Ally we're talking about. She'd just get pissed with me, and it would complicate things."

"You're being a jerk, Rob. Get over yourself."

Rob didn't answer and Jackson headed out. He'd said all he was going to say, and it was up to Rob to make sense of it. Jackson smiled as he opened the door to his truck. And if Rob messed up again, Jackson wasn't going to let Ally go.

Ally walked into the coffee shop and smiled at Nadia, who was manning the counter. It was quiet in the place for a change. The morning rush was over, and the evening crowd was not yet desperate for the caffeine they needed to see them home.

"Hi, Nadia, can I have a small black coffee, please?"

"Sure." Nadia got busy with the pot. "How are you doing, sweetness?"

"Fine, thanks." Ally pointed at the blueberry muffins in the glass pastry case. "I think I'll take a couple of those muffins, please."

Nadia winked at her. "Huh, big spender today."

"I owe one of them to Jackson Smith, and the other is for me as a treat. I got paid today." She grinned at Nadia and waved a ten-dollar bill at her.

"You lasted a whole week? The entire town has been taking bets on how long you would stick it out." Nadia retrieved the muffins and put them in a paper bag. "Half of them think you're doing some reality TV thing and it's a big joke."

Ally groaned. "I wish." She studied Nadia carefully. "I suppose everyone has been filling you in on my escapades."

"Well, I have heard some stuff, but you know what? I don't like gossip and I like you." Nadia handed the coffee and the bag over with a wink.

"Thanks, I appreciate the support."

Nadia smiled. "And if a job comes up here, I'll keep you in mind. I pay the same as Lauren, but it's not so messy, okay?"

"Okay." Ally took her coffee and turned back toward the street. Nadia was not afraid of speaking her mind, and Ally liked that. At least she wasn't whispering behind Ally's back like most people. She was glad she wasn't permanently at the front of the house in the diner. The comments she got and the outright curiosity from some customers as she cleared tables were quite enough to deal with.

Heat burned through the thin soles of her frayed sandals, and she searched for her sunglasses in her pocket. After her shift, she'd stayed too long in town, returning her books to the library, getting essential food supplies, and loitering in the coffee shop. As if she sensed something was going on, Lauren had been extra-sharp with her this morning. Ally sighed. Or maybe that was her guilty conscience.

She needed to talk to Rob and was not too keen on the idea at all. She glanced down at the bag in her hand. But she had an excuse to visit the sheriff's office, didn't she? She owed Jackson a muffin, and she was going to stuff some cash in the bag to repay him for the repair he'd done on her truck whether he wanted the money or not.

It was a relief to step out of the heat and inside the old Victorian building. She asked for Jackson and waited in the cool shadowed hall for him to appear. She smiled as he strolled toward her, and she remembered his hands on her, the feel of his palm on her ass, his cock buried deep inside her.

He met her gaze and she saw he remembered too. Blushing, she held out the bag. "I owe you a muffin."

"Yeah?"

"Last week I ate the one Rob got for you."

His smile was slow and lit up his face. "I wondered where that had gone. It was you, was it?"

"Sorry. But here's a replacement."

He took the bag and stared down at her, then lowered his voice so that only she could hear it. "You okay, Ally?"

"I'm good, thanks."

"Not too sore?"

She swallowed as his breath tickled her earlobe. "No."

"That's good." He stepped away from her. "I'm on till late tonight, so I might not see you until tomorrow. Rob's home, though."

Ally held his gaze. "Do you think I should go see him?"

His smile was brief. "No, I think you should wait for him to come to you."

"Do you think he will?"

Jackson shrugged. "He should." He nodded. "Take care, Ally."

"Bye, Jackson."

Ally set off home, pondering Jackson's words as she went. She'd offered herself to Rob, so shouldn't it be her who went to find him? But there should be power on both sides, shouldn't there? Maybe Rob coming to find her was more important.

As if she'd conjured him up, Rob's truck went past her and pulled up on her drive, just as she rounded the corner of her street. By the time she reached the house, he was standing waiting for her. She took her time strolling toward him and admired his tall muscular frame, his light tan, and the calm strength in his pale eyes. His blue T-shirt was stretched tight across his chest and bore the legendary face of Captain America.

She pushed her sunglasses up onto the top of her head. "Hey, Sheriff."

"Hey, yourself."

"Is this an official visit? Shouldn't you be hiding your truck and skulking 'round the back?"

His faint smile died. "Why should I? I don't give a fuck about all the gossips in this town."

Ally opened the front door. "Of course you don't. That's my problem, isn't it?"

He followed her inside and through to the kitchen. He glanced through the open dining room door as he passed by. "Jackson said you found your mom's computer."

"I haven't had a chance to look at it properly yet. Would you like a drink?"

"Ice water would be good. On your paycheck, I don't suppose you have any beer."

Ally opened the creaking refrigerator door and scooped out some cubes from the barely functioning ice maker. "I don't have any alcohol, period. It doesn't agree with me."

Rob sat at the table, one hand wiping his sweat-dampened hair back from his forehead, the other tapping on the scarred oak. He took the tall frosted glass she offered him. "Thanks."

Ally took the chair opposite him. "So, what's up, Rob?"

He studied her over the rim of his glass. "I wanted to apologize."

"For what?"

"For disappearing on you like that last night."

"It's okay. Jackson stayed."

He winced slightly. "Yeah, so he did." He met her gaze. "Did he take care of you?"

"He did everything I'm sure you would've done."

"I should've stayed to make sure you were okay. That's what a good 'dom' does, right?"

"You're asking me?"

"Hey, it's a partnership. We should be on the same page here."

"But I thought you didn't want to do the 'dom' thing." Ally gathered her courage. "You didn't do anything I didn't like, or want, or need, Rob."

"Even bringing Jackson on board?"

She held his gaze. "Rob . . . you know that was just what I've always wanted. Both of you."

He put down his glass, leaving a wet ring on the table. "We should've talked this through properly, set limits and boundaries and—"

She reached over and touched his mouth with her fingertips. "We did fine. You were right about what I crave, Rob. I want as much sex as I can get, and I want it even when I'm tired or sore. I like to be pushed. It just does it for me—you and Jackson just make it all perfect."

He sighed and kissed her fingertips before taking her hand. "Now I feel like an idiot."

"So what's new?"

His smile warmed her. "You think you're cute, don't you?"

She fluttered her eyelashes at him. "I know I am." And how amazing was this? Here she was, *flirting* with Rob and admitting what she wanted without feeling like a freak or a doormat. But then she was admitting it to a man who understood her. Perhaps that was what was different, that connection, that . . . trust.

She caught herself about to yawn and covered her mouth. "Sorry, I had a short sleep and a long shift this morning, but I did get paid. I don't know who was more surprised I lasted a week, me or Lauren."

Rob stood up. "Probably Lauren. She doesn't know how tough you really are, does she?"

Ally stood, too, and smothered another yawn. "I need to shower and sleep for a while before I tackle my mom's computer." She glanced at him. "Do you want to stay?"

"I wish I could, but I've got to put in an appearance at court this afternoon." He hesitated. "Maybe I could come back and bring some pizza or something? I'm not due on until midnight."

"I have to go back at nine, but you're welcome to come over around six, if you like."

"Sounds like a plan." He came around the table and kissed her mouth. "You taste like coffee and sex."

Ally kissed him back. "So do you."

He smoothed a stray strand of hair behind her ear. "We're all straight, then?"

"As straight as you want us to be—apart from all the kinky stuff."

He smiled again, and she loved the sight of him relaxing, the dimple on his left cheek, and the flash of white teeth. She was proud of herself, too, for being able to appreciate him and yet stand her ground. Did he like that too? Was he glad that she'd found the strength to match his?

Ally let him out of the front door and then went straight to the shower. She felt better than she had in months. She had money in her pocket that she'd earned with her own sweat, a place to call her own, and two men who wanted to make her feel good.

But her smile died as she turned on the shower. So what was still bothering her? Something was still wrong between her and Rob, and she couldn't quite put her finger on it.

Ally switched on the power to her mom's computer and sat back to see whether anything would happen. Lights flickered on the newly cleaned gray screen, and something whirred in the box on the floor. She held her breath as a screen saver of pink daisies appeared, and a few desktop icons.

She clicked on the browser icon and waited as the machine continued to mutter away. Eventually a home page formed, and immediately a banner flashed, offering to upgrade her account from dial-up to broadband. Ally wrinkled her nose. Who the hell still had dial-up, and how come her mom's account was still working?

She thought about the desk she'd discovered against the wall of the dining room earlier. Maybe her mom's checkbook and bank account stuff were in there. She'd have to sort all that out soon. But this made things a lot easier. She wasn't going to complain about the Internet access, though, slow as it was. Otherwise she'd been hoping to "borrow" someone else's unprotected wireless Internet.

Worried, in case the Internet suddenly decided to desert her, she logged into her Gmail account and scanned the fifty or so messages that had accumulated since her last visit about a month ago. Most of them were from her lawyer and her only other close girlfriend, Jill, who was also her AA sponsor.

She took out her cell phone and checked the minutes. She'd love to talk to Jill; just the sound of her voice always cheered Ally up. Maybe she could purchase some more minutes at the gas station with some of her paycheck. It would be worth it. She had no idea how the bill was paid on her mom's landline. Yet another thing to check up on. E-mail would have to do for now.

For half an hour, Ally dutifully replied to her mail and hoped she'd set everyone's minds at rest, although somehow she doubted it. No one would be happy to hear she had decided to stay in Spring Falls for as long as it took to set the house to rights. And that was another thing. She'd promised to attend regular AA meetings and had no idea where the nearest one might be.

Ally's stomach gurgled, and she headed for the kitchen for a glass of milk. According to the clock, it was almost six and Rob would be turning up soon. She took her milk back into the dining room and studied the desk on the far wall. Since no one else had stepped forward, she guessed she really was the lone executor of her mom's estate.

For some reason, it took all her courage to open the lid of the old oak desk. She remembered her mother sitting there, her lank hair falling to her waist, a cigarette or a bottle of beer in her hand as she wrote endless letters to a succession of men begging them to return to her. Letters Ally had to mail or worse—deliver in person—to some guy her mother had briefly hooked up with.

To her surprise, the inside of the desk was quite orderly. Checkbooks were stacked neatly in a pile on top of what looked like bank statements, and bills were all laid out on the opposite side. Ally swallowed hard as she saw her mother's scrawling handwriting again and forced herself to pick up the first checkbook.

Not only had it been meticulously kept, but also there was a running total of the balance of the account, which, although it didn't amount to much, at least explained why the utilities, the phone, and the Internet were still on. Ally read the first bank statement and saw her mom had chosen to pay most of her bills by direct debit. She put the paper down and just stared at it.

Since when had her mother gotten so organized? As a child, they'd lived hand to mouth, often just ahead of the debt collectors. Ruth hadn't been above sending Ally to borrow money from anyone she could think of to stave off the debt collectors. When had that changed?

"Ally?"

"Hey."

She looked up to see Rob in the doorway. His gaze swept the disorganized space and then returned to hers. "I see the computer is working. Did you find everything you needed?" He strolled into the room, his hands in his pockets, and stared down at the screen. For some reason, Ally wished she'd turned it off before he'd arrived.

"I found the Internet. That made me happy." She returned the checkbook to the pile and shut the desktop with a bang. "Although it's only dial-up."

"Better than nothing I suppose." Rob waited as she shut the computer down. "You could've used my laptop if you'd said."

"I wouldn't dare." Still oddly ruffled by the new revelations about her mother, Ally manufactured a smile. "I might end up putting stuff on your Facebook page or reading e-mails I shouldn't."

"I haven't got anything to hide."

"No e-mails from Jane? Lauren said you're seeing her."

Rob shrugged. "I see her occasionally."

"Ah." Ally turned back to the kitchen where she could smell the heavenly scent of pizza.

"What's that supposed to mean?"

She turned to smile at him. "Nothing. The pizza looks good."

Rob remained in the doorway, his blue gaze considering. "I could help you clear out some of that stuff if you want."

For some reason, the thought of him finding out things about her mother right alongside her was unsettling. She found some paper plates and napkins and sat down at the table. "Not until I've had something to eat."

He came and sat opposite her and opened up the pizza box. She licked her lips as he revealed a big pepperoni pizza, her favorite. "I got garlic bread too."

"Great." Ally pulled off a hunk of pizza and didn't even mind the melted cheese dripping down her arm. She sank her teeth into the warm gooey mess and chewed. When she'd finished her first piece, she looked up to find Rob watching her.

"You sure enjoy your food."

"I've learned to. I used to hate eating."

"Because of the modeling?"

She half smiled. "That certainly didn't help as a career choice. Ruth always told me I was fat."

"You always looked perfect to me."

Ally realized she was blushing. Rob took another piece of pizza and shoved the box of garlic bread in her direction. She glanced up at him after she selected a piece. "I shouldn't have listened to my mom about anything."

He continued to eat, his gaze fixed on the pizza box. "Ruth was a hard person to like or to understand, Ally."

"Oh, I understood her all right. She was incredibly selfish and couldn't do without a man or some kind of drug to snort." Ally sighed. "I never wanted to be like her in a million years."

"And you're not."

She waited until he looked up at her and calmly held his gaze. "Yes, I am. Why do you think I ended up in rehab?" She sighed. "Once, when I'd spent all day locked in my apartment because I was 'too sick to work,' I caught a glimpse of myself in the bathroom mirror. I thought I saw my mom looking back at me, and I freaked out. When she started turning up in my mirror every day, I knew I had to do something."

"And you did. You admitted you had a problem and got help."

She rested her chin on her hand. "And since I've been back, I found that my mom did that too."

"So I heard. She was certainly off the drugs."

Ally pushed that uncomfortable thought away. "Some people would say I'm acting just like her, though, wouldn't they? Crawling back here, begging you to forgive me, offering to do anything you want sexually."

His expression cooled. "Do you think that's what I want?"

"I think you're a man who'll take what's offered."

"So, you offered. Did you think I'd say no?"

"Rob, I wasn't expecting you to want to talk to me, let alone sleep with me."

"Would you have preferred it if I'd kept my distance and stayed out of your life?"

Ally studied him carefully. "No."

He ran a hand through his short hair. "That's good to know."

Some demon made her continue. "You had no intention of leaving me alone, though, did you?"

He put down his pizza and slowly wiped his hand across his mouth. "No."

"You've always wanted to win at everything."

"You think this is about winning?"

"Isn't it?"

She watched his face, saw myriad emotions flow through his eyes. "Yeah, I suppose it is. I wanted answers and you have them."

"Answers about what?"

"Why you ran, for one thing."

Ally pushed her plate away as her appetite deserted her. "Because you told me to get the hell away from you."

"That's not all it was about, though, was it?"

"No, of course it wasn't. I was too young to know when to stand my ground and when to leave. I felt guilty about Susan, about Jackson, about you..." Ally wrapped her arms around herself. "I felt guilty about everything."

Rob sat back and his chair creaked. "Did you speak to Susan?"

"I had no choice; if you remember, she was trying to scratch my eyes out."

"Not then, but later, just before she died."

Ally grimaced. "Why would I have spoken to her? I was too busy sobbing my heart out and trying to pack to leave town."

"I kind of assumed Susan would have come back to have it out with you."

"She probably would have, but I didn't see her again. I was already on the bus out of town when Jackson called to tell me what had happened."

Rob went still. "Jackson called you?"

"He probably knew I wouldn't have picked up if it had been you, and he thought I should know."

"I bet he did."

Ally eyed him suspiciously. "Are you trying to stir up trouble for Jackson?"

"For Jackson?"

"Trying to prove that he was involved somehow in Susan's death? Did Jane put you up to this?" Ally got up and tipped the dregs out of the coffee jug. "She seems pretty determined to see Jackson tried and hung."

His mouth tightened. "I don't think Jackson had anything to do with Susan's murder."

Ally paused as she scooped out new coffee. "Murder? You think Susan was murdered too?"

Rob shifted in his chair, but he kept his gaze on hers. "Yeah, I do. Some of the injuries don't match up with a suicide."

"So you think Jackson pushed her off that bridge?"

"No, but I think someone did." He stood up and closed the gap between them, dumped the coffee in the filter, and filled the glass jug up with water. Ally waited while he poured in the water and set it to brew, her mind in turmoil as she tried to figure out what to say next.

Rob kept his attention on the coffee. He'd pushed too far, and Ally was starting to get suspicious. She was no fool, and if he didn't shut up soon, she'd figure out that he was still wondering about her mother's involvement in Susan's death rather than Jackson's.

She touched his shoulder, and he turned to see her pale but resolute expression. "Rob, do you think I killed her?"

He blinked at her. Jeez, he hadn't expected that. "As you said, by the time she died, you were on the bus."

"Unless I'm lying and I waited around the house until Susan came back, took her out to the bridge, and threw her off."

"And did you?"

"No, and I didn't talk to her, either, so can we drop this?"

"Absolutely." For now anyway. He really wanted to ask her

about her mother, but even though she had no love for the woman, she was far too on her guard to start that conversation now. And there were far better things to think about.

He cupped her cheek. "Do you want to finish the pizza?"

"No, you've ruined my appetite."

"I'm sorry, honey. Sometimes I need to clock off my job before I turn up here."

"Police officers never clock off. Even I know that."

"I'm willing to try if you can distract me."

She looked up at him, her gray eyes still slightly wary, her teeth biting into her lower lip. "And how might I do that?"

"Make me a cup of coffee?"

She smiled at him for the first time, and he wanted to kiss the smile from her lips and make her moan his name instead. "Is that all you want?"

"I think that's all I'm going to get."

11

—————

"Thanks." Ally smiled as the bank manager, Mr. Sutcliff, escorted her into his office. "It's good of you to see me at such short notice."

"It's not a problem." He glanced at her over his shoulder. "You're a bit of a celebrity around here, Ms. Kendal. Your mom told me all about you."

"My mom did?" Ally sat in the hard chair and tried to keep her expression neutral.

"Yes, she was very proud of your career." Mr. Sutcliff sat down and typed away on his computer for a moment. "I have the details of your mother's accounts here. Her attorney sent us all the necessary paperwork."

"Apparently she wanted me to be her executor." Ally took out the file she'd found in her mother's desk. "I found this among her things."

"I knew that, Ms. Kendal. I believe I cosigned some papers for her during the last few months of her life. She was very keen on leaving everything straight for you."

Ally wanted to disagree with the guy, but he was right. Her

mother had made very sure that Ally knew exactly what was expected of her and what to do. It made her feel weird, as if her mother had changed into a woman she would no longer have recognized.

"From what I could tell, everything looked pretty straightforward."

"Indeed. Your mother owned the house outright and had no outstanding debts, so everything she leaves you is free and clear."

"I'm planning on selling the house."

Mr. Sutcliff looked up. "I can't say that surprises me, but it is still a tough market around here."

"I noticed that, and the house needs clearing out and perking up a little."

"Well, I'm quite sure she wouldn't mind me telling you there is enough money in the three accounts to cover that."

Ally frowned. "Three accounts?" She looked through the stash of documents she'd brought with her. "I thought she had only two, checking and savings."

"She had another savings account. I believe she used it to deposit the checks you sent her."

"She didn't cash them?"

Mr. Sutcliff cleared his throat. "I got the impression that she regarded that money as sacrosanct. I have no idea why. Perhaps she just wanted you to have it back."

"How much is in there?"

Mr. Sutcliff tapped away at the keyboard and then looked up again. "About thirty thousand dollars."

Ally just stared at him with her mouth open. "Are you sure? What did she live on?"

"I can print the information out for you. Your mom had a small fixed income from her parents' estate, which she supplemented with part-time work. She always said she didn't need much." He sat back and smiled at her. "All I need from you now is a copy of the death certificate and your driver's license. The attorney sent me everything else."

"I have both of those, although my license is for out of state. I'm in the process of applying for a new one." Ally produced the two documents and waited while he took a copy of her driver's license.

"Thank you. It shouldn't take too long to settle all this. As I said, your mom kept everything in good order. We have to advertise and then wait at least thirty days to see if any creditors appear out of the woodwork. After that, I can at least put you on the accounts as a joint holder."

Ally gathered up the remaining documents and returned them to her purse. "Thanks for all your help."

Mr. Sutcliff stood up and shook her hand. "It was a pleasure to meet you, even in such sad circumstances. I'll be in touch."

Ally made her way out of the bank and back onto Main Street, her thoughts in a whirl. If Mr. Sutcliff was right, her mother had saved more than enough money to fix up the house, money that Ally had sent her. She wouldn't have to touch her college fund and might even be able to add to it.

Why hadn't Ruth spent the money? Had she realized Ally was trying to pay her to stay away and resented it, or had she developed a conscience at last?

"Ally!"

She glanced up just in time to see that she had reached the diner and that she was late back from her break. Lauren was waiting for her, arms crossed, expression irritated.

Ally sighed. "I'll make it up, Lauren. I got stuck in the bank."

"You'll make it up, all right," Lauren replied. "And this is your last warning about being late. I'm only letting you off because we're shorthanded tonight, and I need you to stay for an extra shift."

Ally washed her hands and tied on her apron. "I can do that."

"I'm not asking you—I'm telling you."

Ally stared at Lauren. "I get that you don't like me, but I'm still entitled to be treated with respect at my workplace. I said I'd make the time up, and I'm happy to work the extra shift, so get off my back."

Lauren sucked in her breath, but Ally refused to back down. Fig appeared at her elbow and put a hand on Ally's shoulder. "She works her ass off, boss, so how about you just chill here?"

Lauren glared at Fig and then stormed back out to the front of the diner. Ally let out her breath and Fig chuckled. "Hell, I love that woman, but she treats you like dirt."

"She has good reason. I dumped her brother."

Fig returned to his station at the grill. "So I heard. But that's ancient history and not really her problem now, is it?"

Ally picked up her bucket of cleaning supplies and an empty tray. She was so not getting into a discussion about Lauren with Fig. "Thanks, Fig."

He saluted her with his spatula. "No problem, babe."

After that, Ally barely had a moment to think let alone talk. One of the waitresses was out sick, so Lauren was filling in at the front. Two of the kitchen guys were down with the virus as well, leaving Ally the lone busboy and general dogsbody.

By five, she was exhausted; by nine she was contemplating crawling out the back door and to hell with her paycheck. She'd gone to bed reasonably early after she'd satisfied Rob's appetite for coffee and sex, but she was still worn out. The sound of the bell chiming as the last customers left was music to her ears.

Lauren appeared in the kitchen with a load of dishes and dumped them on the already full counters. Fig and Ben shut down and cleaned the grills, leaving Ally frantically trying to catch up.

Lauren walked up to Ally. "I have a date. You're going to have to stay and clean up and then lock up."

"Me?"

"Yes, you." Lauren's gaze dropped to Ally's oil-spattered T-shirt. "Get here early enough to unlock the door for me as well, okay? Thanks."

Ally didn't even have the heart to argue. She just nodded, took the keys Lauren gave her and the note about the code for the alarm system, and carried on washing up. Soon she was alone in the kitchen. Fig had wanted to stay and help, but he'd had another commitment. Ally sighed and looked around. At least he'd stayed long enough to make sure that everything in his area had been done—oil filters cleaned, surfaces scraped down and disinfected, vents inspected. . . .

She wandered out to the front of the diner to see how bad it was and wanted to cry. Thanks to Lauren's efforts, most of the tables had been cleared of dishes but not all. And every single surface needed to be wiped down and sanitized. Ally decided to start there and at least clean the area Lauren would care about most.

"Ally?"

She stilled as she heard Rob's soft voice behind her. He came to look over her shoulder and whistled softly. "Still got a lot to do, huh?"

Ally resisted the temptation to lean against him. "I sure do. It seems everyone else has gone to the ball."

Rob chuckled, the sound vibrating in his chest and down Ally's back. He turned Ally around and his smile died. "You look exhausted, Cinderella."

"I've worked all day. I am exhausted."

Rob's expression tightened. "Don't tell me Lauren made you work with no breaks."

"Oh, I got breaks. I'm still tired, though."

Rob took her hand and led her back into the kitchen. "You go take a nap in Lauren's office and I'll take care of this."

"Rob, you can't do that. It's my job."

He cupped her chin. "Honey, she's taking out her hurt on you and it's not right."

"She's not. We were just shorthanded today. She—"

He kissed her, and like a fool, Ally stopped talking and let him hold her for a blissful moment before she pulled herself away. Why the hell was she defending Lauren anyway?

"I can't let you do this, Rob."

"You can't stop me either."

"But you probably won't do it right."

"When Lauren first took over the diner, I did all sorts of jobs for her until she could afford to pay someone else. I can do anything this place needs *and* do it up to her extremely picky standards."

"Rob—"

"Look, how about we make a deal? You sleep for an hour and then you can take over."

A yawn shook Ally and she reluctantly nodded. "Okay, then, wake me up in an hour."

"Deal." He held out his hand, and she shook it. "Now go and take that nap before you fall down."

About an hour and a half later, Rob stood looking down at Ally's sleeping face. She'd curled up on the tiny couch in Lauren's office, her sweater arranged over her like a meager blanket. Rob studied her pale features, the shadows under her eyes, and wished he could just let her sleep on. But a promise was a promise, and he couldn't help but admire both her spirit and her determination not to crack under the pressure of Lauren's dislike.

"Ally," he whispered. "Wake up, honey."

She opened her eyes and stared at him for a long, timeless moment. Something stirred deep in his chest, and he imagined waking up to her beautiful face every morning. She scrambled to sit, and he stepped back to give her room.

"What time is it?"

"It's coming up on midnight."

She peered at him through half-closed eyes. "I told you to wake me up after an hour."

"I got busy. I only just remembered."

"Right." She stood and brushed at her braided hair. "What else is there left to do?"

He headed for the door. "Would you care to inspect my work, my lady?"

"I *am* going to inspect your work, because if it isn't right, I'm the one who'll get into trouble." Ally marched into the diner and studied the space.

Rob waited for her to turn back to him. "It's okay, right?"

"It looks great."

He shrugged modestly. "It all came back to me the moment I started wiping off the menus. Do you want to finish up in the kitchen?"

Ally followed him back out. "What's left to do?"

"A load of dishes. Do you want to wash or dry?"

She glanced at his already damp T-shirt, which clung to his well-defined abs. "I'll wash."

He stood alongside her, manning the dish drainers and the cloth while she rinsed off dishes in one sink and then washed them in the center sink.

After a while, she looked up at him. "Thanks for doing this."

"You're welcome."

"No, I really mean it. You've gone above and beyond."

"I had nothing else to do."

"No sports on TV, no video games to play, no Jackson to chat with?"

"Jackson isn't exactly the chatty type."

"That's true." She handed him the last plate, and he took it and dried it with the cloth. He put the plate away in the correct stack and used the damp dishcloth to wipe down the counter-top before tossing it in the laundry bin. "I think we're done."

Ally sat beside him on the countertop and sniffed the air. "Oh, man, I'm hallucinating. I can smell coffee."

"Oh, yeah, I made some to keep me going. Do you want a cup before we lock up?"

"I'd love one. It might keep me awake long enough to walk home."

Rob got up to man the coffee. "You don't need to walk. I'm taking you home."

"Then I'll definitely need the coffee." She smiled. "I don't feel as bad as I should, though. That nap did help."

"Good. Come and drink your coffee in the diner. The seats are nicer."

Ally slid down from her perch and groaned as her sore feet hit the tiles. "Okay."

He held open the kitchen door and watched the sway of her hips as she sashayed down the aisle between the booths. Even in her filthy work clothes, she still turned him on. All the lights were off in the diner and the blinds were down. Only the faint fluorescent glow from the kitchen and the orange tint of the streetlight permeated the suddenly intimate space.

Rob sat opposite her in the booth and handed her a mug of coffee. She took it and drank greedily. When she put it down, he instantly refilled it. "Is that better?"

"Much, although now I'll never want to sleep."

He smiled at her. "That's okay. I'm sure I can think of something else for you to do."

"I'm sure you can."

He loved that hint of dryness in her tone and how she tried to cover the spark of interest in her eyes. "I got to thinking while I was working." He glanced at her over his cup and saw the way she was leaning toward him, as if in anticipation. "It helped pass the time."

"And what were you thinking about?"

"You, in the diner."

She groaned. "You couldn't have thought about me somewhere warm and glamorous instead, maybe somewhere with a spa?"

He caught her hand. "No, it was here in the diner, except you were serving early breakfast to me and all the truckers."

"That turned you on?"

He ran his thumb over the soft skin of her wrist, felt her tremble. "Sure. You were wearing that stupid pink uniform Lauren picked out for the waitresses, but your skirt was shorter and your blouse tighter. Every time you leaned over me to refill my coffee, I touched you."

"Where?"

Rob smiled and reached across to brush his knuckles across her breast. He watched her nipple harden instantly in response. "Here." He did it to her other breast. "And here. Until everyone could see your nipples through your shirt."

"Everyone?"

"Yeah, everyone who was looking. And then I went a little further."

"And did what?"

He tugged on her hand until she was standing over him and walked his fingers up the side of her shorts. "Touched your pussy, flicked your clit, and when I got you nice and wet, I tried to get my fingers inside you."

She shivered as he undid her shorts and pulled them down. "Like this."

She gasped and leaned into him, allowing him to use his other hand on her breast.

"But people would see."

"Yeah. Eventually. But by then you weren't exactly worrying about it and neither was I."

He pushed her panties aside and slipped two fingers inside her, moving them back and forth until she was soaking wet. She grabbed on to his shoulder for support, her nails digging into his skin.

"But I don't want to be selfish here. I want the other guys to see the sugar I'm getting and want it. And I know you'll want them to see you, too, so I sit you on my knee, turn you to face them, and flip your little pink skirt up so they can all watch me finger-fuck you."

He swung her around to sit on his knees, felt the jolt in his cock as her soft ass pressed against him.

"You want them to watch?" Ally whispered.

He stripped off her panties and dropped them to the floor. "Yeah, I want them to see how hard I need to work you to make you come for me, how hard you like it."

He dug out his cell phone and flipped it open. "Call Jackson. Tell him to get here as soon as he can. He'll like this." He held the phone to her mouth and waited as she relayed his instructions to Jackson.

It didn't take long for Jackson to get there. But Rob held Ally on the brink of an orgasm. Even when she strained against him and begged, he wouldn't let her come until Jackson arrived.

He looked up as Jackson came to a halt in front of them. "We're playing a game. Ally's the waitress, and I'm about to fuck her in front of a diner full of horny truckers—with your help, of course."

"What am I supposed to be? The truckers?"

"No, you can be the law."

"Funny."

"How about you suck her while I finger her?" Rob waited as Jackson got down on his knees beside Ally and licked her clit. "Yeah, that's good. Keep it up." Rob started to move his fingers again, all four of them now embedded in Ally. His thumb met Jackson's questing tongue, and he shuddered as Jackson sucked him, too, felt the answering need in his cock.

"I need to fuck her." Rob kissed Ally's throat. "Do you still see them all there, honey? Watching us touch you, wishing they could touch you too." She moaned his name, and he increased the pace of his fingers until he could hear the wet sucking sound. "We could do that, right? Line them up and make you suck all their cocks while Jackson and I fucked you."

She climaxed and his fingers were almost crushed. Jackson raised his head and met Rob's gaze. "I think she likes the idea." Jackson caught Ally's chin. "You want that? You want more men getting off on you?"

Rob held his breath as Ally's eyes fluttered shut, and he pulled his fingers out of her. "Answer him, Ally, or you're done coming tonight."

She tried to shake her head, but Jackson had her secure. "Please..."

Abruptly, Rob stood up and moved Ally so that she lay across the width of the table. He grabbed her hands and held them by the wrists over her head, which hung slightly off the table, just a breath away from his groin.

"Get ready to fuck her, Jackson."

Jackson moved to the other side of the booth and positioned himself between Ally's legs. Rob unbuttoned his shorts and his cock sprang out.

"Do you want us, Ally?"

"Yes!"

"Then answer the question."

She licked her lips as if seeking his taste. "I like... I like the idea of you two fucking me in public."

Rob met Jackson's gaze and saw the gleam of speculation. "Yeah? You want other people to watch us fuck you?"

"Yes." She swallowed hard. "Now, please, please let me come."

Jackson shifted his stance, a muscle flicking in his cheek as if he was struggling not to shove himself deep. Rob nodded at him. "Fuck her."

Ally moaned as Jackson slid into her, his hands braced on the tabletop. Rob let go of Ally's hands and guided his cock toward her mouth.

"Suck me, Ally." She opened her mouth, and he thrust forward, heard her gasp as she tried to accommodate his thick length from her upside-down position. It felt odd, too, the top of his cock hitting against her teeth, but he liked that, liked it rough. Her body arched off the table as they both pounded into her.

Rob set his jaw and forced himself to look at Jackson. "Don't let her come."

When Jackson stopped moving, Rob eased his cock out of Ally's mouth.

"You'd let them touch you, wouldn't you?"

Ally stared up at him and nodded.

Rob glanced at Jackson. Whatever magic his buddy had worked with Ally while he'd left them alone to fuck, he was eternally grateful. Rob let out his breath, and Jackson started pumping hard, shoving his thick length into Ally while Rob watched. As soon as Jackson finished coming, Rob replaced him, fucking Ally as hard as he could, enjoying how she squirmed and fought him on the slippery hardness of the diner table, how Jackson held on to her arms to keep her in place for him.

He climaxed and emptied himself deep, felt her convulse around him again. He pulled out and gazed down at her, her body striped with moonlight, her nipples still hard. She held his gaze.

"I'm not done, Ally, and neither is Jackson." He helped her sit up on the table and motioned for Jackson to stand beside him. "Make us both hard again. Use your hands and your mouth."

Jackson shuddered as Ally knelt up on the table, her long dark hair coming out of her braid to cover her face and brush against their skin. His naked left hip bone was aligned with

Rob's as Ally took a cock in each hand and wrapped her palm around them. When she started to work his flesh, Jackson wanted to groan with every stroke. The smell of sex permeated everything, and he loved it.

As Ally continued to fondle him, Jackson couldn't help but glance at Rob. His friend's eyes were half closed in a familiar expression of pleasure. Jackson couldn't take his gaze off Rob's cock. He remembered how it had felt to have Rob's shaft so close to his when they'd both fucked Ally, wondered how it would feel to touch him now. . . .

Without thinking, Jackson added his fingers to Ally's and caressed Rob's cock. He flinched as Rob grabbed his arm.

Ally spoke up. "No, don't stop him, Rob. I'd like to see him touch you."

"You would?" Jackson barely managed to get the words out.

"That's a great idea." Rob's hand closed around Jackson's cock and that was it. Jackson lost it completely, surrendered to the two hands on his cock and wanted to scream with the pleasure of it.

"Suck us, Ally," Jackson managed to gasp. "Suck us together."

She tried her best to get both of them in her mouth, and Jackson luxuriated in the feel of Rob against him and the softness of Ally's mouth. Rob's other hand moved around Jackson's hips, pressing him closer. God, Jackson wished Rob would slide his fingers lower and investigate his ass. The thought was enough to make him come, and he choked out a curse, his fingers tightening on Rob until his friend came, too, the flood of their come not contained by Ally's mouth but trickling down between her breasts.

"God . . . ," Rob ground out, and Jackson silently agreed. All three of them were panting now, sticky with sweat and each other's leavings, and he just wanted to start all over again and lick them both clean.

Rob moved away from Jackson and gathered Ally in a hug. "I'll clean up here. Jackson can take you home, okay?"

"Are you sure?"

Rob kissed the top of her head. "We've already had this discussion. Go home."

Jackson found his shorts and hastily pulled them on. Rob handed him Ally's purse and jacket. Either Rob didn't want to talk about what had just happened between them, or he truly hadn't noticed anything—his sexual attention all on taking care of Ally. And hadn't that always been the case? He'd never looked at Jackson the way he looked at Ally.

Jackson headed for the back door, one arm encircling Ally's shoulders. Whatever happened, he couldn't turn back from what he'd started. Rob knew the basics about Jackson's past experience with other guys, but Jackson had never shared the specifics of his complex sexual tastes or suggested Rob should try him out.

Not that he deserved anything from Rob. Maybe it was time Rob knew what kind of a friend Jackson really was and what a shit he'd been to him in the past.

Ally touched his cheek. "Are you okay, Jackson?"

"Yeah."

"Because you look a bit shaken."

"Yeah?" Jackson held the truck door open and helped Ally inside.

She touched his knee. "You can talk to me about anything, Jackson, you know."

"Sure."

Ally sighed so hard he was surprised she didn't blow out his windshield. Jackson concentrated on his driving. He was not talking to her about anything at all. There really was nothing to talk about.

12

Ally groaned when her alarm went off, and she rolled over to silence it. Her whole body was aching, and the thought of getting up and going to work made her want to cry. But she had to do it. She had Lauren's keys, and if the boss lady couldn't get in, no one would get in, and Ally's job would be history.

"Oh God!"

Ally sat up and clasped the sheets to her breasts. But she didn't have the keys, did she? She'd left them with Rob. That was enough to get her out of bed and into the shower. She hurried into the kitchen to grab a glass of milk and some fruit to eat. Had Rob come in later and dropped the keys off for her? She couldn't see them anywhere.

With a last frantic glance at the clock, she left the house. Her only option was to call Rob as she walked to the diner and ask him to meet her there with the keys. If she got there early enough, perhaps Lauren would never know. She called Rob and was surprised he sounded far more awake than she did.

"Hey, do you have the keys to the diner?"

Ally heard him curse.

"I do. Are you on your way?"

"I'll meet you there."

She practically ran the last block and arrived to see Rob's patrol car parked at the rear of the diner and no sign of Lauren.

"Thanks, Rob."

"You're welcome." He handed her the keys and turned back to his car. "I meant to drop them by last night, but I forgot and went straight home."

"It's not a problem." Ally glanced behind her and saw Lauren's white car approaching. "I'd better look busy. The boss is coming."

Rob's car pulled away just as Lauren got out of her vehicle. Her faint smile soured when she saw Ally standing there. "Why didn't you go in?"

"I was waiting to give you your keys back."

Lauren took the keys and walked around to the front of the diner while Ally waited patiently at the back door. A second later, Lauren reappeared and grabbed Ally by the arm.

"What the hell happened here?" She set off back around the corner, forcing Ally to go with her.

"Oh my goodness." Ally covered her mouth as she stared at the smashed window. The inside blind had taken most of the impact, but Ally could clearly see the wicked shards of glass glinting on the diner tables.

Lauren took out her cell phone. "I'm calling Rob and having you arrested for vandalism. I know you didn't want to stay late, but this is no way to repay me."

Ally blinked. "Hang on, Lauren, I didn't do this."

"Who else would? And after all I've done for you, agreeing to give you a job, feeding you, paying you..." She spoke into her cell. "Rob, this is all your fault. Get over here right now."

Ally took a deep breath. "You are completely wrong, you know." She looked around. The other staff members had arrived and were clustered around the diner, whispering and pointing at the damage and avidly listening to the altercation between the two women.

"I didn't do this. I did my work, and I went home," Ally repeated, her voice rising despite herself.

"You did your work, all right," Lauren hissed.

Ally held her temper as Rob's patrol car pulled up, and he strolled toward them, eyeing the damage. "What happened, Lauren?"

Lauren pointed her finger at Ally. "She trashed my diner."

Rob held out his hands, palms up. "Hold up. How do you know that?" He took the keys out of Lauren's hands. "Let's take this inside and inspect the damage, okay?"

Lauren unlocked the front door and followed Rob inside. What looked like a large rock sat on one of the tables surrounded by shards of broken glass.

"I left Ally in charge of locking up," Lauren stated. "She obviously didn't do her job properly."

"Lauren, I wasn't here when this happened, so how can you blame me?"

Lauren's expression took on an obstinate look. "Because you *obviously* forgot to set the alarm. If that had gone off, the police department would've been alerted, and maybe *someone* would have gotten caught." She turned to glare meaningfully at Rob.

Ally shoved her hands into her pockets. What the hell was she supposed to say now?

Rob touched her shoulder. "I locked up, Lauren. If it was anyone's fault, it was mine."

"What?"

Rob moved past Ally and concentrated his attention on Lauren. "You told me to check up on the place last night, so I did. I let Ally out and stayed to lock up. I must've forgotten to switch on the alarm."

Lauren crossed her arms over her chest. "Why did you do that?"

"What?"

"Let her leave?"

Rob sighed. "Because she was exhausted, and I wanted to make sure the place got locked up properly."

"I bet she forgot to give you the code for the alarm and you're covering for her."

"Lauren, she gave me the code. I put it in my pocket, and I forgot to set the alarm. I'm sorry and I'll pay for all the damage, okay?"

Lauren started to say something, but Rob held up his hand. "Just save it, okay?"

"Why, because you can't bear to hear me say bad stuff about your precious little Ally?"

Rob lowered his voice. "Because you're making yourself look stupid, sis. Now, please get over yourself. File a report and claim it off your insurance company, or collect from me."

He nodded at Ally and stepped back. "I'll go get the paper-work started and call the guys to fix the window. I suggest you get this cleaned up in here."

Without daring to look at Lauren, Ally went into the kitchen, found a pair of thick gloves, and returned with a brush and pan to start sweeping the glass off the tables. Lauren still stood there, her high color fading, her furious gaze fixed on the hole in the glass. Fig and Ben appeared, too, and started cleaning up alongside Ally.

When they were certain that there was no glass left, Fig cordoned off the last two booths in the diner with tape and asked Lauren if she wanted to open up anyway.

Lauren seemed to startle to life. "No, let's wait and see if they can fix the window first. I don't want to risk any more damage. They might have better glass-clearing equipment too."

As she was speaking, the twenty-four-hour glass-repair guys

pulled into the parking lot, and Lauren went out to meet them. Ally surveyed the damaged booth. It was the one that she and Rob and Jackson had been sitting in the previous night. She could only be thankful they hadn't been there when the missile had been thrown. Unless it had been meant for her. Even though the blinds had been drawn, they were old and it was not entirely out of the question that someone had peered in and seen what she was doing. . . .

On that unsettling thought, she returned to the kitchen and shook the last pan of broken glass into the recycle bin. But who would want to do that to her? Lauren hated her more than anyone else in the town, and she was hardly likely to destroy her own diner in the process. She'd be more likely to march up to Ally and confront her publicly.

While the window was being fixed, Ally went to find Lauren. She was sitting in her office, elbows on the desk, hands cradling her head.

"I'm sorry about what happened, Lauren."

"Why are you sorry?"

"Because I know how hard you have worked to build up this business, and this must have been a blow."

Lauren swiveled around to look at Ally. "You know what is a blow? The way my brother still comes crawling around to protect you. I thought better of him."

Ally leaned against the door frame. "I know he took responsibility for what happened, but you're right. I was at fault. You told me to lock up, not your brother, and I should've stayed to see that it was done properly."

"Oh, for goodness' sake, Ally, stop being such a martyr."

Ally straightened up, came into the office, and shut the door firmly behind her. "What exactly do you want me to do, Lauren? Laugh at you and say I'm glad? Admit I threw the rock? I didn't throw it, and you just can't handle that, can you?"

Lauren stared at her for a long moment. "Go to hell, Ally."

"I told you before, I've been there and I didn't like it, so I kept going."

"And came back to seduce my brother all over again."

"That's really what this is all about, isn't it? And you couldn't be more wrong. Rob is one of the strongest men I've ever met. I didn't need to seduce him—he was ready and waiting to get back into my pants. He wants me and that's the way it is. Either get over it or lose him as a brother, because treating him like he's a weak fool is one perfect way to drive him away." Ally stopped talking and drew a shaky breath. "And now I suppose you're going to fire me, aren't you?"

"And have Rob on my back again and you suing me for unfair dismissal? Not happening." Lauren turned back to her computer. "Get out, Ally, and be here at five-thirty tomorrow."

Ally walked out past Fig and into the bright sunshine. She realized her knees were shaking, and she turned her steps toward the coffee shop. She'd never been great at confrontations, but she'd had enough of trying to be nice to Lauren. The woman would never like her again, and she would just have to accept that and get over herself.

Nadia saw her come in and brought over a mug of coffee. She patted Ally on the shoulder.

"You looked as if you needed that. I heard what happened at the diner. Who would do such a thing?"

"I don't know." Ally groaned. "And I just shouted at my employer. I think my days as a busboy are numbered."

Nadia chuckled. "Hold on another couple of weeks and I might be able to make you an offer you can't refuse. One of my staff is leaving, and I'll have an opening."

"That's good to know, but I'd probably still need to work two jobs." Ally sipped at her coffee. "The quicker I can get out of here the better."

"I don't think the sheriff would like that."

"The sheriff would be delighted. I've caused him nothing but trouble my whole life."

Nadia squeezed her hand. "Which is why he likes you. All the other women in this town are far too quick to lie down and offer themselves to him. He's an intelligent man who likes a challenge."

"You have no idea," Ally murmured as she drank her coffee and slowly stopped shaking. What a morning, and it wasn't even eight yet. Seeing as she had an unexpected day off, she'd go home and sleep for a while before continuing the cleaning. Hard work might help her put what had happened into perspective or at least tire her out until she stopped thinking about it.

She finished her coffee, waved good-bye to Nadia, and set off back home. How weird was it that Lauren had told Rob to check up on her? She'd imagined he'd come to find her by himself, but he'd been acting on Lauren's orders. If he hadn't had a good reason for being there, would he have stood up for Ally? He hadn't hesitated to defend her, but then he hadn't had any reason not to.

Ally was only glad she hadn't blurted out exactly what she'd been getting up to in the diner before Rob had arrived to set things straight. Would he have been so quick to back her up if she'd told his sister that they were already lovers again? Ally wasn't sure.

Something else occurred to her as she unlocked her front door. Lauren had told Rob it was all his fault before Rob had even admitted to being there. What was that about?

Ally wiped the sweat from her brow and focused her attention on the boxes on the dining table. Whatever was in them weighed a ton. Had Ruth started hoarding cat food or something? It seemed unlikely and didn't jibe with the neatness of her bank accounts either.

Thinking of the bank accounts made Ally go back to the

desk. Beneath all the copies of the bank statements, Ally had discovered five black books that were filled with her mother's handwriting. She forced herself to open the first book and realized Ruth had kept some kind of a journal. The dates on the books were recent, but Ally remembered Ruth scribbling away all her life.

She opened one of the desk drawers and saw it was full of similar black books. Had her mother kept all her journals? Ally's stomach churned at the thought of what she might find out. She closed the drawer with a bang. Did she want to find out about her mother or not?

Eager to do something other than dwell on the idea of reading her mother's personal stuff, Ally turned back to the pile of boxes on the table. She used the bread knife from the kitchen to open the first sealed box and frowned. It appeared to be full of magazines. Mystified, she pulled out the first one, which was a hefty edition of *Vogue,* and checked the date. It was about five years old. There was a bright sticker on the edge of one of the pages, and Ally turned to it.

Her breath caught as she saw a photograph of herself modeling some up-and-coming European designer. Ally surveyed her own printed image. God, she looked so thin and so spaced out. How could anyone have found her attractive enough to book her for anything? But six years ago she'd been at the height of her fame, thin, and wasted on drugs and alcohol and absolutely what some designers wanted to hang their clothes on—a lanky pile of bones.

Ally took out the next magazine and then the next, turning to every marked page to discover yet another appalling image of herself. She sank to the floor, the last magazine clutched to her chest. Tears burned behind her eyes as she thought about all those wasted years when she'd tried to convince herself that she was happy and had only succeeded in almost destroying herself. Had her mother kept every mag she'd ever appeared in? And if so, why?

The front doorbell rang and Ally jumped. She wasn't expecting anyone. Part of her wanted to continue sitting on the floor and contemplate her mother's actions. Only good manners made her go and see who it was.

Ally opened the door and found Jane with a covered dish in her hands. "Hey, Ally. I meant to bring this over for you last week, but I had unexpected company for dinner." Jane blushed and looked sideways at Ally. "You know how much Rob can eat, and he loves my cooking. He demolished the whole chicken pie. I had to make you a new one."

Jane kept talking and walked right past Ally toward the back of the house. She was wearing yellow shorts and a T-shirt with daisies, and her brown hair was drawn back from her face in a ponytail. Ally followed and watched as Jane deposited the casserole dish on the countertop. "Just take the lid off and put it in the oven to reheat for about half an hour and it will be fine."

"That's very kind of you, Jane," Ally said. "Would you like something to drink? I have lemonade or water."

Jane was looking around the kitchen as if she was a prospective buyer come to view the house. "Oh, water will be fine, thanks, Ally. How's the house coming along? I have a friend who's a Realtor who'd be really happy to help you sell the place. But Rob said you still had a lot to do."

"It is a lot of work." Ally handed Jane a glass and sipped at her own. "My mom kept the strangest things."

"Like what?"

Ally shrugged. "Like hundreds of magazines. I'm going to have a truckload of paper to take to the recycling place by the end of the week."

"Maybe she was into recycling and just hadn't gotten around to taking them herself."

"I suppose that could be it," Ally said carefully. "Whatever her reasons, I'm going to have to get rid of the stuff if I'm going to sell the house."

"You're not staying, then?"

"I don't think so." Ally leaned against the old refrigerator, glad of the cold metal at her back.

Jane sipped at her water. "To be honest, I'm kind of glad about that, Ally."

"You are?"

"Because when you're around, Rob doesn't seem to notice me anymore." Jane's smile was resigned.

"I'm sure he does."

"Nope, it's like you put a spell on him."

Ally met Jane's cool gaze. "I'm not trying to get in your way, Jane. Rob and I have a lot of stuff to talk through, but when we're done, he'll be all yours again."

Jane laughed. "Heck, he isn't mine at all. I'm just hoping he might be one day." She sighed. "He's a hard man to catch."

"He's a hard man."

"Rob is?" Jane looked surprised. "I've always found him to be incredibly sweet."

Ally couldn't help but smile back at Jane. "That's probably why he likes you."

Jane looked hopeful. "He told you that?"

"He said he was seeing you."

Jane put her glass down on the tabletop. "It's all very casual. I'm trying not to push him into anything."

"Good for you. Rob's not the type of guy you can make do anything he doesn't want to." Ally's smile felt strained. She felt bad talking about Rob as if he meant nothing to her. She felt even worse that she was fucking him and that Jane, who seemed so sweet, obviously had no idea. But it was only temporary, and she truly meant to leave him soon . . . didn't she?

Jane wandered back out into the hallway, and Ally followed her, pasting on yet another smile.

"Oh my goodness, I see what you mean about the boxes." Jane paused at the open dining room door. "I hope your mother was more organized about her private papers."

"Actually, she was." Ally's gaze settled on her mother's desk. "She left everything in good shape."

"Luckily for you."

Ally smiled. "Yeah, because otherwise it could've taken me years to sift through all this lot for the important stuff, and then I'd never leave."

"There must be hundreds of boxes. If you need help shifting them, let me know."

"Well, actually, Rob and Jackson volunteered to help me, so I should be fine. They both have big trucks."

Jane frowned. "I think you should keep away from Jackson, Ally. Why does he want to be in this house?"

"To help me?"

"More likely to make sure that you don't find anything to tie him in with Susan's murder."

"You think Susan was murdered too?"

"Of course I do." Jane paused. "And we all know by whom."

Ally felt like she was being sucked in to an episode of a TV cop show. "You think Jackson killed her."

"I do."

"What would he gain from murdering Susan?"

Jane raised her eyebrows. "It's simple. He's obsessed with Rob. He found a way to get rid of both of the women who were in his way—you and Susan."

"But wasn't Susan going to dump Jackson anyway?"

"I'm not so sure about that. She was crazy about him."

Ally thought back to the expression on Jackson's face on the previous night when he'd touched Rob so intimately. She'd always known there was something between the two guys, but she'd never considered it dangerous.

She shook her head. "I think you're way off base, Jane. Jackson and Rob are best buddies."

"Think what you like, Ally. I'm not going to change my opinion. But watch out. Now that you're back, Jackson might get busy trying to run you out of town again." Jane started toward the front door and then stopped. "Drat, I left my sunglasses in your kitchen. I'll just go and get them." Her voice faded as she hurried down the hallway. "You can bring the pie dish back anytime. You know where I live, right?"

"Yes, I do," Ally shouted after her. "I have a casserole dish to deliver back to your neighbor, Mrs. Orchard. I can bring them both back at the same time." Ally waited until Jane reappeared with her sunglasses now propped on her nose. "Thanks again for the pie."

"You're welcome and take care of yourself, all right?"

"I will. I promise I won't let Jackson come anywhere near me with his gun either."

"I suppose you think I'm delusional now, but Susan was scared of him, you know? I used to read her diary sometimes, when she wasn't looking, and she was very unhappy at the end."

Ally opened the door, and Jane stepped out into the sunshine. "Bye, Jane, and thanks again."

"Bye, Ally. Take care."

Ally closed the door and leaned against it. Either Jane had a very overactive imagination or there was some truth in what she said. Someone wasn't keen on Ally being back in Spring Falls, but she still didn't believe it was Jackson. She turned back to the pile of boxes. Everything was so unclear she might as well continue with another hopeless task and sort out her mother's stuff.

13

Ally handed Rob a glass of lemonade and led him through to the dining room. He studied her appreciatively. Her hair was tied back, and she was wearing frayed denim shorts that barely covered her ass and a tank top with no bra underneath that made him want to slide his hands under the thin cotton and—

"See?"

Rob paused to survey the opened pile of boxes. "See what?"

Ally took out a pile of old magazines and handed them to him. "There are twenty-five boxes on this table, and they are all filled with these."

"Magazines?"

Ally flipped the pages of the top copy and pointed at the picture. "They are all photos of me."

Rob glanced at her and then flipped through the remaining magazines. "Hell."

Ally leaned against the table. "Why do you think she kept these?"

She looked so tired and miserable he wanted to pull her into his arms and hold her tight. "Because she wanted to?"

"But why? When I lived here, she always made me feel like I was a nuisance and that she couldn't wait to get rid of me. She even..."

Rob tensed as Ally tightened her lips and simply shook her head.

"She even what?"

Ally turned her face away from him and pushed a strand of hair behind her ear. "She never liked me, Rob, so why did she keep all this stuff?"

"Maybe she changed. Maybe she regretted what happened between you. Did she ever try and contact you?"

"In the first year, she contacted me and asked for money. When I was making some, I sent her a check once a year for about six years." Ally walked across to the desk and stood looking down at it. "The funny thing is, Ruth never used the money. She just kept it in a separate savings account."

Rob considered what to say to her. "Sounds like she felt bad about taking your cash after all. And she did clean up her act, Ally. She stopped selling and using, and there were no guys hanging out at the house after you left."

"She blamed me for that, too, you know? She said I was flirting with her guys and that's why they never stuck around." Ally shivered. "Like I really wanted to be fondled by disgusting old men."

A sick feeling tightened Rob's gut. "Did any of them try to get it on with you?"

Ally looked at him for a long moment, a wealth of unpleasant experiences locked in her eyes. "Of course they did. I had to lock my door to keep them out from when I was about ten."

"Why didn't you tell me?"

"What could you have done?" She shrugged her thin shoulders. "And I didn't want you to know how I lived. You were the one good thing in my life. The one person not tainted by my mother."

"She hit on me once. Did I ever tell you that?"

"My mother did?"

"Yeah, I was waiting for you to come down and go to the football game. She was kind of drunk and came on to me."

"While we were still at school?"

"Yeah. When I was a junior and you were a freshman. I was too scared to come into your kitchen after that. I used to whistle for you from the yard, remember?"

Ally covered her face with her hands. "Oh God, why didn't you tell me?"

"The same reasons you didn't tell me anything. I didn't want to spoil what was between us, and I knew you'd be mortified." He hesitated. "I knew what your mom was like, Ally. Everyone knew."

"That she was a drunk, a slut, and a drug user? Yeah, everyone knew that. But you, Jackson, and Lauren were the only people who made me feel like it didn't matter."

Rob tensed as Ally swung around and shoved at one of the boxes on the table. It fell to the floor, and a pile of magazines slid out like a waterfall. "It's okay, Ally."

"No, it's not. I want to hate her, but how can I when I'm in her house, touching her things, seeing . . . this." She gestured at all the boxes. "She's a mystery to me, and I just can't stand it."

Rob walked across and drew her into his arms. She felt so right there, her head on his shoulder, her narrow frame pressed against him. "Maybe when you clean out her stuff, you'll get more of a sense of what she was really like."

She raised her head to look at him. "I found her diaries, Rob. I'm not sure if I even want to read them."

Rob felt a leap of excitement. "Your mom kept a journal?"

"She did." Ally jerked her head in the direction of the desk. "I found all the books in there."

"Are you going to read them?" Rob released Ally, his stance all business. "Because I'd really like to know—"

"What?" Ally interrupted him, her faint smile disappearing. "You sound like a cop now. What are you hoping will turn up? Her drug stash?"

"As far as I know, she stopped using a couple of years after you left."

Ally stalked out of the room back toward the kitchen, from where a delicious smell of chicken pie floated out.

Rob sniffed appreciatively. "Have you been cooking?"

"Don't change the subject," Ally snapped. "*You* say she'd stopped. I have no idea if that is true. I hadn't spoken to the woman in almost ten years."

Anxious to keep her mind off the diaries, Rob was quite willing to take the heat and go down that path. "Do you want me to bring one of the K-9 dogs in?"

"Are you serious?" Ally faced him, her hands on her hips.

"I'm just offering."

"Then stop it." She went across to the cupboards and took out some plates. "Are you hungry?"

"I'm always hungry, and that pie smells good."

"It should. Your girlfriend made it."

"You did?"

"I'm not your girlfriend. I'm just your . . ."

"Fuck buddy." Even as he said it, he hated the sound of it and curled his lips in distaste.

She flicked the dish towel at him. "Jane made the pie."

"Jane Evans?"

"Yes, your girlfriend, and let me tell you I felt awful having her standing in my kitchen bringing me food while I'm seeing you behind her back."

"She's not my girlfriend. She's just a friend I go out with oc-casionally."

Ally turned her back on him and got the pie out of the oven. "So you're not sleeping with her, then?"

"With Jane? No. I reckon she'd want an engagement ring on her finger before she'd let me have my wicked way with her."

"I suppose that makes it marginally better, although I still feel bad, and so should you."

He drew a cross over his heart. "I promise I won't go out with her while you're here, okay?" Rob offered.

"Hmm." Ally plonked the pie onto the table between them, and Rob's mouth watered. He waited while she dug him out a big portion and then sat opposite him.

He took his first taste and almost moaned. "Damn, but she does make a good pie."

"She sure does," Ally said. "And they do say that the way to a man's heart is through his stomach."

"And they are so wrong."

"What's the way to your heart, then, Rob?"

He looked down at his lap and then winked at her. "You know what it is, honey."

"To your heart? I thought that way led to your bed or any other place you want to have sex with me."

"Maybe I don't have a heart."

"Sure you do, and a woman like Jane would be perfect for you."

"Are you trying to hook me up?"

"I'm just saying that there are many women around here who could live up to even your high standards."

He put down his fork and took a long, slow drink of his lemonade. "I don't intend to get married, Ally."

"Aw ... did I ruin it for you?"

He glanced at her. "Yeah."

"I doubt it. You're not the sort of man who'd let a woman dictate his life."

"Lauren likes to try and dictate to me."

He wished she'd stop talking. She had an annoying habit of getting through his defenses and making him want to say ...

what? That she had destroyed him and that he'd never found the courage to love someone like he'd loved her?

Ally's gaze sharpened. "I've been meaning to ask you about something Lauren said yesterday outside the diner. She said that it was all your fault."

"And she was right. I forgot to set the alarm."

"No, Lauren mentioned it before you even got there. Just after she'd lost it with me about giving me a job in the first place." Ally pointed her fork in his face. "What did you do?"

"What the hell are you talking about?"

"You made her give me the job, didn't you?"

Rob sat back and contemplated Ally's furious face. "I asked her if she had any jobs open, sure."

"And told her to employ me?"

"As I said, I can't tell Lauren to do anything."

"Rob, why would you do that?"

"Because you needed the money and—"

Ally stood up. "You felt sorry for me?"

Rob shrugged. "Something like that."

"Because you wanted to give Lauren a sitting target and wanted me to stick around for the sex?"

"Ally..."

"What?"

"Sit down."

She glared at him for a long moment and then sat back in her chair with a decided thump.

"I wanted you to stick around, period."

"What the hell is that supposed to mean?"

He sighed. "When I saw you again, I realized there was stuff I wanted to clear up with you, stuff from the past."

"You can't always make everything neat and tidy in life."

"I know that. I'm a cop for Christ's sake."

"I've apologized to you for what I did. You're getting all the free sex you want. What else can I do?"

"Stay here and talk to me?"

Ally glanced down at her clasped hands. "So, just because you wanted me to 'stick around' to help you sort out the past, you interfered in my life again and got me a job with Lauren."

"I did what I thought was necessary to keep you here, yeah."

"For your own benefit."

Rob tried to cling to the remnants of his temper. "Ally, what do you want me to say?"

She slowly stood up again. "You can't order my life for me, Rob. That's one of the reasons I left in the first place. I can't let you do that anymore."

He set his jaw. "I didn't—"

"You used your influence to get me a job."

"Hell, I used my influence to get Jackson a job, and I don't notice him complaining about it."

"That's not fair. I've fought hard to learn to stand up for myself, to take responsibility for my actions and to regain my self-respect."

Rob stood, too, his hands clenched at his sides. "I know that! I respect you!"

"Do you? Then why didn't you ask me about the job first? Give me the choice as to whether I wanted you to ask Lauren or not?"

"Because..."

"Because it didn't occur to you, did it? You just thought good old Ally would be so grateful that she might hang around longer so that you could have more sex with her."

"It wasn't about the sex."

She held his gaze. "Are you sure about that?"

He glared back at her. "Oh, yeah, I'm sure. Because I gave you a choice about that and you chose to be just where I wanted you."

"On my knees."

"Where *you* wanted to be, so don't blame all this shit on me." He pushed his chair in and turned toward the door. "This is crazy, Ally. You're trying to turn everything into a battle about dominance, and it doesn't have to be like that. You're not the only one who can change. Yeah, I want you to submit to me in bed, but I sure as hell don't want a doormat. I'll even admit I got you the job because I felt sorry for you—where's the harm in that?"

"But I don't *want* you to feel sorry for me."

He kept his back to her. "Trust me, I don't anymore. Jackson was right about that at least. You don't need my help at all, do you?"

She didn't answer him, and he made the mistake of looking behind him. She was furiously wiping tears from her cheeks, and he wanted to groan. "Ally . . ."

"What?"

He turned fully around. "I don't want to fight about this."

"Too late."

He struggled to think of something to say. "I got you the job because I wanted you to stay in Spring Falls. If that was wrong of me, I apologize."

Ally turned around and walked down the hallway toward her bedroom. Rob heard the door slam and winced. He picked up his keys and went out the back. In his chosen career, he'd learned that sometimes it was better to retreat than to force an issue, and he was absolutely certain this was one of those times.

Jackson looked up as Rob came into the kitchen and frowned. "I thought you'd be staying over with Ally."

"So did I." Rob went to the refrigerator and took out a beer. "I pissed her off big-time."

"*You* did? Who'd have thought it?" Jackson raised his eyebrows and waited to see if Rob would say more.

"Ally found out that I got her the job with Lauren."

"Oh."

"Yeah." Rob contemplated his beer for so long that Jackson thought he wasn't going to speak again. "She accused me of trying to manage her life again."

"Again?"

Rob's pale eyes met his. "You know that was one of the reasons she left in the first place."

Jackson took his coffee through to the TV room, and Rob followed him and slumped down on the tattered leather couch. "So you fucked up."

Rob groaned. "I even tried to apologize, and she just walked out on me."

"Women."

Rob finished his beer and put the empty bottle on the rug beside the couch. "The thing is, I was trying to get her off the subject of her mother and walked right into another fucking trap."

"You told Ally you were interested in what her mother was up to when Susan died?"

"I started to, and she got all suspicious on me."

"Now, there's a surprise."

"I was going to do what you suggested and ask her outright, Jackson, and then she brought up all this shit about Lauren and the job and I got into that with her instead."

Jackson studied his best friend until Rob started to shift in his seat. "Do you want me to tell you what I think?"

"Sure, why not? I don't have any answers. She thinks I'm trying to control her entire life."

"Are you?"

"Hell, no! I told her that she needed to separate the sex from the rest of it."

"And how did she take that?"

"She went on about how hard she'd tried to rebuild her life

and . . ." Rob stopped talking and stared at Jackson. "Shit, she's right, isn't she?"

Jackson simply looked at Rob. "I wasn't very grateful when you decided to fix me either. Do you remember that?"

"Yeah."

"It took me quite a while to get over myself and accept your help for what it was—the hand of a friend. For Ally it's going to be a lot harder than that."

"So what the hell can I do to fix this?"

"You can't. That's part of the problem. *You're* part of the problem. You'll have to wait and see what Ally chooses to do about it."

"Thanks for nothing, buddy." Rob rolled over on the couch and buried his face in the cushions.

Jackson raised his coffee mug in a salute. "You're welcome."

Ally jumped as her cell phone buzzed in her pocket. It had better not be Rob or Jackson. It was too late, and she was too tired to start anything with either of them now. She checked the number and clicked to connect.

"Jill?"

"Hey! How are you?"

"I'm okay, I guess. How are you?" Ally settled herself back against the pillows of her bed and tried to picture Jill's smiling face.

"You don't sound okay. And your e-mail worried the shit out of me."

Ally sighed. "I've got to stay here for a while. I have no choice."

"With all that negative energy around you? The plan was that you'd go back, clear up the mess, and leave as quickly as possible. What happened to change your mind?"

Ally cringed as Jill, yet again, asked her the hard questions.

But then wasn't that what AA sponsors were for? "I thought you said it was a good idea, Jill. It's a chance for me to reconcile with my past, or whatever you like to call it." Jill was totally into all the New Age stuff that Ally despised, but they were still friends.

"Don't make light of this, Ally. The idea was that you find closure and move forward with your new life, not to go back and make the same mistakes again. Are any of the guys you hung out with still there?"

Ally closed her eyes and imagined Jill in the guise of a fiery guardian angel frowning down at her. "Actually, both of them are."

"Bummer. So, have you talked to them?"

"Seen them, talked to them, and fucked them both," Ally said flippantly.

There was a long silence. "Oh, shit, Ally. That was not a good idea at all."

"Yeah."

"Do you want me to come and stay with you?"

"And use up all your vacation time? What about Steve and the kids?"

"They'll manage."

Despite her soft exterior, Jill ran her family and her career with a ruthless efficiency that sometimes scared Ally.

"No, I can't let you sort everything out for me."

"That's true. You've changed a lot over the past few years and made some tough decisions." Jill hesitated. "But by having sex with these guys, aren't you just repeating your past mistakes?"

"Well, I didn't have sex with them *together* before, so something's changed. Does that count?"

Jill sighed. "This isn't funny, Ally."

"I know that. But I like to have sex with Rob and Jackson."

"I'm glad you're starting to think about sex in a positive

way, Ally, but are you sure you know what you're doing? And I'm asking that as your friend, and as your AA supporter."

"Honestly, it's been amazing for me to come back here and have sex with two men I trust."

"So, what's different?" Jill asked.

"*Me.* I'm different," Ally said, trying to think it through. "I realized that I could still stay strong in other areas in my life even if I was sexually submissive."

"And?"

Ally sighed. "God, Jill, you make this so hard for me. *And,* admitting what I want sexually—rather than trying to pretend that what I felt was abnormal—has set me free."

Silence followed her confession, and Ally struggled to swallow. "It's just about sex. What's wrong with that?"

Jill's voice got loud. "Ally, listen up. There's no such thing as sex without emotional payback. You could destroy all the gains you've made with this impulsive, regressive behavior."

Ally tightened her grip on the phone. "You don't trust me to get it right this time?"

"It's not that," Jill said. "But I want you to keep questioning your choices. You're still in a very vulnerable place in your life, and you can't rely on Rob or Jackson to make decisions for you."

Ally forced a laugh. "Trust me, they are both very keen on making me choose what I want."

"Well, that's good, but I still want you to call or e-mail me every night and tell me how things are going, okay?"

"Sure," Ally said. The thought of having Jill there to give her advice was comforting.

"You're strong, Ally, believe it. Now just clear the house, sell it, and come back to New York before you start college, okay?"

"Sounds like a plan." Ally pressed the phone to her cheek and found she was smiling. "I'm okay. I really am. I'm glad I came back. It's giving me a chance to get closure. I know you like that word."

Jill laughed. "I do, and so should you." She paused. "Have you sorted out your mom's stuff yet?"

"I'm dealing with that. It's harder than I thought. Apparently, my mom cleaned up her act after I left."

"But that's great! You of all people know how hard it is."

Ally stared unseeingly at the faded wallpaper. "Yeah, I suppose I do." She didn't want to share any more life experiences with her mother, good or bad, but she had a terrible sense that they were treading the same path. "It's kind of weird, though."

"Why's that?"

"Because I thought she would never change."

"You changed, so why shouldn't she?"

Ally bit her lip. "It makes it harder to hate her."

"But that's a good thing, isn't it?"

"Because I need to let go of my anger before I can 'love' her? You know how I feel about that shit."

"Ally, how about you just let yourself get to know her again? Don't push it, but talk to the people who knew her, find out what her life was like since you left."

"I'll try. That's the best I've got for you at the moment."

"Okay. You're trying to get people in town to accept the new you, so imagine how that must have been for your mother."

"Hard, I should think."

"I'm sure it was." Jill paused as if she was listening to something. "I think the boys are fighting again. I'll let you go. Take care of yourself, won't you?"

"I swear I will." Ally glanced at her alarm clock. "I have to get up really early. It was lovely to hear from you."

"Are you sure you don't want me to come down?"

"I'm quite sure. I'm handling this on my own."

"Ally, you are not. You have me, and I'm going to find out a couple of local contacts who can be available for you if necessary, okay?"

"Okay, I get it. I need help."

"That's right, you do. Now go to sleep."

Ally shut her phone and stared down at the patterned yellow bedsheets. She *was* handling it—most of the time. She'd been surprised at her own assertion to Jill that she could be strong and yet sexually submissive. Why hadn't she realized that when she was arguing with Rob?

Even after their argument, she hadn't contemplated leaving Spring Falls, heading for the nearest bar, or quitting her job. Surely that showed she had changed and that she had staying power? A small pocket of pride blossomed in her chest.

But was Rob right? Was she overreacting to his attempt to help her out? She'd just made a declaration of intent to Jill, and yet she'd already undermined herself in her argument with Rob. He'd been the one to point out that accepting a helping hand from him didn't mean she had to be a doormat—or that he wanted her to be one.

Ally punched her pillow. She'd wanted a job and had been prepared to do whatever it took to get one. The fact that Rob had helped her shouldn't really rankle, but it did. She rubbed a hand across her tired eyes. Was it possible she had overreacted just a little? She groaned and thumped her pillow again. She'd have to talk to Rob again, and that scared her to death.

14

Ally gathered her courage and rang the doorbell of Rob and Jackson's home. Rob opened the door and stared down at her, his blue eyes narrowed and his hair ruffled. He looked like he hadn't slept well either. Ally held up the plate of pie.

"I brought a peace offering. It's the rest of Jane's chicken pie. Can I come in?"

Rob stepped back and Ally followed him inside, through the untidy family room and into the big kitchen at the back. She placed the pie on the countertop and turned to face Rob, who had leaned up against the sink.

"I think I might have overreacted to something you said last night."

Rob raised an eyebrow. *"Might?"*

"Okay, I did overreact, but I wanted to tell you why."

He held up his hand. "It's okay, Ally. I pushed your buttons; you got pissed. I get it."

"What the hell is that supposed to mean?"

He pushed a hand through his short-cropped hair. "I tried

to tell you how to think. I got you a job behind your back. I did all the things that make you nervous about being with me."

Ally stared at him for a long moment. "You figured that out all by yourself?"

He winced. "With a little help from Jackson, who also regularly tells me to get the fuck out of his face."

"It wasn't all your fault, Rob. I freaked out. I'm trying so hard to be strong and independent that I get a bit touchy when I feel like someone is trying to manipulate me." She tried a tentative smile. "I did want the job."

"But you would've preferred it if I'd asked you first. I get that now. I promise I won't do it again."

He still wasn't smiling and Ally wondered why.

"Would you like a soda, Ally?"

"No thanks, I have to get back to work at three."

Rob opened the refrigerator and got out a can of lemonade and popped it open. "Lauren's still working you hard, then?"

"She is and I'm determined not to let her win. She's stuck with me until I either leave or die on the job."

He took a seat at the table and gestured to the chair opposite. "Sit down a minute, okay?"

She sat and studied him carefully. There was a faint frown on his face and trouble deep in his eyes. "What's up?"

"I've got to go away for a few days."

"When?"

"Tonight. They offered me a spot on the gun-safety procedure course Jackson finished up a couple of months ago, and I really need to go."

"So go."

He reached across the table and took her hand. "I'll only be away for five days."

"It's okay. I think I'll survive."

He tightened his grip. "It's not that." He hesitated. "It's just that in the interest of full disclosure, I want you to let me know if you find anything...unusual...as you clear out your mother's house."

"Unusual?"

His pale blue gaze met hers. "Anything that might seem out of place, or anything your mother mentions in those journals of hers."

"For what reason?"

"Some of that unfinished business I mentioned the other night. I've got a bad feeling in my gut about all this."

"I thought you were talking about us."

"We weren't the only people involved in that mess, were we?"

Ally paused to consider his words. "You want to talk about Jackson and Susan?"

"That's part of it."

"And what does that have to do with me cleaning out my mom's house?"

"Maybe nothing, but I'd be grateful if you'd bear it in mind while you're working."

Ally pulled out of his grasp and stood up, her eye on the clock. "I have to go."

Rob stood too. "And you're not happy with me again, are you."

"It's not that. I'm just confused. Why would you think Susan and Jackson have anything to do with what's at my house?" She put her hand to her mouth. "Is this because my mom sold drugs to them?"

"I don't know, Ally." Rob looked exhausted. "That's why I'm asking you to help me."

"Okay." She moved in close and stood on tiptoe to kiss his mouth. He took control of the kiss, turning it into something far hotter and more visceral than she had intended, so she was soon drowning in it. "I have to go."

He spread his fingers over her ass and drew her against his

rock-hard erection, nipping at her lip. "Let me call Lauren and tell her you'll be fifteen minutes late due to police questioning about the window."

"Rob . . ."

He tightened his grip on her ass. "I fucking need to be inside you right now."

Ally stared at him and then nodded. She let him make the call and admired the calm finality of his voice even as Lauren squawked in protest. She moaned as his finger and thumb closed over her nipple and squeezed hard. He had one hand down her panties even as he clicked off the phone, his mouth plundering hers as his fingers slid inside her already-slick entrance.

He carried her into the family room and brought her down on the couch, moved on top of her, and shoved down his shorts. "Yeah, right now, give it up."

Ally moaned as he penetrated her in one smooth thrust and kept doing it, pounding her into the pillows until she started to orgasm around him and cling on to his muscular shoulders. He kissed her throat, her shoulder, and then took her nipple into his mouth and sucked so hard she climaxed again.

He brought his hand up to cup her head and stared down at her. "I want you to think of me when I'm away. I want you to miss this—miss the fucking and miss me."

"I . . ." Ally gasped as he bit down on her throat, making her arch against him. He gathered her ass into his hands and pumped harder until all she could think about was the hard grinding rhythm of his thrusts, his labored breathing, and finally the heat of his come deep inside her.

He slumped over her for a moment and then rolled onto the floor and pulled up his shorts. Ally lay there and looked at him, too exhausted to think of moving let alone going to work. Rob found her panties and shorts and eased them up her legs.

"I need to shower, Rob."

He kissed her mound, his tongue sliding between her already swollen folds. "You don't have time, and I like you wet like this. I like the thought of you working with my come on you all day."

"You are such a Neanderthal sometimes." Ally winced as he helped her sit up. "I at least have to pee."

"Then do it quick, because you're supposed to be there in five minutes, and you look like you just got out of bed."

Ally cleaned up as best she could and then joined him in the kitchen, where he handed her a bottle of water. He'd changed into his uniform. He picked up his hat and buckled on his belt. "I'll drop you off."

"You don't have to."

"I *do* need to ask you some questions about the break-in. I can ask you on the way, and if we arrive in my patrol car, Lauren won't get suspicious."

Ally cast him a sidelong glance. "It all worked out very nicely for you, didn't it?"

He held the door open for her and patted her ass as she walked by. "Sure, sex and interrogation. My two favorite things. Too bad I forgot to use my handcuffs."

Ally had nothing to say to that; all her energy was focused on trying to look as if she hadn't just been fucked by the sheriff. By the time they pulled up at the diner and Rob got out to escort her inside, he'd stopped smiling and had his cop face firmly in place. Ally envied him his ability to switch moods so easily.

He walked her through to where Lauren was working in her office. "Here she is, sis. Fifteen minutes late."

Lauren ignored Ally and nodded at Rob. "So do I bill you for her time as well as for the window?"

"If you like." Rob stepped forward and kissed Lauren on the cheek. "I'm going out of town for a few days. Talk to Jackson if you need anything. Later, Lauren, Ally."

Ally smiled and moved out of his way. She turned back to find that Lauren was staring at her.

"What would you like me to do first, boss?"

"Get your claws out of my brother?"

"We've already had that discussion, Lauren. He's a grown-up and so am I."

Lauren swung around and presented Ally with her back. "Go and bus the tables and then wash dishes, okay?"

"Sure." Ally turned to leave.

Fig waved at her from the kitchen as she gathered up her cleaning supplies. Even one of the waitresses smiled when she saw Ally coming. Two weeks on the job and she felt quite at home, despite Lauren's lack of welcome.

Jackson parked at the old courthouse, took off his jacket, and walked around the corner to the diner. It was well after closing time, and the lights in the front were off. As he came closer, Jackson sniffed the night air appreciatively. Coffee and fries always put him in a better mood, and the diner smelled of both.

The back door was open, and Jackson could see Ally talking to the other busboy as they carried out the trash. He'd been so busy covering Rob's shifts that he hadn't seen her for five days, so the sight was more than welcome. He caught her eye and nodded slowly. "Hey."

She smiled at him and then went back inside. He wasn't worried; she'd come out eventually. He checked his radio but everything was quiet. Jeff had the late-night shift, and Jackson wasn't due back on until six in the morning. His hand went to his gun as another shadow overlaid his.

"Evening, Jackson."

He took a long, slow breath. Despite all the years since he'd been in Afghanistan, his nerves still jangled sometimes. "Hey, Lauren."

"What are you doing out here?" Lauren came out of the kitchen, followed by Ally and the other guy. Lauren locked the back door and then walked around to the front of the diner.

Jackson followed her. "Just checking up on you."

Lauren keyed in the alarm and shut the front door with a decisive bang. "Did Rob ask you to?"

"Of course."

Lauren checked him out, her lip caught between her teeth. "Are you still on duty?"

"No, I'm off for the night. I've got a meeting to go to."

"That's a shame. We haven't had a good talk for ages." Lauren set off for the rear parking lot.

Jackson was aware of Ally still waiting at the back door, but he kept his attention fixed on Lauren. "We 'talk' now?"

Lauren stopped and looked over her shoulder. "I'm worried about Rob. Since *she* came back he's—" She suddenly noticed Ally. "Why are you still here?"

Jackson cleared his throat. "She's waiting for me."

Lauren made a disgusted sound. "Don't tell me she's messing with your head, too, Jackson."

Jackson held Lauren's angry stare. "She's coming to the meeting with me."

"What kind of meeting?"

"The kind that addicts go to." Jackson held out his hand. "Are you ready, Ally?"

She came around Lauren and took his hand. He noticed her fingers were shaking. "Thanks, Jackson."

He turned his back on Lauren and kept walking. "Are you okay?"

Ally paced alongside him, her long legs easily keeping up with him. Without her heels on, they were exactly the same height. "Are we really going to an AA/NA meeting?"

"Yeah, it occurred to me that you might not know where they were held around here."

"I didn't, but I was going to look them up."

He squeezed her hand. "We don't have to look too far. There's one in the Baptist church hall right here in town twice a week, or if you want to go more often, Jamestown has way more choices."

Ally stopped walking and looked at him. "Why do you go to meetings?"

"Because I'm like you."

"An addict?"

He smiled at her serious expression. "Yeah. Me and alcohol? We don't mix." He kissed her on the forehead. "So let's go show our faces, and then we can have dinner together, okay?"

Ally looked up at Jackson as he unlocked the back door of the house. "Thanks for taking me, Jackson."

"You're welcome." He hesitated beside her, his fingers brushing her cheek. "I know I'm not supposed to tell you this, but I regularly saw your mom at the meetings before she died."

Ally thought about that and tried to smile. "It's yet another piece of the puzzle, isn't it? People keep trying to tell me that my mom had changed, and it's so hard to believe it." She kissed Jackson on the nose and laughed. "And then I wonder why no one believes I've changed and I get all pissed about it. You can never really trust an addict, though, can you?"

"You can try," Jackson whispered.

Ally walked through the garage at Jackson and Rob's house and into the narrow laundry room. It was getting late, but she'd enjoyed her evening with Jackson, especially having his silent support when she'd had to stand up and introduce herself to a meeting hall full of fellow addicts.

Jackson touched her shoulder. "Take off your clothes here and I'll stick them in the wash. They'll be ready for you to wear later."

"Everything?"

His heated gaze tracked down her body. "Yeah."

Ally flipped on the light and watched as he started the machine. As she pulled her clothes off, she dropped them into the foamy water. By the time she was naked and closed the lid of the machine, Jackson had disappeared. Ally left her sandals on the cool tile floor and headed into the dark kitchen.

The only light that was on appeared to come from one of the bedrooms, so Ally kept going. A lamp illuminated the white and brown covers on the pristine bed. Jackson's clothes lay in a heap on the floor. The door to the bathroom was open, and she could hear the sounds of the shower going.

She went into the bathroom and paused to admire the view. Jackson was facing away, stripping off his tight white boxers and giving her a perfect view of his ass and long legs. He stretched his arms above his head and groaned, which made all his muscles ripple like silk. He caught sight of her in the mirror and turned slowly around.

"Let's shower."

She followed him into the small glass shower stall, and he kissed her, his already erect cock nudging her belly. She grabbed the shower gel and poured some on her hands. She couldn't help but start washing his chest. He closed his eyes and leaned back against the wall.

"That's nice, Ally."

She continued to run her hands over his burnished skin and licked at the droplets of water and used her tongue on his tight brown nipples. His hand moved to her ass, and he slid his fingers between her legs, finding the wetness already there waiting for him.

"Rob said you'd be wet."

"Did he."

He drew her head up so that he could look her in the eye. "Yeah. He said I'd need to fuck you while he was away because you'd need it."

"So this is for Rob's benefit, is it?"

His hand tightened on her hair. "I was going to fuck you anyway. Rob just gave me an extra incentive." He brought his lips against hers in a slanting kiss, and she let him slide his tongue into her mouth. He kissed like he had sex, with a focused intensity she found irresistible.

She slid her hand down to his shaft, but he pushed her questing fingers away. "There's no hurry. Let's finish the shower first." He helped her wash her hair, his strong hands making the task easy as he rinsed the soap away.

She put her arms around his neck, and he turned off the shower and carried her out to the bedroom, her legs wrapped around his hips, his shaft sandwiched between them. He dropped her onto the bed and stood looking down at her. "Now suck my cock." He moved closer, and she knelt on the mattress and carefully took his cock into her mouth. He tasted of the shower gel and himself, a salty familiar flavor that made Ally want to devour him whole. "Do it fast."

Ally sucked him hard and used her tongue to torment the wet slit at the tip of his crown. He groaned and shoved himself farther into her mouth. His hand tangled in her hair, keeping her where he wanted her, where she wanted to be.

"Yeah, that's good. I'm going to call Rob now."

Startled, Ally tried to look up at him, but he didn't release his grip.

"I didn't tell you to stop. Keep sucking me."

From the corner of her eye, she saw him flip open his cell, punch in a number, and place the phone on the pillow beside her head. Rob's sleepy voice suddenly filled the room. "Yeah."

"It's Jackson. I've got Ally here, too, but she's busy right now."

"Doing what?"

"Sucking my dick."

There was a hiss of static and then Rob cursed. "And you're telling me this why?"

"I thought you might like to play along."

"While you fuck her?"

"Yeah."

Rob's sigh echoed through the room. "I'm hard just thinking about it." There was the sound of rustling sheets. "Yeah, I'm really hard."

"I'm going to fuck her ass first. She's really wet, and I want her begging for it before I finally take her pussy."

"Jeez." Rob's voice sounded hoarse now. "I wish I was there to help you out."

"Tell me what you want me to do to her, and I'll add it to my repertoire." Jackson rolled his hips just to feel the warm pressure of Ally's mouth on his shaft.

"You do your own thing, buddy, and I'll just listen in and do mine," Rob eventually said.

"Sure." Jackson carefully disengaged his dick from Ally's mouth and found the lube he'd placed by the bed. "Turn over, Ally."

She moved onto all fours, presenting him with the most awesome view of her ass and her sex. Jackson coated his fingers and then his cock and moved closer until the front of his thighs brushed against the curves of Ally's ass.

"I'm going to get her ready for my cock now, Rob." He slid two oiled fingers into Ally's ass and moved them back and forth, heard her moan. "She likes it. Can you hear her?"

"Yeah . . . make her moan some more."

Jackson added more fingers, and Ally arched her back, offering him more. "You want me to spank her, Rob?"

"Shit, yeah. She likes it, don't you, Ally?"

Jackson obliged with half a dozen quick slaps to each of Ally's ass cheeks. He paused to admire the effect, felt the fine trembling running through her as he continued to work her with his fingers. His cock ached like he imagined her skin did, and he wanted to shove himself deep and make her scream his name. The thought of Rob listening in made it even better. He imagined Rob sitting up in his hotel bed, one hand gripping his cock, all his attention on the noises issuing from his cell phone.

"Next time one of us goes away, we should set up a video link," Jackson murmured.

"I'm not sure my heart could take it," Rob replied. "Are you going to fuck her or just talk about it?"

In answer, Jackson removed his fingers and pressed forward with his latex-covered cock, making Ally gasp and writhe beneath him. He closed his eyes as her tight passage enclosed him and struggled to stop from coming too soon. His whole upper body was now curved over Ally's, and his cell phone was closer so that he could hear Rob's harried breathing as well.

"She likes it, right?"

"Yeah, and she's going to like it even more when I start moving."

"I've seen you fuck her, Jackson. I know how good it is."

"You like watching me fuck her?"

"Yeah, I do."

The thought of Rob watching him made Jackson so hard he just couldn't contain himself anymore. He slid one arm around Ally's waist to anchor himself and pounded into her. She started to pant and moan with every stroke of his cock, and he forgot about Rob and thought only of how much he wanted to please Ally. He cupped her sex and rubbed her clit in time to his thrusts, felt her start to fight him to reach a climax, but she couldn't beat him. He was, Christ he was coming so hard his cock was going to explode.

Ally screamed his name as he poured himself deep inside her, and he heard Rob groan. Jackson slumped over Ally until he got his breath back and then slowly peeled himself off her. "Talk to Rob while I go and wash up, Ally."

* * *

Ally couldn't believe it when Jackson thrust his cell phone into her shaking hand and headed for the bathroom. She rolled over onto her back. She could barely breathe let alone speak, and she knew Jackson would be coming back soon, ready to fuck her again.

"Ally?"

She thought of Rob alone in a strange hotel bed. "Did you come, Rob?"

"Not yet, honey."

"Jackson will be disappointed."

"He'll live." She heard him shift around. "I've got one hand wrapped around my dick, and I'm picturing you lying on that bed, naked, waiting for Jackson to come and nail you again."

"Are you naked, Rob?"

"I am now. I took my boxers off the moment Jackson called and said you were sucking him."

"I like sucking you too. I like the way you feel in my mouth and how big you are."

"Ally..."

She kept talking, loving the rough sound of need in his voice, need she'd put there and could add to at will. "I liked it best when I had you both in my mouth. Do you remember that?" She felt her clit throb as if enjoying the memory. "I like it even more when you are both fucking me."

"God..."

She almost thought she could hear the sound of Rob's hand moving on his shaft through the phone.

"I wish I was with you now, Rob. I'd take your hand and your cock and lick and suck you until you came all over me." She looked up to see Jackson standing beside the bed, his gaze fixed on her face. "Then I'd do it for Jackson too."

"Ally, you're killing me here," Rob said.

"It would be awesome. I'd love everyone to see us. Love

them to look at us and be so jealous." Ally shivered as Jackson pushed her knees wide and positioned his cock at the entrance to her sex. "Jackson's about to fuck me now, Rob. The tip of his cock is right up close to my clit."

Rob groaned. "I'd like to be there so I could lick your pussy."

"You'd have to lick Jackson's cock as well, because it's right there too." Ally looked up as Jackson suddenly tensed, and she patted his thigh.

"Hell, I'd lick anything right now if it meant getting us all off. I'm dying here."

Jackson came into her, and she grabbed hold of his shoulders and held on tight. For long, frenzied minutes, she could think of nothing else but the power of his body plunging into hers, the strength of his grip and the thick hardness of his shaft pumping inside her. She climaxed hard and he just kept going, each thrust a smack of flesh against flesh, his fingers biting into her spanked ass, his mouth capturing and keeping hers in a long, drawn-out, salacious kiss.

She came again and clung on to him even more, her body almost limp with pleasure, her mind reeling from the satisfaction he was giving her. His sudden withdrawal left her gasping and reaching for him. He flipped her over onto her stomach and started again. His hands were rough on her breasts and then on her already swollen and sensitive clit.

"Please, I can't..."

He kept going, drawing yet another orgasm from her, narrowing the boundary between pain and pleasure, between flesh and mind, between what she wanted and what seemed unbearable.

She moaned when he pulled out again and flipped her onto her back. He knelt up, grabbed her heels, and positioned them over his shoulders. She couldn't even breathe as he plunged back inside her, the angle so acute that she could do nothing but take it.

She opened her eyes and saw his were closed, his features drawn back in a savage mask of lust as he controlled her with his thrusts and the weight of his body. A tide of extreme pleasure edged with pain radiated through her. She scrabbled to hold on to any part of his flesh apart from his cock and screamed so hard through her orgasm that she hurt her own ears.

Jackson came, too, and his climax seemed to take forever. Each hot spurt dragged out as if he didn't ever want to stop. He collapsed over her, and she took his weight, held his shuddering, twitching body in her arms until he started to relax.

After a while, she remembered the cell phone and held it to her ear. "Are you still there, Rob?"

"I'm . . . here."

"Did you come this time?"

His laughter was edged with desperation. "Yeah. You two certainly give great phone sex."

"It will be even better when you get back."

"Ally, don't say stuff like that. My cock is already getting hard again."

"You'll be back in two more days."

"I will and you'd better be ready for me."

Jackson took the phone from her and held it to his ear. "Yeah . . . Sure . . . Later."

He flipped the cell shut and put the phone on the bedside table. Ally rolled over to study his face. "That was awesome."

His smile flickered. "It sure was."

"Were you inspired by the thought of Rob sucking your cock?"

"Ally . . ."

She kissed his chin. "It's okay, Jackson. I think I've always known what you want from him."

"And he's never wanted that from me, so can we drop the subject?"

"Have you ever asked him?"

"I'm not a girl. We don't talk like that."

"Maybe you should." Ally hesitated as she sensed the tension return to his body. "I don't think he'd be that surprised either."

Jackson lifted her off him and sat up, his burnished skin glowing in the lamplight. "Why do you think I left when you did, Ally?"

"Because of what Susan did?"

"That was bad enough, but there was more." Jackson swung his feet over the side of the bed and sat facing away from her. "I knew that if I stayed, I'd be offering Rob less of an 'I'm sorry for fucking your girlfriend' and more of a 'Can I fuck you instead?' vibe."

"But you didn't stay."

He sighed. "I couldn't do that to you, Ally."

"Because you felt guilty?" Ally crawled over and touched his shoulder. "Did you arrange for Susan and Rob to catch us in bed together?"

He turned to look at her. "Is that what you thought? *Shit.*"

"It's a possibility that had occurred to me."

"Here's the truth, Ally. I sure as hell thought about it, and, yeah, I have a lot to feel guilty about." He got to his feet. "I'm going to check on the laundry."

She watched him leave and worried at her lower lip. Was he suggesting he had betrayed her, or what? But how? After her confrontation with her mother, she hadn't exactly planned on heading over to his house, and she certainly hadn't meant to jump into bed with him. After she'd collapsed in his arms crying, he hadn't been out of her sight for a moment until Rob and Susan caught them fucking.

She washed up, drank a glass of water, and waited quietly for

Jackson to return to her. He'd pulled on a pair of black boxers and halted in the doorway.

"I was wondering if you'd still be in bed."

"You have all my clothes."

"I just put them in the dryer. They'll be ready to go soon."

"Thanks." She patted the rumpled covers. "Aren't you coming back to bed?"

"Do you really want me to?"

She raised her eyebrows. "You didn't betray me to Rob. I'd bet my life on it. You might have wanted to, but you didn't, did you?"

He sighed and came to sit down next to her. "I did enough. You know that."

"You offered me comfort when I needed it."

"I offered you sex."

She squeezed his hand. "I thought that was me."

"I should've taken you back home."

"Because you were older than me?"

"Because you were my best friend's girl. I wasn't upset like you were. I knew what I was doing, Ally."

She let out a long, slow breath. "I knew what I was doing, too, Jackson. Originally I tried to blame you, but lately I've realized that I was trying to break free of Rob and I figured the most awful way to do that was by sleeping with you."

"I don't believe you were thinking that clearly. It's easy to look back and find reasons for stuff we did. You were scared out of your wits that night, and not by Rob."

She met his kind gaze and stared into his dark brown eyes. "You are such a nice person, Jackson."

He grimaced. "Nice."

She slid a finger inside the waist of his boxers. "How long does the dryer take?"

He hissed as her finger brushed over the tip of his cock. "About half an hour."

"Then we've got plenty of time for me to suck your cock, haven't we?"

He placed his hand over hers. "And to fuck."

Her body was already sore, but she still wanted him. "If that is what you want."

"Yeah, I want."

She pulled down his boxers to expose his half-erect cock and licked her lips. Sex wasn't the answer to everything, but sometimes it made showing how you felt for someone so much easier.

15

_____

Ally checked the time on her cell phone and glanced back at the arrivals gate. Rob was due back any minute. When Jackson had been called in for an extra shift, she'd borrowed his truck and volunteered to pick Rob up from the Sacramento airport. It was another hot and steamy day, so she'd worn a simple patterned halter-neck dress and sandals, her hair loose on her shoulders. It was nice not to be cleaning something and having to wear her oldest clothes for work.

A crowd of travelers surged through the gate, and Ally had no trouble spotting Rob, who towered over most people. He wasn't in uniform and had settled for an olive green T-shirt and khaki shorts. Ally waved at him. He instantly turned toward her, his bag slung over his shoulder.

"Ally."

"Jackson was delayed at the last minute. I hope you don't mind me coming instead."

Something flickered in the depths of his light blue eyes as his mouth curved into a smile. "I'd much rather see you coming any day."

Ally found herself unable to look away as his mouth descended on hers and he kissed her as if they were alone and naked in his bedroom. His bag thumped down onto the floor and he caged her in his embrace. She forgot where they were as his hand edged down over her ass and flirted with the hem of her short skirt.

An announcement crackled over the public-address system, and Rob wrenched his mouth away from hers. His expression was grim. "We'd better get going."

"Okay," Ally said breathlessly.

He picked up his bag, took her hand, and started purposefully toward the parking lot.

She tugged at his hand. "I parked inside because of the heat. We need to use the stairs or take the elevator to level four."

Rob changed direction and soon they were climbing the echoing staircase to the parking garage's fourth level. Ally let him lead her, her fingers held firmly in his grasp, her heart pounding. He pushed open the door, and they were in the quiet of the far left corner of the parking garage.

"My truck or yours?"

"Jackson's, actually." Ally pointed it out. "It's over there."

"Keys?"

Ally handed them over, and Rob stowed his bag in the back and then turned back to Ally. She was in his arms before she even realized his intention, his mouth voracious and demanding over hers. "I've been thinking about you all week, thinking about fucking you." His hand slid under her skirt and tugged at the thin lace of her panties. "Are you wet for me?"

Ally tried to see past him to the rest of the garage, but she couldn't, and she didn't really want to. Having Rob touching her in such a public place turned her on, and he probably knew it. "Yes." Two of his fingers plunged inside her, and she gasped and grabbed hold of his arm.

He ripped the seam of her panties and they slid down her legs. "I can't wait, Ally. I need to be inside you right now."

He backed her against the low wall at the edge of the structure and bent her over it. She felt warm air on her ass cheeks as he flipped up her skirt, the sound of his zipper, and then... God, he was inside her, shoving himself deep, making her breathe hard through the sudden impalement.

She opened her eyes and looked down, and was amazed to see that there was no one staring up at them. Rob slid a hand inside the top of her dress and palmed her breast, pinching her nipple hard. She came for him and tried to scream, but his other hand came up to cover her mouth and she writhed in silence.

He kept up the fast pace, slamming his length from tip to balls into her wetter and wetter sex. Even through her desire, she heard the sound of the elevator doors open and voices echoing, coming closer and closer.

Rob took his hand away from her breast and fingered her clit. He nipped her ear and murmured, "You're going to come for me now, while these people walk right by us."

She wanted to argue with him, but he had her pinned to the wall, his big body covering hers, his hands and cock dictating all her emotions. The voices drew closer, and he kept fucking her until she couldn't think of anything else, would have turned on him if he'd dared to stop.

She climaxed so hard she started to shake and writhe under him, her teeth biting into his restraining hand, which made him curse.

"You okay there, sir?"

She closed her eyes as Rob stroked her hair. "Yeah, sure. My wife's suffering from morning sickness. You know what that's like—when you gotta puke, you gotta puke. Sorry to disturb you."

"No problem. We just wanted to make sure everything was

okay." A woman's voice this time, the tone warmer and more concerned.

Rob kissed the back of Ally's neck. "You okay, honey?"

She managed a weak nod and a wave and Rob chuckled. "She's a bit embarrassed. You know how it is."

"I sure do." The woman laughed. "Well, I hope everything goes okay."

"Thanks, ma'am. I'll take care of her."

Their voices faded and Rob continued to stand over her, his cock still throbbing deep inside her. A car started up and moved past them. Ally guessed Rob was giving their unwanted friends a cheery wave. Silence fell back over the space, and Ally started to breathe again. Rob pinched her clit and circled his hips.

"I'm not done yet and neither are you."

Ally groaned as he drew back, until just the crown of his cock was inside her, and then he slammed himself all the way back in. He did it again, his fingers squeezing her clit, and she came. With a curse, he started hammering into her, each stroke lifting her hips, exposing more of her sex to his powerful thrusts.

He climaxed, uttering a low, guttural roar as he bit down on the side of her neck. "Ally . . ." He collapsed over her for a moment and then moved away, scooped her up in his arms, and dumped her into the truck. She sat there quivering while he went around and got into the driver's seat.

Ally blinked as they emerged into the bright sunlight and waited while Rob paid the parking fee. She wondered if she looked as disheveled as she felt, her panties gone and her sex swollen and wet from Rob's ministrations. She glanced across at him as he chatted with the ticket guy. Despite the faint sheen of sweat on his skin, he looked as if he'd been doing nothing more strenuous than walking up a few flights of stairs.

They pulled away and Rob headed for the exit. "Do you have to work today?"

"No."

"Then let's take the long way home." Rob disregarded the entrance to the freeway and headed back under the bridge toward the much smaller and slower back road. Ally sat back in the seat and tried to relax. Rob put his hand on her thigh.

"Open your legs for me."

"I'm going to get Jackson's seat all damp."

Rob squeezed her thigh. "Just do it. I can guarantee he won't give a damn."

Ally relaxed her thighs, and Rob's hand slipped between them. He groaned as he encountered the slick wetness. "I like this, like you being all wet from my come." His fingertip grazed her clit and she shuddered. "I wish you could feel like this all the time."

"Wet with no panties?"

Rob flexed his fingers. "Yeah. Totally naked would be even better."

"I don't think the airport authorities would like that somehow."

He didn't answer, just pushed one long finger inside her and held it deep. "Touch your clit, honey. Make yourself come around my finger." Ally couldn't ignore the dark command of his tone, and her hand slid to her lap. "Move your skirt out of the way. I want to see you."

Ally pulled her already crumpled cotton skirt to one side and stared down, entranced, at his big strong hand, which disappeared between her legs and inside her body. She tucked her fingers under his palm and found her swollen clit.

"Before you start, undo my belt, unzip my shorts, and let my cock out."

Ally hurried to comply, but he didn't even look at her, his gaze fixed firmly on the road in front of them. His cock was already half erect and wet at the tip, and she couldn't help but smooth a finger over it. He shuddered but still didn't look down.

"Stroke your clit, Ally."

She slowly circled her own pulsing wet bud and felt Rob's finger push against the smooth walls of her sheath. She touched herself again, and her hips almost came off the seat. "I'm really sensitive...," she moaned.

"I told you what to do, Ally. Now do it."

She stroked herself again, got into the slick motion, and started to moan with every fresh stab of sensation that seemed to radiate from her clit to his encased finger. He didn't help her, making her do all the work of rising to meet him, of pushing herself against the palm of his hand in desperate supplication.

"Harder, Ally." He pressed his hand down, trapping hers over her clit, and ground his palm into her working knuckles. Her climax made her back arch, and Rob kept rubbing her until she came again. He took his hand away from her crotch and cupped the back of her head. "Now take my cock in your mouth and keep it there."

She fought the constraints of the seat belt as she leaned across his lap and opened her mouth wide to take him inside. She started to suck him, and his grip tightened on her hair. "Just hold me. Don't make me come."

Rob didn't dare look down. Ally had relaxed her mouth as he continued to grow, his thick length crowding down her throat forcing her to breathe through her nose. Every jolt of the truck pushed him farther in and made him want to curse. There was no way he wasn't going to explode soon, and he had an aversion to losing control when he was driving. He saw a sign for a motel and sped up a little.

He pulled off the highway and into the parking lot. The motel looked like it had faded away in the bright sunlight, its paintwork drab, the asphalt gray and the white lines that desig-nated the parking spaces hopeful haphazard dots. He carefully disengaged his cock from Ally's mouth.

"Stay here."

He managed to make himself presentable and strolled into the reception area of the motel, where a lone teenager chewed gum and stared up at a baseball game on the small TV.

"Hey, I need a room."

"Sure." The guy didn't take his eyes off the screen. "Thirty bucks a night."

Rob peeled off three tens and laid them on the counter.

The boy pushed a book toward him. "Sign in here." He pushed a large wooden keychain fashioned in the shape of a ba-nana across the desk. "Here you go, room thirty-two. It's just around the back in the shade."

"Thanks." Rob grabbed the key and headed back to the truck, which he had left running in the heat. He pulled around the low block of buildings and found the room. "Come on, honey."

He unlocked the door and stepped into the faded chintzy orange glory of the seventies. At least everything looked clean, and it wasn't as if they were staying long. He caught Ally by the shoulder and pulled her against him, and his cock immedi-ately kicked up again. He bore her down onto the bed, spread-ing her legs with his as he fumbled with his zipper.

Yeah, this was what he wanted, being inside her, making her scream and whimper and beg him not to stop, to never stop, to fuck her until he ran out of come. She wrapped her legs around him and kept him close until he could no longer hold himself back and climaxed in long, shuddering spurts.

Eventually, he levered himself up on his elbows and looked down at her. "You okay?"

She nodded, her gaze fixed on his. He reached behind her neck and undid the ties of her halter neck. "Take the dress off."

He did most of the work, pulling the now-crumpled cotton over her head, leaving her naked, her skin white against the orange bedcovers. Her long legs rested against his. He drew his T-shirt over his head and took off his shorts. They'd both already lost their sandals on the busily patterned carpet.

Before he tossed all their clothes onto a nearby chair, he slid his leather belt out of its loops. Ally licked her lips, and his cock twitched in anticipation. He knelt over her, the belt folded in his hand. "Hell, I can't decide whether to use it as a collar on you or to spank you a little." She swallowed convulsively, her nipples hardening into tight buds. "When you called the other night, you left me so hard I think you deserve to pay, don't you?"

"What about Jackson? It was his idea to call you."

"Don't worry. Jackson will get his." He pictured his best friend fucking Ally. He of all people knew just how to make Jackson sweat and beg.

"I just did what I was told." She fluttered her eyelashes at him. "I thought you'd like that."

Rob smiled at Ally. "Sure." He reached forward and swirled a finger over her swollen clit and she flinched away from him. He didn't retreat; instead, he did it again and watched as she caught her breath. "We need to work on that."

He bent his head and licked her very gently until she started to relax. "Need to get you so that you can take all the loving me and Jackson want to give you." Then he set his teeth on her clit, and she grabbed at his hair so hard his eyes watered. He backed off, leaving her gasping.

"Hands and knees, honey."

He waited as she turned over and presented him with the sweet curve of her ass. He folded the belt in two and tapped her right ass cheek. "You enjoyed the thought of me alone in that bed thinking about what you and Jackson were getting up to, didn't you?"

"Yes," she whispered.

He raised the leather a little higher and spanked her a little harder. "I was hard all week after that." Her hands fisted on the covers as he kept using the leather on her. He watched her carefully, aware of every twitch and moan, bringing her to a pitch where she was gasping his name with every precise blow.

"Spread your legs a little wider."

He rubbed the leather in the thick wetness between her legs, back and forth, back and forth until she was arching her ass as if seeking his cock. He waited until she stilled and then used the leather belt right against her sex.

"Rob, oh God..." She screamed his name again, and the sound went straight to his groin. He smacked her pussy again, this time using the flat of his hand. "If you liked that, tell me to do it again."

"Please, do it." Her voice was muffled against the sheets, but he heard her just fine and obliged, a little harder this time. She started to climax, and he grabbed her hips and pulled her back, impaling her on his shaft, felt the strength of her climax squeezing him like a fist. He hammered into her again, aware that she hadn't stopped coming and that he was gritting his teeth against the inevitable climax that was gathering in his balls.

With a groan, he held her tight and released into her. He had no energy left to hold himself up, and he fell on top of her, pushing her flat against the covers. After a while he rolled over, bringing her with him. Sunlight filtered through the partially closed drapes, and he stared up at the yellowing popcorn ceiling. She felt so right there, against his steadily pumping heart, that he didn't want to leave.

His eyes started to close, and he threaded his fingers through her long hair, only to groan and bring them both to an upright position.

"Damn it, we've got to get back. Jackson will need his truck."

Ally stayed curled in his lap, her breathing even, her face tranquil as if she hadn't quite come down yet from the place he'd sent her, the place where her sexual needs were met by his dominance. He kissed the top of her head and carried her into the small bathroom.

"Ally, we need to wash up."

"Okay."

She smiled up at him, and the trust in her gray eyes made him feel half proud and half ashamed. He'd given her what she wanted in bed. Could he ever give her what she wanted in life? He wasn't even sure if he knew anymore. She'd seemed set on getting out of town as fast as possible, and he hadn't said anything to persuade her otherwise. But could he survive it if she left him again?

He turned on the faucets with more force than they needed, and water cascaded into the shallow peach sink. Ally bent forward to splash the water over her face. He'd promised himself that he wouldn't push her into making decisions, and he intended to keep to that. Forcing her hand wouldn't achieve what he wanted, but would he ever find the right words to make her stay?

Ally glanced across at Rob as he drove the truck into the deepening sunlight. He hadn't said much more to her than the basic necessities. Within twenty minutes, they'd showered, put on their clothes, and gotten back in the truck to continue the journey. Ally stifled a yawn behind her hand, and Rob glanced at her for the first time.

"You want to go stretch out on the backseat?"

"No, I'm fine. It isn't far now."

"Yeah, about another five minutes."

Ally gathered her resolve. "Are you okay, Rob?"

"Sure."

"You seem a bit quiet."

"I'm tired, honey. I've been traveling all day."

"And then you had to fuck me as well."

"That was a pleasure."

"Really?"

"Sure."

Ally fought a sigh. Men were so hard to have a conversation with. Rob's lovemaking overwhelmed her, turned her into a needy, sex-obsessed woman, and she loved it. Loved what he could do to her with his hands, his mouth, his cock, his leather belt . . . She squirmed in her seat. Did he even care?

Rob stole a glance at her. "Are you sore?"

"A little."

"But you're okay with it."

"Sure."

"Now you sound like me."

Ally smiled and looked out the window as the outskirts of Spring Falls appeared. It wasn't even that late, about six according to the clock in the cab. "You can drop me off at the corner."

"Hell, no. I'll take you to your door."

"Even if Jane sees you?"

He patted her knee. "I'm done with hiding. If anyone wants to talk to me about my relationship with you, I'll meet them head-on."

Ally bit down hard on her lip. "We don't have a relationship. You told me that. You said it was all about sex and revenge."

He turned the corner into her street, his keen gaze fixed on the houses. When he shut the engine off, the silence was deafening. He got out of the cab and came around to help her out. His expression was difficult to read, the grip on her arm more definite. He towed her around the side of the house and approached the back door, his key already out. She went past him into the kitchen and stood in the middle, her arms crossed over her breasts.

He swung toward her and then stopped and shoved his hands in his pockets. "It was never just about the sex, Ally. You're the one who said you were going to run off again, not me. What kind of fool would want to get involved with a woman who has already made up her mind to leave?"

After Rob left, Ally couldn't settle and found herself standing in the dining room staring at her mother's desk. Something made her pick up the last of the journals and take them through to her bedroom. Even though she'd understood where Rob was coming from, his words had still hurt her. It was as if he still didn't understand her at all.

She stared at the matte-black face of the journal. But was she any better? She'd steadfastly refused to believe that her mother could ever change, but from what everyone in Spring Falls was trying to tell her, maybe Ruth had. Reading a few of the entries in Ruth's journal, painful as it was sure to be, might at least help solve that mystery once and for all. She opened the book in the middle and settled down to read. The entry was dated about three years previously.

I'm wondering what's happened to Ally. She seems to have disappeared. If I try and contact her, I know she won't answer me, and that's my fault not hers. I'm worried, though, because in her pictures she's been looking thinner and thinner and her eyes... her eyes look as dead as mine used to. I'm afraid she might be harming herself. And it's my fault. It's all my fault.

The words blurred and Ally realized she was crying. How dare Ruth be concerned about her? It *was* her mom's fault, and she had no business making Ally feel bad as well. Ally swiped at the tears on her cheeks with the back of her hand and threw the book onto the floor.

She reached for a tissue, blew her nose, and stared at the journal. But it wasn't all her mom's fault, was it? The choices she'd made were her own, not Ruth's, and she'd paid for them just as Ruth had.

"At least I didn't have a kid or anyone who needed me," she whispered. But was that true? She'd let her friends and her business acquaintances down. Wasn't that just as selfish? Maybe not, but it hadn't been very nice.

"Mirror, mirror on the wall, am I turning into my mom after all?" she murmured, and then found herself smiling at her own bad rhyme. Ally leaned over and picked up the book. When exactly had Ruth changed? Despite her tiredness, she knew it would be impossible to sleep. She replaced the book on the bedside table and went back to check out the desk in the dining room.

She switched on the lamp at the side of the desk and took a deep breath before starting to sort through the journals. They started when Ally was quite young but were very patchy and incomplete. Ally found a journal that covered the period from about two years after she'd left, and she sat down on the dusty carpet to read.

It's stupid. Ally's gone and I feel like there's nothing left in my world. I thought it would be easier not having her around criticizing me all the time, but the weird thing is I miss it. At least she cared enough to try, even though I didn't like to hear it.

I can't even say it's her fault I drink anymore either. I just like to drink. I'm going to talk to Dr. Shalvis tomorrow. Things have got to change.

When Ally closed the book, her eyes were stinging again. How weird that Ruth's words echoed Ally's earlier ones. It seemed that her departure had eventually led to Ruth deciding to quit alcohol and drugs for good. It hadn't been an instant moment of revelation, but a gradual progression of her mother realizing that without Ally's presence, there was no one who really loved her.

Ally stuffed the journal back into the drawer and shut it with a bang. As if Ruth had ever cared that Ally had loved her... She'd never seemed to notice. And she'd stopped loving Ruth anyway...hadn't she?

Too exhausted to think anymore, Ally made her way to bed. Despite everything, she knew she was going to keep on reading. Her mother's words might open up old wounds, but she'd learned that sometimes that needed to happen in order for a person to move on. She was trying the same thing with Rob and Jackson, wasn't she? Ally halted at the dining room door and looked back at the darkened room. If she'd replied to Ruth's messages, would she and her mother have found peace? Pain seized her heart. It was too late to find out. Her mother was dead.

16

Jackson rang the front doorbell and waited expectantly for Ally to appear. It was only ten in the morning, but she'd told him she'd be back from the diner and ready for him. Rob was already at work and, judging from the expression on his face over breakfast earlier, wasn't in a very good mood. It wasn't hard to figure out why. Getting involved with Ally again was never going to be easy.

Ally opened the door, and Jackson smiled at her. She wore her usual outfit of shorts and a skimpy top, both covered in drips of white paint. "Hey. You ready to take some of that stuff to the dump?"

"Absolutely. Come through to the kitchen," Ally said. "I don't have to go back to work until nine, so we have plenty of time to get it done."

Jackson followed her into the kitchen and inhaled the welcome smell of coffee. Ally held up a mug. "You want some?"

"Sure. Thanks." He accepted the mug and leaned back against the countertop. Taking his first really good look at Ally, he frowned. "You okay, Ally?"

She sighed. "I'm not sure. This town seems to bring out the worst in me."

He felt himself tensing. She wasn't going to leave again, was she? "What's up?"

She touched a black book that lay open on the table. "I've been reading my mom's diary."

He grimaced. "That bad, is it?"

"Worse. She turned out to be a nice person after all."

"And what's wrong with that?"

She turned away from him, her shoulder hunched. "Don't you get it, Jackson? She became a nicer person after I left, which seems to indicate that I was the problem all along."

"I don't think that's true." He regarded her closely. "Your leaving probably shocked her into making some major changes."

"I don't know what to think anymore. She started volunteering for stuff, attending AA meetings, making friends...." Ally tucked her hair behind her ear and dumped her coffee mug in the sink. "Everything's different here now—my mom, you, Rob...."

"And you." She met his gaze, her gray eyes startled. "Don't forget, you've changed, too, Ally. We all have the ability to start again and make things right."

"Even my mom."

"Yeah, even her."

Ally sighed. "I've put up with a shitload of attitude from half this town, and I've held my tongue and just let them have their say."

"I know."

She put her hands on her hips. "And?"

"And you must've known that was part of the risk of coming back."

"It doesn't exactly encourage me to stay, though."

"You've thought about that?" Jackson asked carefully.

She avoided his gaze and fiddled with the coffeepot. "As you said, I'm entitled to change my mind as well."

He let out a slow breath. "I'd like you to stay."

"Really?"

Her skeptical tone stung. "What's that supposed to mean?"

"Surely it would be better for you if I left again so that you could bring Rob around to your way of thinking?"

"It wouldn't work, Ally. I tried that once before, remember." He heard the bitterness in his voice and winced.

"We both tried to get away from him, didn't we?" Ally paused. "And we both came back because we realized he wasn't going to come after us."

Jackson stared at her. "I never thought of it like that before, but you're right."

"Do you think Rob wants me to stay?"

"You'd have to ask him."

Ally came around the table and kissed his cheek. "You're a good friend to us both, Jackson. I suppose the only person I can ask that question to is Rob."

"He probably thinks you're going to leave because that's what you told him."

"This is all such a mess." Ally put Ruth's diary in one of the drawers and headed for the door. "Let's move some boxes."

Jackson was quite happy to follow her out. They'd come way too close to the heart of the problem for his comfort. Rob definitely needed to talk to Ally and straighten stuff out. But would he do it when he'd been kicked in the teeth once already? Rob liked to fix stuff for everyone; but it seemed that he struggled to know how to fix himself.

Jackson was no longer sure either. He felt like his teenage self again, stuck between Ally's and Rob's emotions, always trying to make things right for them—usually at his own expense. No wonder he'd gotten resentful, but what had that achieved? Ally had left Rob, and nothing had been the same again.

On that depressing thought, Jackson opened the front door and then went to his flatbed truck. Ally was right—a bit of hard physical labor lugging boxes was much better than thinking about anything.

By the time they got back, Jackson was sweating in his black T-shirt and Ally's face was flushed. They'd shifted about fifty boxes from the dining room and the spare bedroom to the re-cycling facility, and the sun was setting behind the garage. Jackson parked in the driveway, and Ally opened the front door.

"I think we deserve a cold drink after all that work, don't you?"

Jackson wiped at the sweat on his forehead. "We sure do."

Ally was walking ahead of him and he almost fell over her when she abruptly stopped by the open door of the dining room. "What the hell happened in here?"

Jackson looked over her shoulder and went still. Someone had ransacked the few remaining boxes and opened up all the drawers in the desk. The contents spilled out onto the floor. He grabbed Ally's arm and stopped her from walking into the room.

"Don't go any farther. I'm going to call Rob."

He found his cell phone and punched in Rob's number. "Hey, Ally's house has been broken into."

He snapped the phone shut and nodded at Ally. "He's on his way. Now stay behind me and I'll check out the rest of the place."

He moved cautiously down the central hallway, checked the bedrooms, and ended up in the kitchen. Nothing had been disturbed there. He rattled the back door, but it was locked.

"I don't see any signs of a break-in. Did we leave the front door unlocked or something?"

Ally shook her head. "We didn't. I lived in New York for years. I would never forget to lock up."

"And I'm a cop." He studied the unbroken glass panels of the door. "So how did the person—or persons—get in?"

The doorbell rang and Ally went to answer it. Jackson heard Rob's voice and then Jeff's, the other deputy. He walked up to meet them. Ally stood in the doorway, her arms folded across her chest, an anxious expression on her face as Rob carefully entered the dining room.

"Do you think anything has been stolen, Ally?"

"I can't tell yet."

"How about from the desk? Did you keep any financial stuff in there?"

"My mom did, but I took all the important stuff out of there, and I've been keeping it with me."

He beckoned her into the room. "Anything else that appears to be missing or different?"

"It's hard to tell when we only just moved all those boxes out. But I don't remember leaving the computer on. Why didn't they steal that?"

"Maybe you and Jackson interrupted them."

Rob crouched down to survey the mess and touched one of the black books. "What are these? Account books?"

"They're my mother's journals." Ally squinted at the handwriting. "At least I think that's what they are. I haven't been through them all yet."

Rob caught Jackson's eye and nodded. "How does the rest of the house look?"

Jackson answered him. "I can't see any other damage, and none of the windows or doors were open either."

Rob frowned. "Hey, Jeff, can you go and grab the paperwork from my car? I might as well get started on it."

Ally shifted her stance to allow Jeff past her. "Aren't you going to call in your forensic team and a detective?"

Jackson smoothed a hand down her arm. "This isn't New York. We don't have those kinds of resources in this small town. It's basically up to us to investigate everything, and to be honest, there's not a lot we can do here."

Ally looked up at him. "Why would anyone want to do this?"

Rob stood up and walked toward them. "Let's have something to drink and talk this through in the kitchen."

Ally tore her gaze away from the pile of books and papers and went into the kitchen. Despite her shaking hands, she fixed a fresh pot of coffee and retrieved some ice from the freezer to add to the water glasses. Rob and Jackson sat at the table, their expressions grim as they waited for Jeff to return.

"Let me do that. You've had a shock."

Ally almost jumped when Rob took the glasses out of her hands.

"Why would anyone want to break into my house and go through my stuff, Rob?" she whispered.

He put the glasses on the table and squeezed her shoulder. "Give me a minute to write up this report, and then I'll be more than happy to answer all your questions."

Ally took a seat, aware that Rob had his professional face on and that she would get nothing more out of him until he'd completed his job to his satisfaction. That was one thing she'd always both admired and hated about him—his ability to compartmentalize his life.

Of course, it took more than a minute to survey the damage and write the preliminary report. Ally stayed put at the table as the three officers divided up the tasks and got on with it.

A knock at the back door made her jump. Jackson rose to answer the door, and Jane came in, her face flushed. She ignored Jackson and came to stand in front of Ally. "I came by to retrieve my pie dish. What's going on? Are you okay?"

"Someone broke into my house."

Jane gasped and pressed her hand to her chest. "Oh my word. Have you called Rob?"

"He's here with half the sheriff's department."

Jane glanced across at Jackson. "I can see that." She hesitated. "I won't keep you, then, but can you just show me where my pie dish is?"

Ally pointed at one of the cupboards on the wall. "It's in there, Jane. I'm sorry I didn't get it back to you sooner."

"It's not a problem, Ally, honestly." Jane opened the cupboard and went up on tiptoe to try and reach the dish. Without a word, Jackson came up behind her, plucked the pie dish from the shelf, and handed it to Jane with a flourish. She continued to ignore him, her mouth pinched, her expression outraged. "Thanks, Ally. Let me know if you need any help."

She shut the kitchen door behind her with a bang.

"You're welcome," muttered Jackson, and Ally turned to look at him. "You know she only came over to nose around. If I hadn't been here, she would've gone straight into the dining room trying to prove I'd committed a crime."

"I know." Ally held her head in her hands. "I'm just glad you were here when I came in. Maybe I should've told Jane that and set her mind at rest."

Rob came back into the kitchen carrying a clipboard. "That's about it, Ally. Jeff's gone back to cover the office. I need you to read through this and add anything you think might be missing."

While Ally read and checked the details, Rob helped himself to a mug of coffee and sat down with them at the table. "This doesn't make any sense."

"What do you mean?"

"It's not like your normal burglary for cash, is it? Nothing appears to have been taken. It's more like whoever it was, was searching for something."

Ally looked up to find Rob's keen gaze on her. "Like what?"

"You tell me."

"But I don't know! Maybe it's someone who still thinks there are drugs in the house and doesn't know Mom has passed away."

"That's a possibility."

"Why do you sound so skeptical?"

"Because whoever it was had a key, Ally. That puts a whole new slant on things."

"I don't imagine my mom ever changed the locks, so I suppose it could've been someone from her past. Is that what you are trying to say?"

Rob sighed. "It's a possibility."

Ally shivered and gripped her coffee mug. "It's as if my coming back has shaken everything up. Someone doesn't want me here, do they?"

Rob's gaze met Jackson's and Ally stiffened.

"It might not be directed at you, Ally. It's far more likely to have something to do with your mom."

"Why do you keep saying that?" Ally knew her voice was rising, but she couldn't seem to help herself. "You told me she was a different person, so why are you still treating her like a suspect?"

"Because . . ." Rob took her hand. "Look, this may be about drugs, but there's also the matter of what happened to Susan Evans on the night you left town."

"She killed herself." Ally felt bad as Jackson winced. "Everyone knows that, apart from Jane, who thinks Jackson murdered her."

"Ally, the last time anyone saw Susan alive, she came into this house and was seen leaving with another person." Silence fell over the table, and Ally couldn't seem to break it. "Afterward, your mother wouldn't allow the sheriff's department to search the place without them getting a warrant. Then the coroner decided Susan's death was a suicide, and the police had to move on."

Sick realization dawned in Ally's head. "But you didn't move on, did you, Rob? You'd never allow any department you worked for to have an unsolved case."

"It wasn't unsolved, Ally. The verdict was suicide," Rob said.

"But that wasn't good enough for you, was it?" She slowly stood up and gazed at his hard face. "I know why you're so interested in what's in this house. You're hoping to find some evidence that my mother went out with Susan and pushed her off the bridge, aren't you?"

Rob didn't say anything, but she saw the truth in his eyes.

"My God, you really are a piece of work. Was this all about your case? Fucking me? Convincing me that you really were a nice guy after all? Was the 'stuff' you wanted to discuss with me all connected to convicting my mother of murder?"

"Ally . . ." Jackson's low voice intruded on her rage.

She waved it aside. "That's it, isn't it, Rob? Revenge and sex. You even told me that!"

Rob shook his head. "You've got this all wrong. I—"

Ally pushed in her chair. "I get it. Now get out of my house."

She turned on her heel and walked out, shut her bedroom door, and locked it firmly behind her. Nausea churned in her gut, and she wanted a drink so badly she knew she had to call Jill right now. Instead she curled up into a ball and let herself cry.

Jackson stared across at Rob, who remained sitting at the table, his hands clenched in front of him. "Do you want to go talk to her?"

"You think she'd be interested in anything I had to say?"

"At this moment, probably not." Jackson stood up. "Let's

take this back to the station and work out what we need to do to fix it."

"The case or Ally?"

Jackson opened the back door. "Both." He glanced back at Rob, who had the look of a man who'd just been punched in the gut. "Rob, come on. There's nothing else you can do here."

Rob slowly rose and used his hand to push himself away from the table. "I get that."

There was nothing else to say. Jackson knew it wasn't the time for recriminations. Rob knew he'd fucked up, and Jackson had no intention of reminding him.

It took all Rob's concentration to drive the short distance from Ally's house to his office at the old courthouse. Jackson had offered to drive, but Rob had curtly refused. What did Jackson think he was going to do? Cry like a baby? Rob swallowed hard. There was nothing to cry about. Ally had a right to be pissed, but he had just been doing his job.

Jackson followed him into his office and left the door open. Jeff appeared with a sheaf of papers relating to the break-in, which he passed over to Rob to fill out. It always amused Rob that he could reach anywhere in Spring Falls and deal with a crime quicker than he could fill in the resulting paperwork. He concentrated on the mundane, let Jackson bring him some coffee, and waited for the sick feeling in his stomach to settle down.

"So what do you think is going on, Rob?" Jackson asked.

"With Ally?" He shrugged. "I think she's right. Something sure stirred up the waters around here, and she walked right into it."

"But what?"

"I'm hoping it's drug-related."

"But I thought you were intent on solving the mystery of Susan's 'murder'?"

Rob glared at Jackson. "What is it with everyone? What I feel for Ally and what might have happened with Susan are two completely separate matters."

"You can't fool another cop, Rob. There is no way in hell that you didn't even consider that Ally or I might have killed Susan."

"Of course I fucking considered it! But I knew from the timing that neither of you could've done it. The only other possibility is Ally's mom."

Jackson looked unconvinced. "You're shouting at the wrong person. Ally's the one you need to convince, not me."

"Ally's the one I'm trying to protect, although no one seems to give me any credit for that at all."

"Why the hell should they? You're like a man obsessed, and I just don't get it."

Rob set his jaw. "Look, that night, I was the one who found Susan's body."

Jackson blinked. "*You* did?"

"I was heading for Ally's house." Rob shrugged. "I just wanted to see her and make sure she was okay. But I didn't get that far. I found Susan first, draped over the rocks in the creek. The water was really low, so I was able to work out that she was dead before I ran like hell to call the police."

Jackson nodded. "No cell phones for teens then, right?"

"Right. I tried to tell the cops and the medics that it looked like she had bruises on her upper arms, but as far as they were concerned, I was just a kid who didn't know shit about anything. They reckoned all the bruising was the result of her fall from the bridge. I could tell from their conversation they'd already decided it was suicide."

"Well, shit. Why didn't you mention this before?"

"Because I didn't want to stir up even more crap for you and Ally."

Jackson shook his head. "So this is something of a personal quest for you too."

"If you want to put it like that, then yeah."

Jackson sat forward in his seat, his expression all business. "Then listen to this. The way I see it, there are three reasons for anyone to target Ally's home. One, it's related to her mother, and maybe there's a drug connection. Two, someone just wants to drive Ally out of town. And three, someone wants to cover up something about Susan's death. Do you agree with me?"

Rob let out a slow, steadying breath. "Yeah, I do."

Jackson rose and headed for the whiteboard on Rob's wall. He wrote *Ruth, Ally,* and *Susan* and looked expectantly at Rob. "So whose names need to go down in each column?"

17

_____

"Hey, Ally? Don't hang up. It's Jackson."

Ally stared at the phone and considered cutting him off but knew it wasn't going to happen. "What's up?"

"Just in case you're worrying about talking to me, this is an official call."

"It's okay, Jackson. I'm not going to burst into tears or anything."

She heard him sigh. "I want to know if I can bring a K-9 team to your house this afternoon."

"Why would you want to do that?" Ally transferred the phone to her other ear and pulled her muffin out of the toaster. Her appetite had completely gone, but she was determined to eat something.

"Because we're looking at several motives for your house being broken into, and we'd like to search the place for drugs."

Even though she'd been clean for several years, Ally still felt a kick of adrenaline and fear shoot through her at the thought of her possessions being searched. "Are you trying to convince me that I was wrong about Rob's motives for hanging around with me?"

He paused long enough to make her clench her teeth. "I'm trying to do my job, Ally, and so is Rob. Is it okay to bring the dog around?"

"Why not, if it makes you feel better."

Jackson didn't bother to reply, and she was left listening to empty air. How dare he try and make her feel bad? She was the one who had been deceived. As usual, Rob had played her like a violin, used her own sexuality against her until she'd been his willing slave.

She buttered her muffin and sat down at the table. When exactly had Rob intended to come clean with her and suggest that her mom was a murderer? That was one hell of a leap, even for Rob. But maybe he hadn't made that leap; maybe he really did just want to know what had happened to Susan in this house that made her want to kill herself. . . .

Dammit, it hurt. Ally chewed on her muffin and tried to swallow. But if her mom wasn't involved, why hadn't she let the police inside to search the house? Ally dropped the muffin and ran through to the dining room. Her mom's journals and other books still littered the carpet. Was the truth about what had happened to Susan buried somewhere in her mother's diaries?

With trembling hands, Ally sat on the floor and started to sort through the books. There were at least forty of the black books scattered around and some still in the open drawers along with loads of other items. Ally started to assemble them by date ordering them backward in time.

Jackson rang Ally's doorbell and waited for her to appear. She opened the door, and he wasn't surprised to see that she looked almost as rough as Rob did. When would they realize that it had never been just about sex or a police case? Jackson had a strong urge to bang their heads together and lock them in a room to sort it out once and for all.

"Hey, Ally, this is Javier. He's going to bring his dog in, okay?"

Ally stepped out of the way, and Javier moved forward, his German shepherd, Topher, trotting quietly by his side. "Afternoon, Ms. Kendal. I'll try to be as quick as I can."

"Sure. Be my guest."

Jackson wondered if Javier had picked up on Ally's distinct lack of welcome, but he didn't seem bothered. In his line of work, he was probably used to it. Ally glanced up at him. "Are you coming in or not?"

Jackson stepped into the welcoming cool darkness of the hall and took off his hat. "Thanks. I'll try to keep out of your way, too, all right?"

She touched his arm. "Are you pissed at me?"

"I'm on duty." Jackson stared straight ahead at Javier, who was kneeling on the floor talking to his dog. "If you want to talk to me later, give me a call."

"Fine."

Inwardly Jackson groaned. Any man knew that when a woman said "fine," she meant the complete opposite, but he couldn't talk to her now. He didn't want to. He was tired of being stuck in the middle of her and Rob, fucking sick of it.

Ally retreated to the kitchen. Jackson decided to follow Javier at a discreet distance as he and the dog moved through the cluttered ranch house. It was also a pleasure to watch the man and dog work together, their movements so coordinated you'd think they could mind-speak to each other.

After what seemed like a relatively quick search, Javier came back to Jackson. "I'm not finding anything. Do you have any idea what we might be looking for or how long ago the stuff was planted here?"

Jackson lowered his voice. "The woman who owned this house previously used to have a lot of drugs here and a lot of visitors. We were concerned that the recent break-in might have been orchestrated by someone who didn't know she was no longer alive."

"So it could've been a while, then?"

"Yeah, maybe as long as three to five years."

Javier sighed and leaned down to pat the dog. "Then anything that wasn't properly protected has probably gone moldy or turned to dust by now."

"Well, thanks for checking. It was a long shot, but it was something we had to eliminate from our lines of inquiry."

Javier turned to go, and Jackson saw him out through the front door. The K-9 units had their own special vehicles, so Jackson's patrol car was also parked on the drive. He shut the door and went back into the kitchen, where Ally was getting herself a glass of milk. She didn't offer him anything, and he could sense hostility coming off her in waves.

"I thought you'd like to know he didn't find anything."

"Thanks." She continued to sip at her milk and regard him over the rim of the glass. "So now we're back to my mother being a murderer?"

"We have to consider all scenarios."

"You mean just that one, don't you?"

He struggled to maintain his composure. "No. We are actively investigating other avenues."

"Yeah, right."

"Yeah." Jackson took a step toward her. "In case you've forgotten, there are a lot of people in this town who would be pleased to see the back of you."

"You think someone might be trying to scare me into leaving?"

"It's highly possible."

"I did wonder about that when the diner window was smashed." She swallowed hard. "Did you realize that we were sitting right there earlier that night?"

Jackson regarded her carefully. "That's true. Is there anyone you'd like to mention as being particularly malicious toward you?"

"Like Lauren, you mean? She's hardly likely to destroy her own diner just to get back at me. As if Rob would lift a finger against her."

Jackson put on his hat. "As I said, Rob will do his job or he'll hand the case over to someone who can do it better."

"He'll never confront Lauren." Hurt flickered in her gray eyes. "Maybe he has a special category just for me." She bit down on her milky lower lip, and Jackson wanted to pull her into his arms and hold her tight. She walked away from him, her narrow shoulders hunched. "Look, there is something I want to share with you and Rob. Can you call him over?"

"He didn't think you'd want to see him."

"He's right. I don't want to see him, but I think he needs to see what I found."

"Can't you just show me?"

"And have Rob think I'm trying to get you on my side? I'm not putting you in the middle again, Jackson. As far as I'm concerned, you and Rob are both at fault."

"What did I do?"

She raised her chin. "Like you didn't know what he was up to."

He wanted to tell her that he'd tried to make Rob set things straight with her and that he'd told him it would end badly, but Ally's hostile stance made him unwilling to break Rob's confidence. "Okay, I'll call him."

Rob pulled up at Ally's house, and the fist knotted in his chest seemed to tighten even more. What the hell did she want to see him about? When Jackson had called, he'd almost turned tail and run. But he had to continue the investigation. His job and his pride were all he had left at this pathetic moment in his life.

Jackson opened the door and led him down the hallway to

the dining room where Ally was pacing the dusty carpet. She looked so tired and worn out that he wanted to grab her, make her look at him and tell her that everything was going to be all right. But he'd tried the bully tactics once before, and all he'd done was make her run away.

"Ally."

Ally barely bothered to acknowledge him, and it fucking hurt. She went to stand by the table where a pile of black books had been stacked.

"I went through all my mother's journals earlier to see if I could find one relating to the time period when Susan died."

A leap of excitement jolted through Rob. "That was a great idea."

"Except that the diary for that time period is missing."

Rob glanced at Jackson, who'd take up a position by the open door where he could see out into the hallway. "Are there a lot of journals missing?"

"No just that one." Ally looked down at the floor. "They'd all been tipped out of the drawers and scattered around. It took me about an hour to go through them and put them in order."

"So whoever came into the house was looking for something very specific."

Ally raised her eyes to stare at Rob. "And unless my mother managed to survive death, it can't have been her."

He held her glare and gave it back to her. "She could've had an accomplice, Ally. According to the original police reports, there were at least three men living in this house during that year. I'm currently trying to trace them."

"You're so determined to prove that my mom did it, aren't you?"

The anger he'd tried so hard to repress tore through his professional demeanor. "And you're so keen to prove she wasn't involved that you won't even listen to me. She might have cleaned up her act in her last years, and I'm glad for you that she did, but that night? That night when Susan died, your mom was a drunk and a drug addict, and who the hell knows what she was thinking or feeling or capable of doing."

"That's not fair."

"No, you just don't want to hear it. It's easier to carry on blaming me than to deal with the fact that your mother hung out with some very unsavory people and that she might have been an accessory to murder."

Ally's face paled and she steadied herself on the edge of the table, her fingers white.

Rob struggled to lower his voice. "I just want the truth, Ally. That's all."

"And you don't care who gets hurt in the process, do you?"

"I'm doing my job."

"And so you'll agree that my mom might not be the only suspect."

"I never said she was. You just jumped down my throat the moment I mentioned her."

She couldn't even look at him.

"I know she was your mom, but let's not forget she was one of the reasons you left Spring Falls in the first place." He sighed. "Look, I'll do my best to find out who is doing this."

"And you won't just focus on my mother?"

"Ally, the person who is after you now is very much alive and has a key to your house. That fucking terrifies me."

"I'll get the locks changed."

Jackson stirred. "I'll get that started first thing tomorrow, Ally, okay?"

"You do that," Rob said. "I reckon she should spend the night with us, don't you?" He almost wanted to laugh at Ally's outraged expression.

"At our place?" Jackson didn't look quite so convinced.

Ally squared up to them both. "I am not staying anywhere near you."

"In a town as small as this, where else can we guarantee your safety?"

"The hotel?"

Rob shrugged. "Only if one of us stays in the room with you. You'd be much safer at our house, though."

She glared at them for a long, tense moment. "Fine, I'll pack my things."

Rob exhaled as she pushed past him and Jackson and headed for her bedroom. He lowered his voice. "I didn't think she'd go for it."

"I'm not sure it's a good idea."

Rob slammed his hand down on the table. "What else am I supposed to do? She's not staying here, and I'm not leaving her alone in some fucking hotel."

Jackson shook his head. "Rob...you are being way too pushy."

"You haven't seen the half of it, buddy." Rob nodded at the kitchen. "Go check that everything's locked up and I'll meet you out front."

Rob settled into his truck and waited for Ally and Jackson to emerge. The light was fading, and the sky was an uncertain mix of red and purple, like a gigantic bruise. Was Jackson right? Was he in danger of pushing Ally over the edge again? For someone who was supposed to have all the answers, he felt so fucking powerless right now. He beckoned to Jackson, who had followed Ally out of the house. "I want you both in here with me, okay?"

"You want me to leave my patrol car on the drive?"

"It can't hurt. It might put our perp off for another night if he thinks there's a cop staying here."

"Okay, but Ally's not going to like sharing the ride with you."

Jackson turned back to Ally and ushered her toward Rob's truck. Rob saw her instant refusal and his gut tightened. Jackson kept talking and persuaded her to get in the back. She kept hold of her backpack and set it on her knee. Rob started the engine and glanced at her in his rearview mirror, but she wasn't looking at him, her gaze fixed out the window.

Rob drove the short distance to his street and stopped at the corner. "Hold on a minute, guys."

He walked up to a darkened house and knocked on the door until a familiar face appeared. After a few seconds of conversation, he came back. "Ally? You can stay with Jeff. He and his wife would be happy to have you."

Ally's startled face looked up at him as she hurried to get out of the car. He didn't dare touch her or he'd never be able to let go.

"Why did you change your mind?" Ally said softly.

"Because I don't want you to run." Rob sighed. "Ally, I know I've fucked up, but please, honey, don't leave town, okay? And give me a call in the morning before you return to your house so someone can accompany you."

She stopped on the porch and studied him. "Okay." She stood on tiptoe and cupped his cheek. "Thanks."

He watched her walk into the welcoming warmth of Jeff's family home and turned away. Hell, it was hard to stop himself from overprotecting someone he cared about. Hadn't that always been his problem? And hadn't he learned that it was the surest way to force the people he loved to leave him?

Jackson had gotten out of the car and stood on the sidewalk, staring at him. "You did the right thing, Rob."

"Maybe." Rob looked across at Jackson. "I'm in love with her, Jackson."

"So am I." Jackson slid into the passenger's seat. "So we'd better get this shit sorted out, hadn't we?"

18

"It's okay, Ally, go on in."

Ally turned the new key and went into her house, Rob right behind her. Everything looked the same. Nothing else had been touched in the twenty-four hours since she'd left. She let out her breath and walked into the kitchen. The faucet was dripping, and the refrigerator buzzed like a chronic asthmatic, but that was nothing new.

Rob put a new set of keys on the table. "Here you go. There are two new back door keys and two for the front. I've got a set as well, which I'll return to you as soon as this is all settled. The guy who came to change the locks says he'd also recommend getting some window locks and an alarm installed."

"I'm sure he did, but I can't afford to do that right now." Ally picked up one set of the keys. "How much do I owe Jackson anyway?"

Rob shrugged. "I don't know. You'll have to ask him yourself." He held out his hand. "Do you want me to put those new keys on your key ring for you?"

"I can do it myself, thanks." Ally struggled to remove her

old front door key and broke a nail in the process. She frowned down at her key ring. "Where's my back door key?"

"Don't you have it?"

Ally tried to remember. "I know you returned it to me after you made those copies, but what did I do with it then?" She stared at Rob. "If I lost it somewhere, that might be how the person got in."

"When did you last use it?"

Ally started to pace the small kitchen, checking the work surfaces and bowls as she passed. "I don't remember. The last couple of times, you guys have unlocked the doors for me."

Rob shifted his weight. "Can you think about it some more? It might be important."

Ally stopped walking and closed her eyes. "I'm *thinking*."

"I suppose it doesn't matter too much anymore, seeing as you've changed all the locks, but it might give us some idea about when the key was taken."

"I probably just lost it, Rob."

"Maybe, but I've got to consider all the worst scenarios."

"I suppose you do."

Rob took a step toward her. "Look, Ally..."

She held up her hand. "I'm not sure I want to hear anything you have to say to me, Sheriff, and I have to get to work, okay?"

She picked up her new keys and walked out the back door, hoping to hell he'd get the message and keep away from her, even if it was just for a little while. She knew he'd never let it go and would be back demanding stuff from her, but she was not going to let him hound her into making decisions quite yet.

"Ally." He'd followed her out, and she reluctantly looked back into his determined blue eyes. "I need your help to solve this."

"And I don't want to be anywhere near you."

He winced. "Yeah, I get that, but you might be in danger. Someone's trying to hurt you, and I just can't let that happen."

"Oh, right, because you're a cop."

A muscle twitched in his cheek. "Because despite everything, I care about you, and I want to make things right."

Ally swallowed back the sting of tears. "Stop pretending you 'care about me' and just do your job."

Rob looked like he wanted to argue about that, but after a long moment he continued. "How about you just give me a list of all the folks in town who you think might have a grudge against you or your mother."

"You can just pull out the electoral roll and use that."

He didn't smile. "I'd appreciate it if you could be more specific."

All traces of emotion had gone from his voice, and he was now pure cop. That was what she'd wanted, wasn't it? So why did it hurt? "I'll do that. Anything else?"

"Manpower permitting, we'll probably have someone drive by the property regularly, especially when you are on the premises."

"Okay, I can deal with that."

"And, Ally, if anything freaks you out, even the smallest thing, you call me or Jackson right away, okay?"

"I'll definitely call Jackson."

Rob rubbed his hand over his unshaven jaw and suddenly looked more tired and defeated than Ally had ever seen before. "Whatever works for you—just promise me you'll do it."

"I will. Now I really have to get to work."

"I'll drive you."

"No thanks." Ally turned on her heel and walked away from him, her heart thumping, her knees threatening to give way. It wasn't fair that she still wanted to do everything he told her to do, that her stupid body wanted to fling itself into his arms and beg him to make everything right for her.

* * *

For a change, Lauren didn't bug Ally too much on her shift and just let her get on with her work. While she cleaned tables, Ally thought about Rob's request for her to write a list of all the people in town who had a big fat grudge against her. The trouble was, the most obvious candidate was working right alongside her in the diner and just happened to be the sheriff's sister.

Ally thought it was far more likely to be one of the losers her mother had allowed to live in the house in exchange for sex and drugs. She couldn't remember the names of all the guys Ruth had slept with, but some of them might have stayed around and become upstanding citizens in Spring Falls. Perhaps they were worried that Ruth had mentioned them in her journals or something. She'd never made a secret of her diaries.

She scraped a half-eaten egg into the trash. Why had Ruth kept the journals? It was surprising that in her later years when she'd gotten clean she hadn't thrown out any reminders of her past. But maybe she'd left them for Ally. To help her . . .

"You can take your lunch, Ally."

Ally looked up to see Lauren waving at her from the diner. "My lunch?"

Lauren looked exasperated. "Your break, then—just take it now and make it last half an hour, okay?"

Ally glanced at Fig, who raised his eyebrows at her and muttered, "Just take it, dude. She's obviously in her happy place."

"Okay, I've got to go to the library, anyway, and I'll grab a sandwich at the coffee shop." Ally took off her apron and kept her gaze on Lauren, just in case she was about to change her mind. "See you later, guys."

Rob waited until Ally left before he walked back through the kitchen to Lauren's office. He'd asked Lauren to get Ally out of the diner while they talked, aware that in the small space, loud voices would carry. And he suspected it was going to get loud. He knew he was walking a fine line, taking on his sister himself, but he couldn't allow anyone else to do his dirty work. If there really was a case to answer, he'd do his civic duty and hand it over to another officer to investigate.

Lauren was waiting for him, so he closed the door behind him and took a seat on the couch.

"What's up, big bro?" Lauren asked, her brown eyes narrowed, her foot tapping against her desk.

"I want to talk to you about Ally."

"What's she done now?"

"Did you know that someone broke into her house a couple of nights ago?"

"Into that dump? Whatever for?"

"That's what I'm trying to establish." Rob took out his notebook, and Lauren stiffened. "Can you tell me where you were on Sunday evening?"

"Are you serious? Do you really think I'd waste my time breaking into her crappy home? If I did get in there, I'd be more likely to suffocate her in her bed and get rid of her once and for all."

"Is it any wonder I'm asking you these questions when you talk about her like that, Lauren? Everyone in town has heard you bad-mouthing her."

"And that makes me a suspect?"

He met her gaze head-on. "Yeah, it does."

Her mouth dropped open. "You're serious, aren't you? What the hell has she been saying about me?"

"Ally's said nothing. But every single person I've talked to about this has mentioned your name."

"So because I tell it how I see it, I must be guilty?"

He shrugged. "Sometimes the most obvious answer to a question is given by the person who shouts the loudest."

"I didn't break into her house, Rob, and you know it."

Rob hardened himself against the outrage in her eyes. "Then tell me where you were that night and we're done."

"Fine, I was at home in my apartment."

"All evening?"

"Yes!"

"Is there anyone who can vouch for you?"

"My cat."

"Unfortunately, I don't speak cat. Anyone else?"

"The pizza-delivery guy from Alfredo's came about seven."

Rob wrote that down. "Cool, I'll check into that." He stood up. "Thanks for being so helpful, Lauren."

Lauren shot to her feet too. "I don't get it, Rob. Why are you doing this? I'm beginning to see why Ally walked out on you in the first place."

Suddenly, Rob felt weary. "Well, at least one good thing has come out of this, then."

She grabbed his hand. "You don't need her!"

Rob sighed. "I do, Lauren. I'm sorry but I do. I haven't felt the same about anyone else since she left. You *know* that. How many women have you introduced me to over the years? Have I ever wanted any of them for anything except a few dates and a quick fuck?"

"That's not true, I—"

Rob put his hand on her shoulder. "I'm a big boy now, sis. I can take care of myself, and I want Ally."

"And what if she doesn't want you?" Lauren whispered.

Fear coalesced in Rob's gut. "If she doesn't, it's my own damned fault." He squeezed Lauren hard. "I've gotta go. Thanks for the help, Lauren, and please, lay off Ally, will you? Some-one's trying to hurt her, and the last thing she needs is you on her back as well."

Lauren bit down on her lip. "I'm not going to do that."

Rob carried on as if she hadn't spoken. "She's so strong, Lauren. Strong enough to get away from her fucked-up mother and survive a drug addiction. I didn't appreciate her enough before, but I sure as hell do now." Lauren's eyes flickered, but she didn't say anything. "At least give her credit for growing up." He shook his head. "You're a better person than that, sis. Maybe it's time for you to grow up, too, and get over this once and for all."

He nodded, opened the door, and left before she could say anything else.

Ally glanced back down the street at the diner and thought she saw the flash of a white patrol car. Was Rob looking for her? If so, he was going to be unlucky, and she was pretty sure that Lauren wouldn't help Rob find her. As she walked, she tried to work out how much longer she needed to get the house fixed up and whether she stood a chance of avoiding Rob for that long. Neither calculation came out well.

With a sigh, Ally went into the coffee shop and smiled as Nadia immediately poured her a cup of coffee and held it out. "You want a muffin with that, Ally?"

"Yes, please, Nadia."

"Did I tell you that your mom worked here for a while when we first opened?"

"You didn't." Ally managed to smile.

"She gave her notice because she thought her presence here tainted our new business, and she didn't want to make it fail."

"Yeah, I hear she was thoughtful like that," Ally muttered.

"Yes, she was. You are much like her." Nadia paused. "Hey, do you knit?"

"Yeah, I do. How did you know?"

"Ruth knitted as well, and a little bird told me that you've been getting pattern books from the library. I run a knitting circle on Wednesday nights. Do you want to come?"

"That would be awesome," Ally said quickly. She'd taken up knitting in the rehab place when she'd needed something to do with her hands and had come to love it. "I didn't know my mom knitted."

Another link to Ruth and, perhaps more importantly, an opportunity to get reacquainted with some of the town residents who might have stories to offer about Ruth to help her understand her mom better. And she needed to do that. She realized it now. Perhaps coming back to Spring Falls hadn't been all about Rob after all. . . .

Nadia was still speaking. "Don't forget about the job, either, will you? I don't think this town would survive now without my baked goods and my husband's coffee." She patted Ally's arm. "I don't want this nonsense to make you leave again. It will all settle down. I'm sure of it."

Ally wasn't quite so certain, but she took the muffin and coffee and found an empty seat in the corner. Yet another example of a mother she didn't know and had never been allowed to know . . . She checked the time and blew hard on her coffee. Lauren had given her half an hour, but she still didn't want to be back late, and she had to check the library for the book she'd requested online.

"Hey, Ally."

She looked up to find Jackson smiling down at her.

"Hey." She tore her gaze away from his and stared at her coffee. He didn't seem to take the hint and instead pulled out the chair opposite her and sat down.

"You're still mad."

She flicked a glance at him. "Well, duh."

"And if I tell you you're overreacting?"

"I'd tell you to mind your own business."

"It is my business. I'm part of this. I'm not going to let you or Rob take over again."

"Rob's the only one who does that."

"You're both behaving like idiots."

"He used me, Jackson."

"And have you let him explain anything?"

"What is there to explain?"

"How did you feel when he wouldn't listen to you on the night you left?"

"I felt awful. That's one of the reasons why I ran so far and didn't come back until now."

"And now you're doing the same to him? Shutting him down before he can explain? Getting your own back before you walk out on him again and break his heart?"

"It's not like that. He only wanted sex. He told me so."

Jackson reached across and took her hand. "Ally, you know that isn't true."

"What do you want me to do, Jackson? Go and kiss his ass and tell him he's right and I'm wrong? I can't do that."

"I don't expect you to. I just want you to think about talking to him before you make any firm decisions about leaving. Is that too much to ask?"

Ally looked into his dark eyes. "This is such a mess. I didn't mean to drag you into this either."

His smile lit up his face. "You have given me my life back. I don't want you to leave town." He squeezed her fingers hard. "Do you want to stay?"

"How can I?"

He stood up and put his sunglasses back on. "You can—you just have to want it."

Ally stared at his back as he went up to the counter to get his coffee. How dare he make it seem so easy? She knew what he really meant. She should forgive Rob and everything would be fine again. Well, she couldn't do that. Rob had stepped over the line one too many times for her liking.

She bit into her muffin and envisaged leaving town, the house sold, and enough money in her pocket to do whatever she wanted. But all the people she truly loved were right here in Spring Falls. Ally almost choked on the crumbs. She didn't love

Jackson and Rob; she was just using them for sex like they were using her. Even her conscience laughed at that lie.

Ally stood up, her stomach churning and her mind in chaos. She didn't want to love anyone. Love hurt like crazy, and she didn't want to go through that again. She threw the rest of her muffin in the trash and walked out, her coffee gripped in her hand. Outside, she breathed in the hot, dry California air and fought to regain her composure.

In the distance, she watched Jackson cross the square and head into the old courthouse. He was right about one thing: She would have to make some decisions soon, and all of them would require some sort of compromise.

She turned to the library, which faced the courthouse across the square, and made her way through the wide oak doors. As usual, Mrs. Orchard manned the front desk, her poppy-patterned blouse a riot of color over her imposing bosom.

"Good afternoon, Ally, and how may I help you?"

"Hi, Mrs. Orchard. I ordered a book online, so I've come to pick it up."

"Slide your card for me dear and I'll check." Mrs. Orchard tapped away on the keyboard and then nodded. "It's here. I'll go and find it for you."

Ally waited patiently at the desk, the quiet solitude of the library easing her mind and making her relax.

"Here you are." Mrs. Orchard waved the book at her. "Now here's a funny thing, Ally. The last person to get this book out was your mother, Ruth."

Ally glanced at the title of the book; it was one Jill had recommended. "My mom read *Stop Repeating the Same Destructive Relationships and Become the Woman You Were Meant to Be?*"

Mrs. Orchard lowered her voice and leaned in closer to Ally. "She read a lot of these kinds of books. I don't really believe in them, but they certainly seemed to help her. She became a much better person after you left."

"So everyone keeps telling me."

"Now, Ally, I know you had it rough, but at least your mom tried to turn her life around at the end."

Ally managed a tight smile before she walked out. Anger sat like a lead weight high in her chest. She didn't want to hear about what a great person Ruth was ever again. Ruth had been a terrible mother and hadn't even protected her own daughter from harm.

Ally veered off the path and took a detour into the small grassy sitting area in the center of the square. She clutched the library book to her chest and sank down on the grass, her back against one of the old oak trees. The light dazzled her eyes, and she closed them tight, bringing up memories of her childhood and of her mother.

With a groan, Ally wrapped her arms around her knees and rested her forehead on them. What weird instinct had made her jump to defend her mother when all the evidence suggested she might at least have been involved in what had happened to Susan? Just because she was identifying with her mother's struggle with addiction didn't make them exactly the same. Ruth hadn't been aware of much that went on in her own house, hadn't listened when Ally had desperately begged her not to allow some of the men to stay.

Logically she knew Rob had a point, but it was difficult to hear her mother being vilified again. She'd tried so hard to pretend that everything was normal and that her mom wasn't a crazy, spaced-out mess. She'd even wanted to believe in the new Ruth, the clean, drug-free friend to all. But she couldn't. She just couldn't. Ally raised her head and stared at the old courthouse. And that meant she needed to grow up and help Rob sort this out.

19

"You don't have to do this, Sheriff." Ally glanced behind her as Rob followed her into the kitchen. "When you said you were going to keep a close eye on my house, I didn't think you meant this close."

"I'm just going to walk through the rooms with you to make sure everything is secure, and then I'll leave, okay?"

"I was just about to go to bed."

His measured blue gaze swept over her. "So I see. By the way, that's my T-shirt."

"I'll wash it and give it back to you."

"Whatever." He sounded way too calm and reassuring for her liking, but she couldn't deny that it was kind of comforting to have an officer of the law looking out for her on such a personal basis. She waited by the table until he moved past her, the scent of his lemon aftershave a tantalizing breath away.

"Do you do this for all the town's citizenship?"

"If I can. Spring Falls is a small town."

He kept moving up the central hallway and stopped at each closed door to open it and survey the contents of the room. By the time they came to her bedroom, Ally was right behind him. She reached for the door at the same moment he did.

"I think I can take it from here, Sheriff."

As she opened the door, something clattered against the glass. The next moment she found herself pinned under Rob's weight on the bed. She managed to look up to see that one of the windows was slightly ajar.

"Rob, get off me. It was just the blind banging against the window." He didn't move, and she shivered as he buried his face in the crook of her neck and simply breathed her in. "Rob..."

He placed both his palms on the bed on either side of her and levered himself away as if he were doing a push-up. "I don't want to get off you. I want to take off my belt and use it to tie your wrists together and secure them on the headboard. Then I want to fuck you until you beg me not to stop."

Ally tried not to breathe as she imagined him doing what he suggested and found her body responding despite her best efforts to remain still.

He bent his head and nipped her throat, his voice a low, rough sound that barely reached her ear. "You'd let me, wouldn't you? I bet you're wet now just thinking about it."

He shifted his stance and climbed off the bed. Before she could roll over, his knee drove between her thighs, spreading her legs. His fingers drifted over her wet core, and he sighed her name. "Yeah, you're wet. I could fuck you right now without any foreplay and you'd take me easily."

He stepped away from the bed. Ally rolled over onto her back and stared up at him. He met her gaze, his own somber. "But that's not going to work, is it? I can't keep you tied up and naked all the time. I can't make everything right with sex." He nodded to her. "Good night, Ally. Call me if there are any problems."

Long after he'd gone, Ally still stared at the door, her mouth open and her emotions in a riot. Rob had backed off even though he'd known he'd won, that she wanted him despite everything. Ally curled up into a ball. Had he tried to show her that he now understood the difference between binding her to him with sex and allowing her to make that choice with her head and her heart?

Ally punched her pillow. "Damn you, Rob Ward." She didn't want to believe that he'd meant it, because if he understood that, then he really did own her, and there was no reason for her to hate him at all.

Jackson paused at the entrance to the family room and stared down at Rob. His house buddy lay stretched out on the couch, wearing a pair of tight white boxers, a bottle of beer in one hand, watching baseball on TV.

"You okay, Rob?"

There was no answer, and Jackson abandoned the doorway and came farther into the room. At least three empty bottles lay on the carpet, and Jackson breathed in the seductive smell of alcohol and imagined the beer sliding down his throat. He pushed that dangerous thought away. "Are you drunk?"

"Not drunk enough."

Jackson sat on the other end of the couch right up close to Rob's bare feet. "Four's enough. You've got to work tomorrow, right?"

"Yeah, at six, but I don't think I'll be able to sleep, so I might as well get wasted first and then walk it off."

"Why won't you sleep?"

Rob took another swig of beer. "Because I just walked out on Ally, and I'm so fucking horny I can't see straight."

"Ally hates your guts."

"But she'd still let me fuck her."

"And you know that, how?"

"Because I was just at her place and she made it very clear that she'd let me."

"And you walked out."

"Yeah, because I was trying to prove a stupid point, that it's not just about the fucking, it's about everything."

"That was very . . . noble of you."

Rob glared at him. "Sure. Laugh."

"Actually, I meant it." Rob held Jackson's gaze, his blue eyes widening. Jackson's thumb connected with Rob's ankle bone, and he made small soothing circles on it. "Ally's got herself all mixed up about this shit with her mother. She's so used to defending the woman that she does it automatically."

"And?"

Rob didn't pull away from Jackson's touch, so Jackson kept it up. "And you did the right thing. You gave her space to sort it out for herself. We all need space sometimes."

Rob glanced down at Jackson's moving fingers. "Like you're giving me now?"

"I'm . . . a fool." He went to move his hand, and Rob stopped him. Jackson slowly raised his gaze to meet Rob's pale blue stare. "I've been so busy telling you and Ally to be honest with each other that I've forgotten to be honest with myself."

"About what?"

"About you."

Rob's fingers tightened over his. "What about me?"

Jackson exhaled. "How I feel about you, and what I want to do to you when you tell me you're hard."

"I thought you just fucked other guys." Rob cleared his throat. "I was beginning to think there was something wrong with me."

"I like fucking." Jackson hesitated, trying to find the right words. "But with you? It would be a lot more complicated than that."

"Because we're buddies?"

"Because if you turned me down, I'd lose you as my friend, and I convinced myself I'd rather not risk it."

"Yeah, I can see that." Rob nodded and took his hand away. "You should've seen Ally, Jackson, wearing just my old T-shirt, her ass raised in the air, her pussy all wet..."

Despite the sudden change of subject, Jackson's cock kicked against his cotton shorts at the salacious image. He managed to mutter a reply. "I wish I'd been there."

"She'd probably have let you fuck her."

"I'm not sure about that."

Rob shifted in his seat and cupped his balls. "I'm so fucking hard, Jackson."

Jackson glanced at Rob's groin and then looked away. "Yeah, I can see that."

"Seeing as how I was so noble, I guess you should repay me somehow."

Jackson went still. "Like how?"

"You could suck my cock."

"Didn't we just touch on this and you brushed me off?"

"I'm not brushing you off. I'm asking you to help me out."

"And what about what I said?"

"About this meaning something to you?" Rob stroked his thumb along the hard ridge of his arousal, and Jackson practically salivated. "I get that it's a risk, but it's one I'm willing to take." He hesitated. "It's not as if I hadn't guessed how you feel. It's just not the sort of thing a guy can bring up in conversation, is it?"

There was a challenge in Rob's stare that made Jackson shake with a mixture of excitement and dread.

"You'd let me suck your cock?"

"Sure."

Immediately Jackson's shaft went from semierect to painfully aroused. But this wasn't about him; it was about Rob. He surveyed Rob's position on the couch and wanted to moan with anticipation. He turned sideways and knelt between Rob's outstretched legs.

He leaned forward and kissed his way up the growing bulge behind Rob's white boxers. Rob groaned and his hips rose off the couch. Jackson used his tongue to dampen the cotton and clearly outline Rob's thick, pulsing cock.

"Yeah, that's fucking good, Jackson."

Rob was watching him, and that made Jackson even harder. He licked Rob through the cotton again, felt his friend's shaft grow even more as the wet purple crown tried to force itself out of the tight waistband.

"Nice," Jackson murmured, and swirled his tongue over the wetness, until Rob grabbed his hair. Jackson slid his tongue into the slit, and Rob's grip on his hair became painful.

"Take it out—put me in your mouth."

Jackson was more than willing to oblige. He pulled Rob's boxers down and off and settled between his thighs, licking a slow, wet line down the thrusting shaft of Rob's cock and then nuzzling his balls.

Rob tugged on his hair again. "In your mouth, suck me."

Jackson levered himself onto his knees and bore down on Rob's cock, swallowing him deep and hard until Rob groaned. He loved the taste and texture of Rob's heated flesh, the way the blood pumped so close to the surface, the urgent way Rob thrust upward, drilling himself farther down Jackson's throat.

Yeah, this was everything he'd ever dreamed of. Jackson closed his eyes and simply lived the moment; he brought his hand up to cup Rob's balls and massage the soft skin between his ass and sac with his thumb. Rob groaned out some obscenity and started thrusting upward. Jackson took it all. Setting his teeth lightly on Rob's flesh, he held him deep until his friend climaxed, his come so far down Jackson's throat that he hardly tasted it.

"That was fucking awesome."

Jackson slowly released Rob's cock from his mouth and moved away from him, one hand rubbing over his lips to keep that scent and taste with him when he...

He couldn't speak. Jackson nodded at Rob and got off the couch. His cock ached so bad he needed to attend to it right now, and no way was he begging Rob to touch him. He'd never expected this to be reciprocal.

Jackson stumbled into his bathroom and turned on the shower. It took way too long to ease his shorts down over his swollen shaft. The water still wasn't that warm when he got in, but it didn't matter. Hell, he needed cooling down. He braced one arm against the wall and rested his forehead against the coolness of the tile. He grabbed the soap and stared down at his pulsing cock. He licked his lips, tasted Rob there, and wrapped a shaking hand around his shaft.

Rob watched Jackson disappear and hurriedly sat up. "Hey, wait."

But Jackson either hadn't heard him or didn't want to hear him. Rob glanced down at his cock, which was still throbbing with pleasure. Jackson's touch hadn't felt weird at all; in fact, he'd fucking loved it, that strong mouth, Jackson's fingers on his balls....

And just like that, he was hard again. Rob got up and stormed after Jackson. He could hear the sound of the shower going but barged right on in. Through the steamed-up glass, he could see Jackson about to yank himself stupid. Without allowing himself to overanalyze it, Rob stepped into the shower and turned it off.

"I'm not good enough to touch you, then?"

Jackson raised his dark gaze to Rob's face, his black hair dripping from the shower, sending rivulets of water down over his muscled chest. "I didn't ask for anything in return. I just wanted to make you feel good."

Rob looked down at Jackson's cock. "And if I want to play with your dick?"

Jackson tried to turn away from him, and Rob followed him, shoving his buddy up against the shower wall. Rob slid his hand around Jackson's hip and wrapped his fingers around Jackson's shaft. It felt right in his hand. Jackson groaned as Rob started to move his fingers, hard, sharp thrusts that made Jackson tremble. Rob moved in closer, his erect cock pressing against Jackson's ass.

"God, I'm coming, Rob."

Jackson's hoarse shout made Rob tighten his grip until he felt Jackson's hot come drench his fingers. He didn't release Jackson, just stood there, his face buried in Jackson's neck while his friend panted and shook under his hands. Yeah, it felt right, and he wanted it, wanted more. Reluctantly he took his hand away, and Jackson stirred.

"Thanks, Rob."

There was a note of finality in Jackson's tone that made Rob tense. He set his teeth on Jackson's ear and bit down. "We're not done."

"You want me to suck you again?"

Rob circled his hips against Jackson and heard the hiss of his breath. "How about we take this into the bedroom? You've got condoms and lube, right?"

"What?"

"You don't want me to fuck you?"

Jackson gave a strained laugh. "Hell, I've *always* wanted you to fuck me."

"Then what's the problem?" Rob nuzzled Jackson's throat. "I want it; you want it—let's do it."

Rob followed Jackson back into his bedroom and waited as his friend found what they needed. He was hard again, and the thought of having Jackson like this suddenly seemed as natural as having Ally. Why hadn't he understood this before? That the three of them were meant to be together in every way possible.

Jackson glanced up at him, his expression still a mixture of anticipation and fear. "Are you sure, Rob? It's okay if you change your—"

Rob climbed onto the bed and put his hand over Jackson's mouth. "Stop talking and get on your hands and knees." For a moment, Rob wondered if Jackson would rebel against his less-than-conciliatory tone.

Rob knelt behind Jackson and smoothed his hands over the curve of Jackson's spine, over the indentations of his hard abs and the tight muscles of his ass. He stroked Jackson between the legs from his balls to the pucker of his ass, until Jackson lifted his hips in supplication. Rob took a moment to slide a condom over his erect cock.

"God, Rob."

Rob lubed up his fingers and slid the first one deep into Jackson's ass. He used his other hand to locate Jackson's dick and lightly stroked the wet tip. "You like that, Jackson? You want more?"

"Yeah."

Rob smiled as he added another finger, keeping his touch on the crown of Jackson's cock so light that he could almost feel Jackson's frustration. He moved his fingers back and forth, easing his way deeper inside, watching Jackson as carefully as he watched Ally when they fucked. He was in charge of their pleasure, and he'd make damn sure they got what they wanted—when he wanted to give it to them.

"More, Rob."

"What's the rush, Jackson? Maybe I want to make it last all night. Maybe I'll push my cock deep inside you and just stay put until you are begging me to fuck you." He added two more fingers and held them still inside Jackson. "Maybe I'll make you come and come until you're screaming for it, and you'll let me take you so fucking hard you'll be sore for weeks."

Jackson shuddered and arched his back. Rob circled his finger in the wetness pouring out of the slit of Jackson's cock. "You want it hard like that, Jackson? Like Ally does?"

"Yeah."

"Yeah? Is that all you've got for me?" Rob took his hand off Jackson's cock and wrapped it around the base of his own shaft. "How about a please?"

"Rob . . . fuck me—please. I need—"

Rob pulled his fingers out of Jackson's ass and shoved his cock all the way in, making Jackson groan his name. He pulled almost all the way out and then with one thrust of his hips, went deep again. He closed his eyes and pounded into Jackson's ass, fumbling a hand around to Jackson's dick and pumping that in time to his urgent thrusts.

It was amazing. He didn't need to worry about crushing Jackson. His friend was well able to take everything Rob wanted to give him. And he wanted to fuck him hard, to make up for all the wasted years, all the wasted time when they could've been doing this together.

Jackson's come spilled over Rob's fingers and set off an answering spasm in Rob's balls that had him climaxing long and hard. Fireworks dazzled behind his closed eyes, and he slumped over Jackson, bringing his friend down to the bed with him. Rob inhaled the combined scent of satisfied lust, condom, lube, and sweat and smiled against Jackson's shoulder.

After a long time, he licked a slow, wet path along the edge of Jackson's ear. "That was awesome."

Jackson shivered at his caress. "Yeah."

"Back to saying nothing, then?" Rob bit down on Jackson's earlobe and eased his cock free of Jackson's tight passage. "Let's get cleaned up."

They showered together, keeping it short and to the point.

Neither of them bothered to dress again. Jackson paused as they reached his bed, and Rob punched him in the arm. "I'm not leaving yet. You might not want to talk, but for once, I do."

He climbed into the bed next to Jackson and lay on his back, one arm cradling his head.

"What is there to say, Rob? I know you fucked me because you couldn't have Ally."

Rob sighed. "And I knew you were going to say that. I fucked you because I wanted to. I've always wanted to, but I didn't want to make things even more complicated than they already were."

Jackson rolled up on one elbow so that Rob could see his face. "What the hell does that mean?"

"Look, that night I found you and Ally together? Things kind of fell into place. First off, I was mad at her but I wasn't really surprised. Then I was mad at you, and that scared me half to death. I kind of knew you wanted her as much as I did, but I didn't know I wanted you."

"I just thought you were mad for the usual reasons. No one wants his best friend fucking his girl," Jackson answered him, his voice low and rough in the darkness. "I got involved with Susan for all the *wrong* reasons, and I think she was starting to figure that out. Finding me in bed with Ally made it all too clear for her, and she couldn't take it."

"She sure was livid."

Jackson sighed. "That night when she found us together? She was fucking furious with me and determined to move on." He paused and his voice cracked. "I could never understand why the next thing she did was go jump off a bridge as if I'd destroyed her."

Rob reached out and put a comforting hand on Jackson's shoulder. "We were all kids. How else were we supposed to handle it? It's easy to look back and say I should have realized that I could have you both, that we could all have each other and just sort it out from there, but none of us were capable of making those kinds of sexual decisions then, were we?"

"No." Jackson cleared his throat. "It wasn't all Ally's fault, you know."

"What wasn't?"

"Her ending up in my bed. I took advantage of her."

"I know you did." Rob grimaced. "It just took me too damn long to work it out."

"Ally was all messed up because of something else that happened, Rob. She decided she wasn't good enough for you and that I was her way out. And I didn't try and change her mind. I just took the opportunity and ran with it. I was jealous of your relationship, and I wanted to see what you'd do."

Jackson shifted restlessly on the sheets. "I'm not proud of myself. I let Ally take all the heat and then ran away myself. What a fucking loser."

As he thought it through, Rob continued to rub his fingers over Jackson's muscled biceps. He'd always wondered what had driven Ally into Jackson's arms, always feared deep in his heart that his sexual aggression had caused it, that that was why he'd lost his two best friends.

"And I thought it was all about me. I was so sure I was the center of the universe in those days."

Jackson shrugged. "Don't we all at that age?"

"No, I mean I thought Ally hated me and I didn't know why."

Jackson stroked Rob's unshaven face. "She didn't hate you. She doesn't hate you. Don't beat yourself up. We were all too busy dealing with our own issues to see the big picture. We were just kids."

Emotion crashed over Rob, and he turned his face into Jackson's hand and kissed Jackson's palm, heard his friend's soft curse. Very slowly he moved his lips again and sucked Jackson's thumb, felt his own cock jerk in response. "I want to suck your dick."

Jackson's low laugh warmed him. "You think I'm going to say no?"

Rob took a deep breath. "And then I want you to fuck me."

Jackson stroked his cheek. "You don't have to do that."

"Yeah, I do. I want to. If we get Ally back, I want us all on equal footing. We all get to fuck whoever we want."

"And if we don't get Ally back?"

"Shit, I can't even think about that."

Jackson hesitated. "*This* can end right now. I'd never stop you from finding another woman."

"You're a lot more patient than I am."

"I've had a lot of practice."

Rob sat up. "I haven't and I want it all, you—Ally, and me together at last." He leaned into Jackson and found his friend's cock already erect. "Now tell me how you like it."

20

Ally ate her way through her bowl of granola and contemplated the day ahead. It was the weekend, so she didn't have to work. Lauren had some other lucky employee who got to work all the busiest shifts. She glanced at the calendar from the local Chinese takeout she'd stuck on her refrigerator. One more week before Nadia might have a job for her. One more week to decide whether she wanted to blow off her job at the diner and tell Lauren what she really thought of her or maybe keep two jobs.

Someone hammered on the back door, and Ally jumped. She put down her spoon and approached the frosted glass with caution. She unlocked the back door and stared at her employer. "What's up, Lauren?"

Lauren swept in through the door, her nose held high, her normally tied-back blond hair around her shoulders.

Ally braced herself. "Look, if you've come to fight with me, I'm not interested, okay?"

Lauren took a seat at the table and drummed her fingernails against the wood. "Do you really think I'd bother to break into your house?"

Ally remained at the back door and held it open. "Lauren, this is a police matter. It's not up to me to speculate about what happened."

"I asked you a question."

"And I'm not at work, and you are invading my privacy. So either shut up or leave."

"Rob said you didn't directly implicate me. He said that a lot of other folks did, though."

There was a slight tremor in Lauren's voice, which made Ally pause, shut the door, and walk around the table to see Lauren's face. "When did Rob tell you that?"

"Don't pretend you don't know."

Ally sat down. "Believe it or not, he doesn't tell me everything. What did he do?"

Lauren's eyes flashed. "He freaking interviewed me as if I was a potential suspect!"

"You mean he asked you some questions?"

"Not in a nice brotherly sort of way. In that overbearing, 'this is official police business' tone, complete with a request for an alibi and all that shit."

Ally simply stared at Lauren. Rob had done that? She'd doubted he would ever call Lauren on anything. "I suppose he was just doing his job." Ally realized she was echoing Rob and wanted to smile at her own hypocrisy.

"Do you really think I would do that to you?"

Ally met Lauren's gaze full-on. "Actually, I don't. I know you don't like me, but I reckon if you had gotten in here, you would probably have shot me or something, not just messed up the place."

Lauren's face crumpled. "When you left, Ally, Rob changed. He became someone I didn't even recognize. So I lost both of you, you see."

Ally reached for her hand and Lauren let her. "I never meant for that to happen. I thought that if I left, Rob would get over me pretty fast."

"But he didn't."

"So he says." Ally sighed. "I understand why you are angry with me, but I can't make it right for you, Lauren."

"Rob told me to grow up."

Ally hoped her surprise didn't show on her face.

"He said that you had dealt with a whole load of shit in your life and had moved on, so why couldn't I?"

"Rob has a terrible habit of telling everyone how to get on with their lives. You don't have to believe him or do what he says."

"But he made me think. He's never talked to me like that before in my life. He's always tried to protect me, and maybe it's time he stopped." Lauren squeezed Ally's hand and then got to her feet. "I've got to go. I just wanted to make sure you knew it wasn't me doing all this stuff to you."

"It's okay. I never thought you'd smash the window of your own diner."

Lauren looked startled. "Rob thinks that was about you too? Well, if you find out who it was, let me know so I can stick them with the bill."

Ally swallowed down a laugh as Lauren headed out the back door, her nose still in the air. Well, they hadn't exactly ended up the best of friends, but it still felt as if a bubble had been popped and that Lauren's hostility would lessen as time went on. Ally went back to her granola. She still couldn't believe that Rob had found the nerve to interrogate his own sister. It really did seem as if he could separate his emotions out from his job after all....

Apart from when it came to her, of course. Ally groaned and chewed on her cereal and her thoughts. Okay, so she'd panicked herself into protecting her mother, had assumed that Rob was targeting *only* her mother, and had brought everything between them crashing to a halt.

And why was that? Despite all her efforts, did she still really believe that at her center she was a useless child scrabbling to pretend that all was right with her world, terrified that she'd be taken away from her mother if she let on how bad things really were? Was she still terrified of the feelings Rob stirred in her?

If that was true, she really had learned nothing. Ally jumped up from the table and went to find her cell phone. She punched in Rob's home number and got his voice mail.

"Rob? It's Ally. I'll help you find out how Susan died, okay? Just tell me what you want me to do."

To work off her tension while she waited to hear back from Rob, Ally set to work on the dining room. She stacked the last of the boxes in the garage, polished the furniture, and vacuumed the ratty carpet. By the time she finished, the room looked about a million times better than it had before, and Ally was exhausted.

The sun was low in the sky now, light streaming through the kitchen windows and warming up the countertops. Ally pulled the blinds and made herself a tuna sandwich on rye. She sat at the table and poured herself a big glass of milk. She frowned at the glass. If he turned up, would Rob bring beer?

If he turned up.

Ally got up, put the milk carton away, and rummaged in the cutlery drawer for a pair of scissors. She couldn't find one and yanked the second drawer open. Stuffed into the drawer was one of her mother's black journals. Ally held her breath as she retrieved the book and saw the scissors underneath it.

She vaguely remembered shoving the book into the drawer to avoid one of her visitors seeing it, but she couldn't remember which one. She'd been surprised that anyone had bothered to come and see her. Mrs. Orchard had popped in with brownies,

Nadia with freshly ground coffee, and even Mrs. Ford, one of her neighbors, had brought her a casserole.

With shaking hands, Ally returned to her seat and checked the date written on the inside cover of the book. Was this the book she'd thought was missing, and what should she do if it was?

When she realized it was a much later journal, the last one her mother had written, she tried to relax. She'd started reading it a while back and never finished it. Ally found her place and started again, eating her sandwich as she read.

I just got back from the specialist's office and it's not good. I have breast cancer. They're going to try all that chemo and stuff on me, but I don't think there's much hope. I could see it in their faces, and I know it in my soul. I can feel it, the cancer, creeping through me. The only thing I'm sorry about is that I can't tell Ally. Nadia says I should call her, but I can't. I don't think all is well with Ally, and I don't want to burden her with all this crap. Why should she have to put up with a dying woman out of duty? I have friends here who will help me through. I have friends. I'd rather Ally kept away.

Ally gritted her teeth. Would she have come back? She checked the date on the top of the page. Hell, she'd been in rehab at that time, hardly able to do anything for herself, let alone for anyone else. She swallowed back tears. Dammit, she was not going to cry again.

Unbidden, a memory of going to the zoo with Ruth surfaced. For once, her mother's attention had all been on her. They'd had snow cones, bought food to feed the elephants, and laughed together at the antics of the penguins. On the way back, she'd snuggled up against her mother and fallen asleep, a new cuddly teddy bear clutched to her chest.

When they'd arrived home, the man her mother had kicked

out two weeks previously met them at the door, and Ruth had run straight into his arms. Ally had made her own supper and taken herself to bed, knowing even at seven that her mother wouldn't notice her again for days. Eventually she'd stopped hoping that Ruth would notice her at all....

The ring of the front doorbell made her jump and close the book. It was dusk now, and she was reading in the dark, her glass of milk grown warm beside her. She made her way up the hallway and recognized Rob's distinctive shape through the glass. For a moment she paused. Did she want him here? She'd much rather have this conversation over the phone.

She opened the door, and Rob inclined his head. "Hey."

"Hey, would you like to come in?"

"Sure."

Ally stood back so that he could precede her into the hall. He was wearing his brown uniform and his cop face, and she couldn't decide if that was good or bad. If he was able to keep things separate, so could she.

"So what can I do for you, Ally?"

She invited him to sit down, but he refused, which meant she had to keep looking up at him. She wrapped her arms tightly around herself.

"As I said in my message, I'm willing to help you catch whoever broke into my house."

He nodded. "And do you have any further information you'd like to share with us at this point?"

"Are you suggesting I know who it is and just haven't gotten around to mentioning it yet?"

He simply stared at her, his blue eyes devoid of emotion. "Any information would be welcome at this point."

"I haven't got anything new to tell you, but I did want to offer my services if you need to set a trap for this person."

"Set yourself up as bait?"

"If that's what it takes."

Rob regarded her for a long moment. "That's very generous of you. I'll keep it in mind."

"Okay, then." Ally tried to keep her voice light. What had she expected? That the moment he saw her, he'd instantly understand that she'd changed her mind and beg her to come back to him? With the history of their relationship, she could hardly expect that. If she wanted him—and even thinking that terrified her—she'd have to do all the work, and she was so scared of being rejected. With a small sigh, she turned back toward the front door. "I'll see you out."

The kitchen clock chimed nine times just as they reached the front door, and she put her hand on the new latch only to have Rob reach over her head and gently close the door again. She turned to look at him and found herself pressed up against the wall while he thoroughly kissed her.

When he was done, he stepped back and wiped his mouth. "My shift just finished."

"So you kissed me."

He rubbed his thumb over her lower lip. "I know how you like me to keep my private and public lives separate."

"About that..."

He pressed his thumb over her lips and shook his head. "Let's not go there, okay? Let's keep this professional."

"But you just kissed me."

He raised his eyebrows. "That was an aberration. I won't do it again."

She bit his thumb and he cursed. "Rob, I'm trying to be brave here and sort things out with you, and you don't want to hear me?"

His gaze softened. "Honey, I could listen to you all night, but I'm serious. Let's sort out these problems one at a time, okay?"

"And if we can't solve them?"

"Ally, I've been a cop for quite a while. In my experience,

once someone crazy gets all stirred up over something, they usually can't stop even if they want to. And the more frustrated and angry they get, the harder they'll try to achieve their aim."

"Which is me leaving town."

"We don't know that for sure. It might just mean you leaving this house. Whatever secrets it conceals might be better staying hidden."

"But you just said that the person who started all this won't stop no matter what I do."

He stared down at her. "It's okay. We'll keep you safe. I can promise you that."

"But you can't, can you?" Ally whispered. "Because we don't know who this person is or exactly what they want."

He cupped her jaw. "We'll keep you safe."

She leaned into his palm like a cat seeking a caress and nuzzled his palm, drawing a rough sound of need from him. But this wouldn't do. She couldn't just give up and expect him to protect her every minute of the day. She was a grown-up. She reluctantly moved away from him and opened the front door.

"Thanks, Sheriff. Let me know when you need me."

"Ally..."

She manufactured a bright smile. "I promise I'll call if I'm the slightest bit worried, okay?" She gently pushed him out the door and shut it in his face. She pressed her hand to her heart, which seemed to be aching, which was quite ridiculous.

It seemed to take forever for Rob to start his engine and pull off the drive. Ally waited until she was sure he was gone and then walked back down to the kitchen. She'd make herself some hot chocolate, finish reading Ruth's journal, and put herself to bed.

Ally yawned and glanced at her bedside clock. It was past eleven, and she had to work in the morning. She put her empty mug on the nightstand and set her alarm. She'd almost finished the last journal. Ruth's struggle to accept that she was dying had kept Ally's attention despite herself, and she felt even more sympathy for her mom.

Just as she switched off her lamp, she heard a crash that seemed to come from the rear of the house. With shaking hands, she wiggled back into her shorts and shoved her feet into her flip-flops. She checked the pockets. Where the hell was her cell phone? She could only find her front door keys. Had she left it in the kitchen to recharge? There was no way she was heading back there to find out.

Ally tried to calm her panic and rationalize her actions. Yeah, she was scared, but no one could get in, could they? She had new locks on her doors. But what if someone had broken the glass and gotten in through the window? That thought was enough to propel her out of bed and to the door of her room, where she crouched down to listen.

She couldn't hear anyone, but that didn't mean there wasn't anyone there. She opened the door a crack and peered down the hallway toward the kitchen. Moonlight caught shards of glass glinting on the floor, and Ally's stomach did a peculiar flip. She definitely wasn't stupid enough to wander on down to the kitchen. She would do what any regular woman would do and run like hell.

She crawled on her hands and knees in the opposite direction toward the front door and knelt up to open the latch. She half turned her head so that she could still see down the hallway, and something skittered across her vision. The door latch clicked as she opened it, but she didn't care. As it swung back into its lock, she sprinted away from the house and headed for Rob's. There was no logic to her decision; she just knew she had to get to him and Jackson.

It seemed to take forever to get there and bang on the back door. Jackson opened up and she fell into his arms.

"Ally, what the hell?"

She let him guide her farther into the house, heading for the only lit room. She hesitated as she saw Rob sitting up in Jackson's bed, his hair disheveled, his skin gleaming with exertion. Ally inhaled the scent of sex and clung on to the door frame as her world took yet another crazy swing.

"I didn't mean to interrupt anything."

Jackson put his hands on her shoulders and brought her firmly into the room. "You're not interrupting. Now, what's going on?"

Jackson's calm voice steadied Ally. "I think someone was trying to break into my house." She laughed hysterically. "What a night. And here you two are, sharing a bed. Am I supposed to scream at *you* now, Rob? Or will you tell me it was all Jackson's idea?"

Rob reached out and drew her into his lap. She could smell Jackson on him, and the musky scent of come. "Ally, we'll get to that in a moment. Now tell me what happened."

She leaned into him as he stroked her back. "I was just going to bed when I heard something that sounded like glass breaking at the back of my house."

Rob looked up at Jackson. "Call Jeff. He's out on patrol. Ask him to take a look and report back."

Jackson disappeared, and she heard him talking on the radio. Suddenly she felt so tired that she couldn't even pull free of Rob's comforting grasp. She closed her eyes as he stroked her hair back from her face.

"You did the right thing by getting out of there, honey."

"I'm not one of those stupid chicks in the movies who just has to go and check out the cellar, you know."

His quiet chuckle rumbled in his chest. "I know that. I'm just glad you're okay."

Jackson reappeared, his expression grim. "Jeff says the kitchen window is broken, but there's no sign of entry. He's going to stick a piece of plywood over the hole so everything's secured, and he'll keep an eye on the place for the rest of the night."

"Don't I need to go and check it out?" Ally asked.

"You're in shock, honey. You'd better stay with us and we'll all take a look in the morning."

Ally started to pull away from Rob's hold. "No, it's okay. I don't want to be in the way."

Jackson appeared on her other side, effectively blocking off her exit. "You're staying right here between us, where you belong."

God, she didn't have the strength to argue anymore, because he was right. At this moment, there was no other place she would rather be. Jackson got into the bed, and Rob drew the covers up over them all. Ally lay on her back between the two men, who both had an arm around her. She felt her eyelids begin to droop as their combined warmth and solidly reassuring presence surrounded her. But it was no good.

"Can we talk about this?"

"Don't you just want to sleep?" Jackson murmured.

Rob groaned. "She's a woman, Jackson. She won't sleep until everything has been sorted out to her satisfaction."

Ally put her hand on Rob's chest. "When did you two get together?"

"When Jackson finally got over himself and begged me to fuck him."

"I didn't beg."

"Yeah, you did. You wanted it real bad."

"Sure, I wanted you, but I wasn't that desperate."

Ally put her other hand on Jackson's chest. "I'm not surprised that it happened. I'm just wondering *when* it happened."

Rob shifted his weight, and Ally became aware of his erection prodding her hip. "Recently. Which is why Jackson can't keep his hands off me."

"Like you're any better."

Ally realized Jackson was also erect. She resisted the temptation to slide her hands lower and squeeze both of their cocks so hard that they stopped all the man talk and gave her the truth. She struggled to sit up.

"I want to go home."

Both the men went still. Rob recovered his voice first. "You can't, honey. It's not safe."

"Then I want to sleep by myself. I can use your room, Rob, seeing as you've moved in here." She shot Jackson a look. "Perhaps Jane had it right after all and you really do want Rob all to yourself."

Jackson's face went blank. "That's not what I want, Ally. I want you both—I swear it."

Ally managed to scramble out of the bed. "Good night, guys. See you in the morning."

Rob started after her. "Ally, don't do this."

She held up a hand to stop him. "You were the one who said we should leave all the personal stuff alone until we solved this case. So let's do that, shall we?"

She made her way to Rob's bed and cuddled up in his lemon-scented sheets. She couldn't deal with all this right now; her mind seemed to be spiraling out of her control as if she were looking down on herself from a great distance. She hugged Rob's pillow and stared into the darkness as shivers racked her body. She couldn't believe how much she wanted to crawl back into bed with Jackson and Rob. Had they decided she wasn't worth the risk and consoled each other? She shied away from the thought that they didn't need her anymore and were just being kind. She just couldn't deal with it.

Rob lay back on the pillow and stared up at the ceiling. "Well, fuck."

Jackson sat on the side of the bed, his expression unreadable.

He smoothed the rumpled bedsheets with his long fingers. "If you want to go to her, I'm okay with it."

Rob scowled. "No, we've already been through this. We're all in this together. Ally's just had one too many shocks in one night."

"And what if she doesn't get over it, Rob? What do we do then?"

Rob understood the tension in Jackson's voice all too well. He knew how hard it had been for Jackson to finally give in to his desire for him. "She'll get over it. She loves us both." He patted the sheets. "Now get into bed and let's try and get some sleep."

He woke up suddenly in complete darkness and heard the faint sounds of Ally crying. He got out of bed and went to her, picked her up, and brought her back into Jackson's bed. She didn't seem to be quite awake, so he kissed her and soothed her with his mouth and hands until she started to kiss him back, her mouth hot and desperate against his, her fingernails scraping at his flesh.

"Honey, it's okay. Just go to sleep, all right?"

"But I want..."

God, Rob wanted it, too, but this wasn't the right moment. They'd be taking advantage of her whether she realized it or not. He kissed her forehead and guided her back down onto the pillows. "Just sleep, okay?"

She murmured his name, turned her face against his shoulder, and started to relax. He could feel the wetness of her tears against his chest, and it made him want to forget all his obligations to keep citizens safe and rip apart whoever was hurting Ally with his bare hands.

Much later he woke up to see slivers of light coming through the blinds. Ally was touching him again, and his cock was already responding. He couldn't stop her this time; he just couldn't.

He sensed Jackson waking up, too, and guided his friend's hands and mouth onto Ally as well. She seemed to welcome the urgency they felt and grabbed Jackson's hand and pressed it between her legs. She began to move against him. Rob kissed her neck and then moved lower to her breasts, tugging hard on her nipples as Jackson buried his face between her legs and licked and suckled her there.

Rob closed his eyes to experience everything better, the wet sounds of Jackson sucking Ally's cunt, her moans and soft cries as Rob teased her breasts. He dragged her hand down to his cock and then wrapped his fingers around Jackson's. They all moved together as if they'd practiced such erotic exercises countless times.

God, he wanted to fuck them both, wanted them both to fuck him so badly. Ally tugged on his cock, and he fell forward until she took him deep into her mouth. Jackson moved as well and slid his cock inside Ally. When Jackson made her climax for the third time, Rob touched Jackson's shoulder and they changed places, Rob now inside Ally's sex and Jackson in her mouth. Hot and wet and gripping him like a fist. Rob luxuriated in the feel of Ally's sheath, and he drove into her.

And then they moved again. Jackson was now on his back with Ally straddling him. Rob groaned when Jackson grabbed him by the dick and licked the crown of his cock. He groaned even harder when Jackson twisted around to take him fully into his mouth. Rob felt Ally watching him and kissed her, connecting them all, making them all scream together when they climaxed.

And then Ally settled between them, her body boneless with pleasure, and that, perhaps, was the best thing of all. Rob's arm crossed over her hips, and he could still touch Jackson. And Jackson did the same. Rob let his eyes start to close. Ally was safe—at least for the next few hours. He'd worry about all the other stuff in the morning.

21

Even though she was sandwiched between Jackson and Rob, Ally managed to wiggle out of the bed and head for the bathroom in Rob's part of the house. She studied her ravaged and swollen face in the mirror and wanted to groan. She also surveyed her clothes. How the hell could she go straight to work wearing a pair of shorts and a thin top with no bra?

She shut the door to the bathroom and turned on the shower, waited until the water ran hot, and stepped inside. How she had ended up back in Jackson's bed with both men making love to her was still a mystery. The last thing she remembered was trying to sleep and fighting off the desire to crawl back to the guys. Maybe that was what she'd done? But, no, she had a faint memory of Rob carrying her, his voice soothing as he kissed away her tears.

Ally closed her eyes and rested her forehead against the wall, letting the water stream down her back. She'd woken up from a hot dream of them fucking her and just carried the dream into reality. Their lovemaking had been as fierce and raunchy as she wanted, both men responding to her desire to blot out the fear and take her to another place where all she'd been able to think about was what they were doing to her.

Someone tapped on the glass door, and she jumped and spluttered in the water.

"Ally, you okay?"

It was Rob. He was naked and tousled, his blue eyes full of concern as he studied her.

"I'm fine."

He nodded and pressed his palm against the glass as if he wished it weren't separating them. "I'll take you home so you can check out the damage, okay?"

She nodded at him, too overwhelmed to speak, and for once he didn't press her. Ally finished her shower and got dressed in the only clothes she had. When she reached the kitchen, Rob was making breakfast. He pointed at a seat at the table.

"Eat."

Ally sat and he put a mug of coffee and a piece of brown toast in front of her. She concentrated on forcing the toast down while Rob took another mug of coffee that she assumed was for Jackson back through the house. She swallowed hard. Jackson probably didn't want to see her after the awful thing she'd said about him last night.

Rob came back in and buckled on his heavy belt. "You ready to go?"

Ally managed to speak. "I'm supposed to be at work."

"I know. Jackson's going to talk to Lauren before he clocks in for his shift."

Ally stood up and looked uncertainly down the hallway. "Is Jackson okay?"

"He'll get over himself."

"I didn't mean what I said," Ally blurted out.

"I'm sure he knows that, honey." Rob held the back door open. "Are you coming?"

There was nothing else to do but follow Rob out into the bright morning sunshine and get into his truck. Ally huddled down in the seat and watched the houses pass by. Someone in Spring Falls didn't want her there, and it could be anyone. A rock could come right through Rob's windshield at any moment.

Ally shivered and Rob's narrowed gaze flicked over her again. "You cold?"

"A little." She tried to smile. "I'll need to get some clean clothes before I go on to work."

"Sure."

Ally tensed as they pulled into her driveway. From the front, the house looked its normal shabby self. Rob shut off the engine and walked around to open her door.

"Do you want to stay in the truck? I can check out the damage and get you some clothes if you give me your new keys."

Ally fished out her keys. "Oh, God, Rob, we changed the locks. That's why the person couldn't get in and smashed the glass instead."

"Yeah, that makes sense." Rob held out his hand. "You coming?"

Ally took a deep breath. She refused to let this beat her. She took Rob's proffered hand and he smiled.

"Good girl."

She ignored him and went toward the side gate, her fingers entwined with his, her heart beating erratically. She could hardly bear to look.

"Yeah," Rob said. "Someone couldn't get in and pitched a hissy fit all right." He walked closer and removed the plywood that was duct-taped over the gaping hole in the back door's glass panel. "Threw one of your plant pots right through the glass to try and get to the new lock."

Ally peered over his shoulder. "At least the damage isn't too bad."

"It isn't. You'll be fine once you've cleaned up a bit and I fit the new glass." Rob nodded at the door. "Why don't you open up so that we can see the damage?"

With shaking hands, Ally unlocked the back door and let it

swing open. Rob touched her arm. "Let me go in first. I've got boots on. I'll get the vacuum and brushes, okay?"

Ally let him crunch through the broken glass to her storage cupboard and waited until he returned with the cleaning stuff. She moved forward to help, and he held up his hand. "Look, let me do this while you go get dressed."

"Are you sure?"

His smile made her heart turn over. "It's the least I can do."

"Are you going to check for fingerprints or anything?"

Rob was crouched down on his haunches, the dustpan and brush in his hand. "Jeff checked the outside last night before he boarded it up, but I'll see if there are any fragments of the flower pot big enough to dust." He cleared his throat. "Trouble is, there's soil on everything and it's extremely hard to get prints off terra-cotta anyway."

Ally inched past him and headed to her bedroom. As she changed, she could hear the sounds of Rob clearing up, the clattering of glass, the low hum of the ancient vacuum cleaner. She repaired her face as best she could and brushed out her hair before braiding it again. She put on her jeans and a stouter pair of shoes and went back to join Rob in the kitchen.

He looked up at her from his position on the floor. "You got any gallon-size ziplock bags, Ally?"

"Sure." She maneuvered around him to the right drawer and handed him the box, noticing that he'd pulled on a thick pair of gloves he must have gotten from his truck. "What did you find?"

"A few big fragments of clay pot. They might yield nothing, but at least we can have a look."

The kitchen clock chimed seven times, and Ally winced. She was almost two hours late for her shift, and Lauren was not the most forgiving of employers.

"Ally, why don't you go on in to work? Take my truck. I'll finish up here and bring your keys back to the diner."

She spun around to stare at Rob. Sometimes it seemed he

could read her mind. "Thanks, but it's okay. You'll need your truck. I can walk in."

He frowned. "Are you sure, honey? I could ask one of the guys to drive by and pick you up."

She met his stare head-on. "I think I'd like to walk. It's only ten minutes. I can't hide forever."

Rob stood up and walked across to her. "You're a brave woman, Ms. Kendal."

"No, I'm not. Look what I did last night, running to you and Jackson like a screeching baby."

He kissed her nose. "I'm glad you came to me and so is Jackson."

Ally hesitated. "Look, if there really is something serious going on between you guys, I'm okay with it. Jackson's always wanted you, and I'm kind of glad that he's finally getting what he wants."

A smile kicked up the corner of Rob's mouth. "I'm kind of glad too."

Ally patted his smooth cheek. "To be honest, I never thought you'd go for it."

Rob shrugged. "Jackson's a special case. I guess I knew what he wanted all along, but I could never get my head around it until you came back." He paused. "It's like something inside me knew it would work if we were all together again."

"That's great." Ally tried to keep her voice from trembling. She would be glad for them, she *would.*

"I realized a lot of things." He lightly kissed her lips. "We'll be talking about some of them as soon as this case is cleared up, so don't even think about leaving town."

"But if I went, you and Jackson could be happy together."

"Yeah, right." Rob's faint smile died. "We'll talk about it, okay? Now get to work before Lauren gets on my ass."

Ally stood on tiptoe to kiss him and then turned away, her thoughts in turmoil, her emotions completely gutted. Could she really walk away and leave Rob and Jackson to their happy ever after? She put on her sunglasses and walked down to the corner of the street.

She should leave. Maybe her presence in Spring Falls had done some good after all. But what about her? Where would she go, and what did she have to look forward to? Ally swallowed a lump in her throat and looked resolutely toward the town center. She had friends. She had a place at college, and she would make damn sure she passed every single exam and aced every paper to fulfill her dream of becoming a teacher.

Jill would welcome her back to New York with open arms and put her up for as long as she needed. She could even look up Dave and go backpacking around the country. Surely after facing Spring Falls, she could face anything?

By the time she reached the diner, she was way too hot and glad to duck inside the kitchen, which was hot in a different way, but at least had some air-conditioning. Fig waved his spatula at her, his face flushed as he flipped half a dozen pancakes.

Ally put her apron on and headed for the front of the diner. She hated how vulnerable she suddenly felt, like any of the folks eating their breakfast might jump up and try to throttle her.

"Everything all right, Ally?"

Ally almost jumped out of her skin as Lauren came up behind her. "I'm sorry I'm late."

Lauren frowned. "Jackson said someone smashed your kitchen window in." She touched Ally's shoulder. "Are you okay?"

Ally blinked at Lauren. "I'm . . . fine, thanks. I can work the two extra hours after the end of my shift."

Lauren waved a hand. "There's no need. You go home and rest up, okay?"

Ally stared after her boss. What had just happened? Had Lauren actually been pleasant to her? She grabbed her spray bottle and hurried toward the first booth.

"Good morning, Ally." She turned to see an elderly couple

who lived down the street from her ensconced in the next booth. They came in every weekday morning to take advantage of the senior specials. "You're late today. Did you have an appointment?"

"Morning, Mr. and Mrs. Ford." Ally smiled. Living in a small town meant any changes in your routine were always noted and commented upon. "Just a problem with some broken glass I had to clean up before I left the house."

Mrs. Ford nudged her husband in the ribs. "I told you I heard something last night. I thought about calling that nice sheriff. Did you get burgled, dear?"

"No, thank goodness. I had new locks installed last week."

"Now that's an excellent idea." Mrs. Ford nodded and poked her husband again. "We should do that, George." Mr. Ford grunted something and returned his attention to his eggs. "Well, I'm glad that you're okay, Ally dear. We wouldn't want anything to hurt you. It's always a treat to see your smiling face."

Ally turned back to her work, aware all at once that no one in New York would ever notice or care if she came into work on time or not. Spring Falls had its downside, but perhaps everyone wasn't out to get her after all.

Ally left work around one and walked back through the mainly deserted streets. It was approaching ninety-five degrees, and most sensible folks had retreated into their air-conditioned homes and cars. She couldn't begin to imagine how anyone had survived out here back in the gold rush days of the last century.

Rob had left word with Lauren that it was all clear to go home, although he hadn't left her back door keys. As she walked up the street, she studied the bland façade of the ranch house. Did it feel like a home? She felt as unsafe and unsettled there as she had when she was a kid.

Outside the actual house, there had been good times with Rob, Jackson, and Lauren. She'd been lucky to have them as friends. They'd been her family, and they'd made her life far more bearable. Ally gripped her keys in her fist and approached the peeling cream paint on the front door. The door opened easily, and she went into the cool darkness of the hallway.

The house would have to go.

The thought crystallized in Ally's brain, and she let out her breath. Even if she kept a base in Spring Falls, she couldn't live here. With the money her mom had left her in the bank, she could put the house on the market and take the best offer available without worrying about every cent. It was time to call a Realtor and talk about putting it on the market.

Ally progressed farther down the hall and into the kitchen. The glass in the door had been repaired, and there was no sign of any damage. A note from Rob was propped up against the ancient toaster. She read it out loud.

" 'All clear here. But come over and spend the night anyway—Rob and Jackson.' " He'd added three *X*s and three interlinked hearts; that made her smile, which was probably exactly what he'd intended.

She propped the note up on the table and hesitated by the phone. Hadn't Jane said something about having a friend who was a Realtor? Maybe she should call Jane and get the number now while she was still determined to sell the place. She looked around the countertops. Where the hell was her cell phone? Had Rob put it somewhere safe for her? After a quick fruitless search, she used the landline to dial Jane's number, which she'd found stuck on the refrigerator under the pizza delivery service flyer.

"Hey, Jane?"

"Yes, it's me. What can I do for you, Ally?"

Ally propped her hip on the edge of the table. "I was wondering if you had the number of that Realtor friend of yours handy."

"Alison Haymore? Yes, I'm sure I have it here somewhere." There was a rustling sound. "Have you decided to sell the house already?"

"I'm thinking about it."

"You're leaving town?"

Ally smiled at the hope in Jane's voice. "Well, I'm not sure about that yet, but I really want to get rid of the house."

"Why's that?"

Despite the heat, Ally shivered. "Because it's full of ghosts."

There was a pause before Jane replied, "Darn it, I can't find the number. I'll go look for it, and then I'll bring it over, okay?"

"Sure. I'm not going anywhere until nine tonight."

"Great, well, I'll drop in later, then. Bye!"

Ally disconnected and then got herself a cold glass of water. She'd shower, finish reading Ruth's journal, and wait for Jane to turn up.

Two hours later, Ally was almost finished reading. Ruth's struggle with the cancer that had eventually killed her made Ally sad. She was just about to close the book when she noticed there was another page of text, and it was addressed directly to her. She turned the page and started to read.

Dear Ally, I hope you get to read these journals of mine and don't just throw them in the trash. There's a lot of junk in this house, and I can't seem to stop it growing. My friends want to help me clear it out, but if I let them do that, things might emerge that I'd rather not deal with. I'm hoping you'll deal with them for me, Ally, which is a lot to ask from a mother who sucked at mothering and let you down. But then, I've always been a coward. Perhaps you can set things right. Do you remember when you were a little girl and I taught you how to play hide-and-seek with that favorite teddy of yours? You didn't realize I'd stuff my drugs in the back of the teddy so that if we got busted, the cops wouldn't look there. Pathetic, I know. I'm almost ashamed to write it. But there it is. Find the teddy, find the truth, and do what you think best.

Ally closed the book and studied the black cover, her mind scrolling back through the years to picture the ragged teddy her mother was talking about. It was the bear Ruth had bought her at the zoo. She closed her eyes and evened out her breathing. Where had she hidden the thing? Her mother had always told her the best places, and Ally hadn't realized why.

What was her mother talking about anyway? What had she concealed, and why? Ally raised her head and stared blindly at the wall. It all made a terrible kind of sense now. Someone was after something in the house, and her mother was suggesting she had something to hide, but what?

The doorbell rang, startling Ally. She put the book away and went to open the front door. Jane was there, her smile beaming, her flowery pink dress making her look as fresh and cool as a morning breeze.

"Hey, Ally. I was going out, anyway, so I thought I'd bring the phone number by." Jane walked down the hall and into the kitchen, her head bent as she riffled through her large flowered purse. "I have a flyer here somewhere with a discount on it."

"That's great, Jane." Ally followed her guest, her thoughts still far away.

Jane glanced at the back door. "I see you got everything fixed up nicely."

"Yeah, Rob was very kind and did the glass for me."

"Rob did?" Jane put her purse on the table and continued to rummage through it. "Darn it, I know I put the thing in here." Her gaze fell on the note Ally had left on the table. "Oh."

For some reason, Ally wanted to snatch the piece of paper away before Jane finished reading it.

Jane abandoned her search. "Why would Rob invite you to stay at his house when you're leaving?"

Ally shrugged. "He's just doing his job."

"You think he invites everyone involved in a crime scene to stay over?"

Ally sat down at the table. "Rob and I have been friends for years. He's a bit overprotective."

Jane took the seat opposite Ally, her cheeks now flushed, her mouth set in a firm, unyielding line. "You're seeing him again, aren't you?"

"I'm . . ." Ally wanted to squirm in her seat. "It's not like we're going out or anything, Jane. We just have a few things to sort out before I leave." Wow, that sounded lame even to Ally.

"So you're going to sell this house and move in with Rob?"

"That's not what I said. Selling this house has nothing to do with him."

Jane fiddled with the handles of her purse. "I suppose I should've seen it coming, really. I know what you're doing with Rob, Ally. I've seen you."

"And I know you won't believe me, but it doesn't mean anything."

"Because it's just sex?"

"Yeah." Ally felt awful. "I know for you there's probably no difference between being in a relationship and just having sex, but for Rob and me, it's different."

Jane's lip wobbled. "That's a lie, Ally. The kinds of lies men tell themselves so that they can get what they want from women. My dad was like that with my mom. I never thought I'd hear you use the same perverted logic."

Ally couldn't answer. Trouble was, it was a lie. Ally knew she'd never been able to separate the sex from the love with Rob or with Jackson. She knew that whatever he claimed, Rob felt the same too.

She took a deep breath. "You're right, Jane. I didn't come back here to hurt anyone. I came to make amends, but I've realized that I do care for Rob."

"And now you won't be leaving." Jane opened her purse and pulled out a tissue to dab at her eyes.

"I'm not sure what I'll be doing yet. I'm still intending to go to college in the fall. That's the truth, Jane."

Jane sighed and dropped the tissue back in her bag. "Well, you've made things very complicated for me, haven't you?"

"I'm sure if you just talk to Rob, he'll tell you how he really feels."

"It's not just about Rob." She gestured at the note. "That message has two men's names on it."

Something in Jane's tone made Ally look up from her contemplation of the table. "Well, I know you don't approve of Jackson, either, but that doesn't have anything to do with your issues with Rob, does it?"

"You're sleeping with both of them, Ally. Of course it does."

"How do you know that?"

Jane made a tiny gesture of distaste. "I saw them both pawing you through the window of the diner."

A cold lump formed somewhere in the region of Ally's chest. "You were watching us?"

"I was walking my dog like any other citizen has a right to do and had to put up with that porn show."

Ally felt herself blush. Jane must have gotten up pretty close to see through the blinds. There was nothing she could say about that night that wouldn't infuriate Jane. The most obvious question as to whether Jane had hurled a rock through the window to express her disapproval screamed danger.

Needing something to do to stave off her agitation, Ally got to her feet and went across to the refrigerator. How the hell could she contact Rob or Jackson without her cell phone? "Would you like a drink, Jane? I'm parched."

"I don't think so, Ally."

Ally turned back to Jane, and her throat went dry. Jane had produced a rather wicked-looking knife from her purse.

"I think I'd rather you tell me the truth."

22

Rob sighed as he crossed out the name on the whiteboard. It was late afternoon, and his shift was almost over. Despite the blinds being closed, it was still way too hot in his small office, and he was sweating. He and Jackson were staring at the incident board on the wall. He crossed out the name, Ted. "That's the last of Ruth's lodgers accounted for. He's in San Quentin."

Jackson frowned at the board. "So who does that leave us with?"

"No one—or the whole town. Take your pick."

"This makes no sense at all, does it?" Jackson looked. "We've eliminated all the suspects, including your sister, and we're still turning up blank."

Rob sat down heavily behind his desk and shoved a hand through his damp hair. "Maybe it is just random acts of vandalism after all. Some kids who've heard the old stories and thought it would be fun to mess around with Ally now that she's back."

"I suppose that could be it, but it feels way more personal to me. Do you get that?"

Rob nodded. "Yeah, like someone really wants to hurt her." He grabbed his hat. "I'm going to talk to Lauren one more time, and then I'm going to take Ally her keys."

"Try and persuade her to come to our place tonight."

"I already asked her." Rob paused in the doorway. "You okay with that?"

Jackson grimaced. "I'm hoping she didn't mean that shit she said about me."

"I don't think she did. She was worried about you this morning."

"Yeah?" Jackson smiled. "Good to know. I can work with that."

"Then I'll catch you later."

Ally swallowed hard and stared at Jane's smiling face. "Um, Jane? What's with the knife?"

"Oh, I brought that because I thought you might not want to talk to me. It's quite sharp."

Ally retreated slowly toward the back door. "I'm happy to talk to you, so could you just put it away?"

"The back door is double locked, Ally, and you don't have the key—Rob does. I saw him leave with it. You won't be able to unlock it before I get to you."

Ally went still. "Okay, so can we just talk?"

Jane patted the table. "Come and sit down, then."

Ally didn't really want to go anywhere near Jane, but she had little choice. As she took her seat, she scanned the counter-tops again for her cell.

"Ally, I'm not stupid. I took your cell phone when I broke the glass last night. I wasn't very happy to see you'd changed the locks, but at least I got that. I thought it might come in handy."

Ally studied Jane's pleasant face. "So this was about Rob all along?"

Jane smiled. "Not all of it. He's obviously not the man I took him for if he's hooked up with you again, is he?"

"So, what else?"

"I think you know, Ally. Why else did you mention *ghosts* on the phone? Taunting me like that was not a good idea. I refuse to be blackmailed by scum like you."

Fear curdled in Ally's gut, but she concentrated on looking relaxed. Surely the longer she kept Jane talking, the more likely she'd find a way out of this nightmarish situation.

"I'm not sure what you mean."

Ally jumped as Jane pointed the knife straight at her. "Don't lie to me." Jane paused to push a stray hair back from her face. "Rob was coming around to the idea of marrying me quite nicely before you turned up with your slutty ways." She sniffed. "I'm not surprised Jackson was sniffing around you, but I thought better of Rob."

"Why don't you like Jackson?"

Jane opened her eyes wide at Ally. "I told you why. Because he wants Rob all to himself."

"You also told me you hated him because he killed Susan."

Jane shrugged. "Well that was just to make you suspicious of him. Unfortunately, it didn't work, but I had to try."

Ally bit down hard on her lip. She felt as if she'd strayed into an alternate universe. Jane seemed far too calm and relaxed to be contemplating harm, but she had a knife. . . .

"So this *is* all about Rob. Don't you think you're being a bit overdramatic? Can't we all just sit down and talk it through like adults?"

Jane's smile disappeared. "It's about my life and my future with the man I love, Ally. I don't think that's being melo-dramatic at all."

"I really don't know what you're after, Jane. If you wanted to scare me into leaving Spring Falls, you've pretty much achieved your aim. I'm terrified."

Jane leaned forward. "You'll be leaving, one way or another, but not until you give me what I'm looking for."

"Which is?" Ally hissed when the tip of the knife cut her cheek. She instinctively recoiled and pushed herself away from the table.

Jane stood up and looked reproachful. "I want the journal."

Ally held her hand to her burning cheek and edged away from Jane. "Didn't you already take that?"

"I took your mom's journal where she talked about that night, but the pages I wanted were ripped out."

"What pages?" Ally glanced at the doorway into the hall. Could she reach that before Jane and get to the front door? She wasn't sure.

For the first time, Jane looked agitated. "Your mom was writing stuff about me and what happened to Susan." Her frown deepened. "After Susan's death, I came back here and told your mom that if she talked to the police about me being there, I'd tell them that *you* were with Susan when she died."

Ally stretched out her hand for a piece of paper towel to mop up the blood rolling down her face. "But I had an alibi."

"Your mom was so drunk, she didn't know anything, so she agreed to keep quiet. But now you're back disturbing everything, and I just know you're going to find those pages and give them to Rob, and I can't have that."

There was a slightly hysterical note in Jane's voice that made Ally want to run like hell. Instead, she edged toward the doorway. "Then I think I might've found what you're looking for in the dining room. You can have the pages, okay? I don't want them. I really don't care what they say either. My mom wasn't exactly the most reliable witness in the world."

Jane blocked her path and brought the knife up to Ally's throat. "Nice try, Ally, but I'm coming with you. We'll retrieve the pages together."

Keeping the knife angled against Ally's neck, Jane picked up her purse and nudged Ally forward. "Where exactly did you find them?"

"They were down the back of the drawers. I found them when I was putting all the stuff back after you broke in."

Jane stiffened. "I didn't 'break in.' I just borrowed your back door key in case I needed to get my pie dish and you weren't home."

Ally had nothing to say to that. Apparently Jane could justify the craziest actions imaginable.

"Did you read them?" Jane asked.

"No." Ally tried to sound relaxed. "I only found them this morning, so I haven't had a chance. If you take them, you'll be the only one who knows what's written there."

"I can't take that chance, Ally. Your mom probably told you all about it."

"I haven't spoken to my mom in ten years."

Jane put her purse on the now-cleared table, right next to the monitor and keyboard. She gestured Ally forward to the desk. "Give them to me."

Ally hated having to turn slightly away from Jane, who was fishing for something in her purse again. It seemed that no one was coming to save her, so she'd have to do something to help herself. She opened the second drawer, which was full of her mother's black journals.

"Give me a minute, Jane. I put it right under all these books."

She picked up a stack of about ten journals, spun around, and threw them at Jane's face. As Jane shrieked and lunged for her, Ally shoved the nearest chair across Jane's path and ran for the front door. She flung it open and spotted Rob's patrol car pulling into the drive.

Jane was behind her now, the knife blade glinting in the sun as she raised her arm. Ally saw Rob's startled face as he flung open the door of his car and faced them, his gun leveled at Jane.

"Put the knife down, Jane."

"Or you'll shoot?" Jane smiled and grabbed Ally's braid, yanking her closer. "Shoot Ally. She deserves it, not me. I'm just trying to clear up a few things around here."

Rob remained still, his pale gaze fixed on Jane. "Let Ally go and drop the knife. Then we'll talk, okay?"

Ally swallowed convulsively as Rob's gaze flicked over her and then fixed unerringly on Jane. "Drop the knife, Jane."

"Well, for goodness' sake, there's no need to get so serious, Rob!" Jane tossed the knife away and released her hold on Ally's braid. Ally fell to her knees and forced herself to breathe. "Ally's just overreacting!"

Another patrol car rounded the corner at speed, and Jane's gaze narrowed. "I hope that's not Jackson. If he'd gotten here sooner, I might have held on to that knife so he could watch me stick it in you, Sheriff."

Rob moved forward and kicked the knife away toward the gutter. "You going to come down to the station quietly, Jane?"

Jane frowned. "Why do I need to go anywhere? Ally's going to give me the pages, so everything's okay now. I didn't really hurt her. It's just a scratch."

Rob stared at Jane. She sounded so normal, it was downright weird. He held open the door of his car. "Humor me, okay?"

Jane sighed. "Well, can Ally get my purse? I left it in the dining room on the table, and I hate not to have it with me."

"I'll make sure you get your purse." Rob motioned her toward the car. "I just want to ask you a few questions."

Jane got into the back of the car and then froze and tried to grab his arm. "But Ally hasn't given me the pages. I can't go yet." Rob pushed her back into the car, expertly handcuffed her wrists behind her, and shut the door. Her face contorted with rage as she realized she couldn't get out, and she started banging her shoulder against the glass.

Rob moved to where Ally still sat on the driveway, hugging her knees. "You okay, honey?"

"I . . ." She looked at him and shook her head. "What the hell is up with that woman?"

"I have no idea, but she sounds completely nuts to me." He touched Ally's bloodied face and realized his fingers were shaking. "Do you need to go to the ER?"

A shadow loomed over them, and, thank God, Jackson was there. He had the knife in a plastic evidence bag, which he handed to Rob. "Take Jane in. Ally can fill me in on the details."

Rob helped Ally stand up. Despite the heat, she was shivering. He didn't want to leave her, but he knew he had no choice. "Yeah, take her inside, Jackson, and look after her. She needs it."

"Sure."

Jane was red-faced and screaming now, all composure gone as she banged on the window. When he got into the car, Rob braced himself for a tirade of abuse, but Jane seemed perfectly normal again. He kept himself busy on the short drive, arranging for immediate backup from the county mental health department.

Jackson put his arm around Ally and walked her back into the house. She was shaking so violently he wanted to take her someplace quiet and just hold her. But he knew Rob would expect him to get some of the official details out of the way before he succumbed to his softer side.

She paused at the door of the dining room, and he noted the overturned chair and the journals scattered all over the floor. A big flowery purse sat on the table next to the computer. "So Jane had a knife, and you threw the book at her, literally, right?"

"I threw a whole pile of books at her, and then I blocked her by pulling the chair over. It gave me just enough time to get to the front door before she could get to me."

Jackson squeezed her shoulders. "You did great, Ally. The worst thing to do is to try and get the knife off someone. Unless you know what you're doing, you usually end up hurting yourself."

She gulped in a breath. "I remembered something about that from the self-defense classes I took when I lived in New York. I knew the best thing was to keep her away from me and run like hell."

Jackson kissed the top of her head and set the chair upright. He pulled a thin pair of gloves out of his back pocket and opened Jane's purse. He took out a heavy plastic bag and showed it to Ally.

"Hell, she had a gun in here too." He realized he sounded almost as shaken as Ally did. All-too-familiar gruesome images of what he and Rob might have found at the house if they hadn't gotten there fast enough flashed through his brain.

"Somehow that doesn't surprise me." Ally sat down with a thump on one of the chairs. "She'd probably worked out a plan to shoot me and make it look like suicide or something."

Jackson left the purse and turned back to Ally. She looked exhausted and no wonder. She'd had a hell of an afternoon. He crouched down in front of her and touched her knee. "I know you probably don't want to talk about this right now, but I need to know what she was after."

"I understand." Jackson waited as Ally visibly composed herself. "At first I thought she just wanted to run me out of town because she's obsessed with Rob." She glanced down at him. "That's why she doesn't like you either, Jackson. But then I realized it was a lot more complicated than that. She thinks my mom wrote incriminating stuff about her and Susan in her journal."

Jackson frowned. "But didn't she take that journal?"

"Apparently my mom had already ripped the crucial pages out, and Jane wanted them back." Ally shook her head. "I feel like such a fool. I *invited* Jane in this afternoon. I had no idea all this crazy stuff was floating around in her head. She thought I'd found the pages and was trying to blackmail her." Jackson winced as her grip tightened on his fingers. "It's got me wondering about whether my mom deliberately made me leave that night."

"Your mom?"

"Jane said she threatened to tell the police that I left this house with Susan on the night she died." Ally studied his face. "Maybe Ruth tried to drive me away to keep me safe."

Ally got up and headed for the boarded-up fireplace. "My mom left me a message in her last journal asking me to set the past straight." She studied the painted-over boards. "When I was a kid, she used to pretend to play hide-and-seek with me so that I learned how to stash her drugs." She winced, and inwardly Jackson cringed with her.

She gestured at the fireplace. "Do you think you could break this open for me?"

Jackson eyed the plywood. "Sure. I've got a pry bar in my car."

It took him less than five minutes to pull the old plywood away from the gaping hole. He stood back to let Ally kneel on the brick hearth. She reached her arm up inside the chimney and felt around for something.

"There's a little ledge right here...." Her expression changed. "Oh God..."

He moved closer as she pulled down a faded pink backpack and laid it on the brick.

"This was my backpack when I was a kid," Ally whispered.

Jackson touched her shoulder. "Let me open it, okay? I have gloves on." He unzipped the top all the way around and peered into the pinkish glow of the interior. He carefully drew out an old teddy bear and a plastic container.

"That teddy was mine," Ally said. She sounded resigned. "It's probably got my mom's drug supply still in the back."

Jackson turned the teddy over, undid the buttons on the back of the dress, and slid his fingers into the cavity beneath.

"Not drugs, Ally. Money." He showed her the thick roll of one-hundred-dollar bills tied with an elastic band. "Interesting place to keep your savings." He put the teddy down and rested the rolled bills on its chest. He turned his attention to the sealed container, which seemed to contain lots of smaller bagged items. When he opened the lid, he grimaced at the faint smell. "That's definitely weed, but it doesn't smell too fresh to me."

Ally squeezed his shoulder. "That's probably why my mom agreed to go along with Jane. She didn't want the police in the house anyway because of the drugs. Is there anything else?"

Jackson refocused his tangled thoughts and picked up the teddy bear again. Something crackled and he pulled out two folded pieces of paper.

Ally let out a long breath. "That must be what Jane was looking for."

"I'd say so."

Jackson got up and grabbed the evidence bags he'd gotten from his car when he got the pry bar. "Let's put all this stuff away until we can get it to Rob."

"Yes." Ally sounded dazed. "I'm not sure I want to deal with it at the moment."

Jackson took her hand and drew her into his arms. "It's okay, Ally. Everything will be all right now."

She didn't say anything, just buried her face into his shoulder and held on. Jackson drew her even closer and rested his cheek on her hair. He was quite happy to stay like that for the rest of his life. Eventually she looked up at him, her expression rueful.

"I'm sorry. I'm behaving like a girl, aren't I?"

"You are a girl, and considering what you've had to deal with recently, you've done good."

She let go of him and headed for the kitchen. "Do I need to go down to the sheriff's department and make a statement?"

"Yeah, at some point that would be great, but there's no rush."

She swung around to look at him, her face resolute. "I'd like to get it over with as soon as possible."

He nodded. "I'll call Rob, tell him what we found and ask him what he'd like us to do." He paused as she kept staring at him. "What?"

"You're always so nice to me, Jackson, and I really don't deserve it."

"I like you." He shrugged, still unable to use the other L-word and not sure she could handle hearing it right now. "I always have."

She reached for him and cupped his cheek, her gray eyes full of tears. "Weird, because I like you too."

He briefly touched her fingers in response and struggled to find the right words. "How about you put on some coffee? Seeing as neither of us can drink responsibly, we need something to get us through this."

Her smile flickered out. "Sure, that's a great idea."

He went to leave and then turned back to her and yanked her right into his arms. He kissed her with a thoroughness that drew an instant response from her, making him hard and ready to fuck her until she clung to him and begged him never to stop.

He managed to pull away. "Shit, I'm sorry. That's not exactly appropriate, is it?"

She licked her lips. "You behaving like a caveman and staking a claim on your woman? Sometimes you and Rob are just the same."

He nipped her lower lip. "I want you to be my woman— mine and Rob's. Do you get that? Do you understand?"

She stared into his eyes. "I hear you, Jackson, but we're all so emotionally screwed up at the moment, what with Jane and my mom and everything. . . . I can't bring myself to just let go, because at this moment if I did, I'd just want you to take me to bed, strip me naked, and fuck my brains out."

Jackson's cock kicked hard against his uniform pants. "Don't say things like that, Ally," he said hoarsely. "Not fair."

"Because you'd do it, wouldn't you? And that goes against everything you've been trained to do, which just illustrates my point that we're not emotionally ready to deal with this yet."

Jackson took some long, slow breaths. "Okay."

"Okay?" Ally raised her eyebrows.

"I'm going to let you go and I'll call Rob right now." Jackson took himself back into the dining room and radioed Rob. The scent of coffee drifted down the hallway to him as he waited to be patched through.

"Hey."

Rob's calm voice steadied Jackson immediately.

"Boss, we found a whole bunch of stuff hidden up the chimney, including pages from Ruth Kendal's journal." Jackson glanced at the bagged-up items on the table and saw the teddy bear. Emotion clawed at his throat at the thought of Susan, who hadn't deserved any of this, hadn't deserved to be treated like shit by him and certainly hadn't deserved to die. . . .

"Jackson?"

He tried to turn his focus back to what Rob needed to hear. "Yeah, so Ally wants to come in and give you her statement. Do you want me to go ahead and bring her?"

"Sure, if that's what she wants. We have Jane secured, so Ally won't have to see her."

"Okay, we'll be there in about half an hour." Jackson shut

off the connection and went back to the kitchen. Ally sat at the table drinking her coffee. She looked up at him when he came in.

"Jackson, what's wrong?"

He sat down heavily in the chair and covered his face with his hands. "What the fuck do I know about loving someone? Look what I did to Susan. How the *fuck* do I dare think I can love you?"

He was aware of Ally moving and then felt her hand on his knee as she knelt in front of him. "Jackson, it wasn't your fault."

"I let her down, Ally. She was so mad at me, and she was right to be mad. She told me that she'd figured out I wanted Rob and that I should've been brave enough to stand up for what I wanted and not drag you and her into my mess." He forced himself to look at her. "She was so fucking smart and honest and funny. I can't believe she went and killed herself. I just can't."

"Susan made her own choices, Jackson. And whatever really happened that night, we can be sure Jane had a hand in it somewhere." Her eyes widened. "Hell, Jane was here, wasn't she? My mom must have written about her. *She's* the person Susan was seen with."

"Yeah, but..." Jackson swallowed hard. "Shit, I..."

Ally wrapped her arms around him, and something inside him, something he'd held so deep through all the long, lonely years, seemed to shatter. He leaned into her shoulder and allowed himself to cry.

"It's okay, Jackson," Ally whispered as she stroked his hair. "It really is going to be okay."

23

Ally couldn't quite believe it was still the same day, but here she was sitting down to a very late dinner of pizza and barbecue wings with Rob and Jackson. She didn't feel very hungry, but she forced herself to eat, found it easier when her stomach remembered she hadn't had anything for at least twelve hours. Rob drank beer, but she and Jackson stuck with soda.

"So how was Jane holding up?" Jackson asked as he refilled his glass.

Rob glanced at Ally, but she gestured for him to answer. "She was eerily calm until she realized we weren't going to let her go home and feed her dog. Then she started ranting about Jackson being a murderer, and the county medical officer authorized her removal to the safe unit at County General for further evaluation."

He grimaced. "They can hold her there for seventy-two hours pending further medical examination. I don't think it will take them that long to figure out she's got a screw loose somewhere."

"You don't think they'll let her out for a while, then?" Ally said anxiously.

"Not for a while. She was quite happy to own up to everything she'd gotten up to—she was quite proud of herself, actually." Rob shuddered. "Jane said she followed Susan to your house later that night, Ally, and that when Susan couldn't find you, she was so mad that she confided in Jane that Jackson wanted me." He glanced at Jackson. "Apparently Jane had a thing for me even then, so you can imagine how that went down."

"Not very well," Jackson replied.

"Jane said she and Susan kept arguing about it, and eventually, Jane got so mad she pushed Susan off the bridge."

"Accidentally?"

"Jane says not. She then left Susan and went back to Ruth's house to make sure your mother didn't say anything to incriminate her."

Jackson nodded and Ally checked him out. Apart from a little redness around the eyes, he looked his normal self. If he felt anywhere near the measure of relief she was feeling for no longer being solely responsible for Susan's death, he was hiding it well.

"Do you think she'll be back here eventually?"

Rob sighed. "I don't know, Ally. They'll evaluate her and determine whether she's a danger to society, examine her claims to have pushed Susan off that bridge, and take it from there. We also have your mom's journal as evidence of exactly what happened that night. My gut feeling is that she won't be getting out for a long while, especially if she still insists she intends to harm you or Jackson."

Ally rested her elbows on the table. "I'm beginning to wonder if my mom engineered that last argument with me to make sure I left for good."

"What do you mean?" Rob asked.

"I think she was trying to protect me after all. She probably knew that Jane wasn't going to let it go, so she made sure I didn't want to stick around."

"We'll never know for sure, but I'd like to think it was true. Ruth certainly did turn her life around," Jackson said quietly.

Ally swallowed hard. "But it sure took a lot to make that happen. I wonder whether it was worth it." She took a deep breath and cradled her glass in her hands. "I'm still going to sell the house."

Jackson glanced at Rob, who cleared his throat. "Yeah? I can't say I'm surprised. I wouldn't want to live there if I'd been through what you have recently."

"Don't you care?"

Rob frowned. "Well, it will make things a bit cramped here, but we do have three bedrooms, so I'm sure we'll be able to fit all your stuff in."

Ally fixed him with her most intimidating look. "You *assume* I'm moving in with you both, then?"

"You know what they say about assuming anything, don't you?" Rob shifted in his seat. "You could just see it as a temporary thing until you find a new property in town."

"Again you're *assuming* I'm going to stay in Spring Falls."

Rob reached for her hand. "You're staying, honey. Jackson and I have discussed it, and we just can't let you go."

Ally snatched her hand back. "You've discussed it." She turned to Jackson. "Didn't you clue him in on that discussion we had earlier about it being too soon to make such decisions when we're all so emotional?"

"I told him," Jackson said. "But he's a stubborn ass. You know that." He hesitated and looked at them both. "Ally, if me getting out of the picture makes your decision easier, then I'm quite happy to leave."

Rob frowned. "You're not going anywhere. We're all in this together."

Ally scowled back at him. "I'm quite happy for Jackson to stay. We understand each other. I love him."

Rob raised his eyebrows. "So you think I'm the problem?"

Jackson stood and held up his hands. "Hey, how about you two have a chat and then call me when you've decided, okay?"

Ally waited until Jackson had left and then turned her gaze onto the empty pizza box. The silence lengthened until Rob cleared his throat.

"Aren't you going to talk to me?"

She shot him another glare. "After all I've been through today, I would think you'd be the one wanting to talk to me!"

"I'm not sure what you want to hear. It's much easier to just keep on blaming me for everything."

"I don't blame you for *everything*—just the parts where you deliberately abused my trust and used sex to get around me."

He raised his eyebrows. "That's all?"

"That's more than enough, don't you think?"

He shoved a hand through his short dark hair and pushed back from the table to pace the kitchen. "Ally, you drive me fucking crazy. You're right. I should never have gotten back into bed with you."

She marched over to him and jabbed him in the chest with her index finger. "Well that's good to know, because I feel exactly the same."

His mouth came down and covered hers, and she didn't stop him kissing her. She let him force his tongue into her mouth and possess her with a thoroughness that told its own story.

He wrenched his mouth away and looked down at her. "Here's the thing, Ally. Let's stop lying. I'll always want to get in your pants, and you feel exactly the same, because at some level we trust each other to make it right."

She swiped a shaking hand across her well-kissed lips. "How can you say that and then not admit to using me?"

"Because it's never been about *using* you. Sure, if I had any sense, I would've kept my pants zipped. But I couldn't. You think I'm using you? How about this? I can't imagine fucking anyone else but you and Jackson ever again—that's how dumb I am."

"And you expect me to believe that?"

He raised his gaze to the ceiling and set his jaw. "Believe what you like. I'm trying to be honest here. At least I'm fucking trying. . . ."

Ally sat back down at the table and studied his clenched fists and defeated expression. She'd been quick to judge him, and his tangled attempts to explain weren't making her feel any better about what he'd done. But she wasn't eighteen anymore, and this time she wasn't going to walk out until she'd gotten to the bottom of the mess. At some level she did trust him; they'd known each other for so long.

She took a deep breath. "When I arrived here, why didn't you just come right out and ask me what had happened at my mom's that night?"

He grimaced. "Because it wasn't the first thing on my mind."

"You thought you'd try and get in my pants instead."

"No!" He took the seat opposite her. "At first the two things were separate. I'm a guy. Touching you, fucking you . . . was just too tempting. The rest of it was my job, something I'd been wondering about ever since I found Susan's body."

"You found Susan's body?"

"Yeah and when stuff started happening to you, I couldn't help but make that connection."

"And I didn't exactly make it hard for you to get what you wanted from me sexually, did I?"

He grimaced. "I fell just as hard, Ally. All that crap we both spouted about it just being about sex wasn't true, was it? I just wanted to get close to you again and took any chance you offered me."

Ally looked into his eyes. "Okay, I'll buy that. But what about my mom?"

"You and Jackson have been looking at this the wrong way. I only made a serious connection between you and Susan's death after I'd started to worry about what was happening to you right *now*. I tried to ask you about Ruth, but you always changed the subject, or we started arguing about something else. Hell, you've never wanted to talk about your mom."

"Okay, I'll talk about her." Ally placed her hands palms down on the table. "That same night, Ruth and I had an argument, and she threatened to tell everyone in town I'd been sleeping around and cheating on you. She said she knew all the kids and that they'd believe anything she said if they wanted her to sell them some weed."

Rob reached across the table and took her hand. "Why didn't you come and tell me?"

"Because I didn't want that kind of . . . filth touching you. My mom could be very convincing when she wanted to be. That's why I went to Jackson. I thought I'd tell him and he could tell you, which was pretty damn immature of me. But things got a bit more complicated, because I forgot Jackson had his own issues to deal with."

"And he ended up persuading you into his bed."

"And it seemed *right*, you know? Because by that point, I thought I would never be good enough for you and that my mom was just going to make everything worse." Her mouth quirked up at the corner. "And there I was, with Jackson, doing exactly what she'd accused me of. It seemed easier to break your heart myself than have my mom do it for me."

Rob contemplated their joined hands. "I'm not sure what I would've done if you'd tried to tell me this then, Ally, and that's being honest. I was already panicking because I thought I'd scared you about sex. When I found you with Jackson . . . it seemed easier to get angry and push you away than admit how I really felt."

Ally looked up at him. "By the time I'd had it out with you and got back home, Ruth had already packed most of my things and was screaming at me to get out. I didn't know Susan and Jane had already been by, so I just ran and barely made the bus."

She studied his familiar face, saw the lines of strain etched on his tanned skin. "It felt like my whole world was crashing down around me."

Rob brought her hand to his lips and kissed her fingers. "When I first saw Susan's body in that creek, I thought it was you. I thought I'd destroyed you, and I knew I'd lost the best thing in my life. I don't think I've ever gotten over it."

He took a deep breath. "I don't want to lose you again, honey. I love you. Please fucking stay." His voice cracked. "I don't think I could survive it if you left me again."

Ally closed her eyes to savor his words. She hadn't believed he would have the courage to ask her. Could she do it? Could she trust him again after all the hurt, the lost years, her own struggle to find herself? Ally took a deep breath.

"I'll stay, Rob."

"Here with me and Jackson?"

"If that's what you both want. But I'm still going to college in the fall."

"Of course you are." His chair crashed to the ground and he came around the table and picked her up. "Honey, that's the best thing you've ever said to me."

She allowed him to hold her, relished his strength even more now that she knew she was capable of standing on her own. "The best thing? Surely 'please get naked with me and Jackson right now' has to be better than that?"

He crushed her against him. "Okay."

She raised her head to stare at him. "I haven't decided if I'll live with you yet. I might rent my own place near the college and just come down and visit."

"Sure, whatever you want, honey. We'll make it work, I promise."

Ally hid a smile against his chest as he shouted for Jackson and strode down the hallway toward his bedroom. She doubted he'd let her leave quite so easily when he calmed down. He'd always want to be in charge, and she and Jackson would have a hell of a time stopping him—although that might be fun. She imagined Rob tied up and gagged while she and Jackson fucked him. . . .

Sharing a home with two guys was bound to raise some eyebrows in Spring Falls, but what did she care? They'd been gossiping about her all her life. At least now what they whispered and imagined would be true.

Please turn the page for an exciting sneak peek of

SIMPLY CARNAL,

the next installment in Kate Pearce's
House of Pleasure series!

1

―――――――――

"May I speak to you, sir?"

"Of course, Ambrose. What is it?"

Christian Delornay looked up from the accounting book he was studying and considered the worried face of his normally unshakable aide-de-camp. According to the clock on the mantelpiece it was already past midnight, but the noise from the upper floors of the pleasure house had not yet abated.

He directed a frown at Ambrose. "Why are you still here? You are supposed to be off duty."

Ambrose shrugged. "Because there were matters that required my attention. Why are you still here?"

"Because my mother is not, and she's left me with all the monthly bills to pay."

"You like it when she's away. You fight less."

Christian found himself smiling reluctantly at that truth, but Ambrose didn't smile back. "What *exactly* kept you?"

"There's a woman in the kitchen."

Ambrose's upper-class drawl held a hint of the warmer cadences of his West Indies homeland that only emerged when he was perturbed.

"There are always women in the kitchen." Christian put down his pen. "Should she not be there?"

"She is asking to speak to Madame Helene."

"Did you tell her my mother isn't here?"

Ambrose hesitated and came farther into the room. "I did not. I think you should see her yourself."

"Why?"

"Because she is sorely in need."

"Of what? A man?" Christian grimaced. "Then she scarcely needs me. There are plenty of willing guests upstairs for her to choose from, no matter what her tastes."

Ambrose shut the door behind him with a definite *bang* and advanced on Christian's desk. "That wasn't the kind of help I had in mind."

"Does she want money, then—or worse, a shoulder to cry on?" Christian's smile wasn't pleasant. "I'm not known for my soft heart. I leave that to my mother and sister."

Ambrose held his gaze, his warm brown eyes steady. "I would still ask that you see her."

Christian leaned back in his chair. "She obviously had quite an effect on you."

"She..." Ambrose hesitated. "She reminds me of myself—how I was before you took me off the streets and offered me a job and a home."

"She's a pickpocket and a thief, then?"

Ambrose's smile flashed out, his teeth white against his dark skin. "I doubt it. She seems to be a lady, but there is something in her eyes that reminds me of how it feels when you can see no future for yourself. I'm not sure if she has the will to last another night."

Christian sighed. "A lady, you say? I can scarcely fail to help a damsel in distress. Send her in."

Her gaze came back to meet his, and he noticed her eyes were slate gray without a touch of blue to redeem their steel.

"I was expecting to meet Madame Helene."

Her voice was low and cultured, with a slight accent under-lining her status as a lady.

"My mother isn't here tonight. I'm Mr. Delornay. May I not help you instead?"

She swallowed and brought her hands together into a tight clasp under her breasts. She had no gloves, pelisse, or bonnet. Her only outer garments were a thick woolen shawl and mud-died half boots soaked through with filth. She'd probably pawned the rest of her clothing. The question was why? What had brought her to living on the streets?

"I need employment, Mr. Delornay."

Christian sat back and studied her. "And you thought my mother might provide it for you?"

"I was told she might, sir."

"With all due respect, ma'am, you look a little frail to man-age either a job in our kitchens or as an above-stairs maid."

She moistened her chapped lips with the tip of her tongue. "I understood that this is a brothel." She glared at him. "Doesn't a brothel always need new flesh?"

Christian slowly raised his eyebrows. "You are a whore?"

"I am whatever I need to be to survive, sir."

Christian poured himself a glass of brandy. "But my mother does not run a brothel. She runs an exclusive pleasure house, which is available to the very rich for an extortionate fee and even then she personally vets every member."

"But surely these men still need women to . . . to . . ."

"Fuck?"

She flinched at the word, and he wondered whether she might run. "If you are indeed a whore, my dear, you should hardly be shocked by my language."

"I've heard that word before, sir. I'm no shy virgin."

Ambrose paused as he opened the door. "You will be
with her, sir?"

"As gentle as I was with you when I caught you pickin
pocket all those years ago."

Ambrose chuckled. "You threatened to strangle me
drown me in the Thames."

"Ah, that's right." Christian nodded. "I promise I will li
to what she has to say. Will that satisfy you?"

"I suppose it will have to. I'll go and fetch her from
kitchen."

Christian returned to his accounts books half hoping th
the woman had taken off, preferably without stealing anythin
too valuable. He was soon engrossed in the complex figure
and it was only when he heard Ambrose gently clear his throa
that he remembered to look up again.

The sight that met his eyes wasn't unexpected. Working, as
he did, on the less salubrious edge of society, he'd seen plenty
of desperate women. But Ambrose was right: She was different,
and he'd been trained to notice the smallest details. Her clothes,
although soiled, were of high quality, and her skin was as pale
and unlined as a lady's. She briefly met his gaze and then raised
her chin as if he was beneath her notice and looked beyond him
to the window.

Her profile was quite lovely and reminded him of a Titian
angel. Christian yearned to stroke a finger down her jawbone
and touch the shadowed hollow of her cheek. Her hair was
dark and braided tightly to her head. She was far too thin, of
course, and probably on the verge of starving.

"Mr. Delornay," Ambrose said. "This is Mrs. Smith."

Christian nodded. "Thank you, Ambrose. I'll call if I need
you."

He received another stern look from Ambrose, but refused
to respond to it, his attention all on the woman in front of him.

"Mrs. Smith, it is a pleasure. How may I assist you?"

"That might be true, but you are scarcely a common trollop, either, are you? You look more like a rich man's mistress." He waited, but she said nothing. "What happened? Did your lover abandon you?"

Her smile was small and desperate. "Alas, I almost wish that were true."

"Then what is the truth?" She pressed her lips together and stared at his desk. "You expect me to employ you without you telling me anything?"

"I was widowed. My husband's family were unwilling to support me, so I left."

"You left?" Christian frowned. "What an incredibly stupid thing to do."

"I had no choice, sir."

"I find that hard to believe."

A small, choked laugh escaped her, and Christian tensed.

"Do you truly believe I would be standing here begging you for the opportunity to sell my body to any man who wants it if I had another choice?"

"As I have already told you, this is not a brothel. No one sells herself. In truth, they all pay a great deal for the privilege of having sex with anyone they want."

"Why would anyone want to pay for *that*?"

Christian smiled. "Because they can."

She shivered and wrapped her arms around her waist. "Then you have nothing to offer me?"

She was shaking now, her whole body swaying like a willow tree in a storm, and he feared she might swoon. "I can offer you a hot meal and a decent bed for the night."

She raised her head to look at him. "Your bed?"

He considered her for a long moment, until a faint blush stained her hollowed cheeks. Then he smiled. "In your present pitiful state, I fear you wouldn't survive the night, my dear."

"But then you know very little about me, don't you?"

She stepped forward until she was almost at his side. "I am quite happy to prove my worth to you."

She started to descend to the floor. Christian reached forward and grasped her by the elbows, bringing her back to her feet. He kept hold of her and stared into her gray eyes. Ambrose was right: There was no hope there, only desolation and desperation.

"I'll keep your generous offer in mind. When did you last eat?"

She blinked at him. "What does that have to do with anything?"

"I can scarcely throw you out on the street in this condition. My mother's reputation would be ruined."

"Not yours?"

"Mine is already beyond redemption." He patted her shoulder and moved away from her to ring the bell. "We will talk again when you are rested."

While he waited for Ambrose to reappear, Christian retreated behind his desk and picked up his pen again. His visitor was visibly shivering now, one hand gripping the back of her chair as if she would fall without the support. He kept a wary eye on her until he heard Ambrose's welcome footsteps in the hall.

"Yes, Mr. Delornay?" Ambrose asked.

"Would you provide Mrs. Smith with a warm meal and a bed in the servants' quarters? I will see her again when she is restored to health."

Ambrose bowed. "Of course, sir." He smiled encouragingly at the woman. "I would be delighted to assist you."

Mrs. Smith continued to stare at Christian. "I'm not sure why you are being so kind to me, sir."

"I'm not being kind. As I said, you appear to be at death's door. I cannot afford to cast you out and have your lifeless corpse found anywhere near my mother's pleasure house. It would be bad for business."

She nodded, and Ambrose took her by the elbow and led her gently out of the room. Christian sat back in his chair and contemplated the silence. Mrs. Smith—and somehow he doubted that was her real name—was a mass of contradictions. Her blunt offer to sexually service him had confounded his previous opinion that she was a well-brought-up woman down on her luck.

And he didn't like being wrong.

He found himself smiling. As Mrs. Smith said, desperation made a hard master, but he wasn't sure how he could help her. Luckily, his circle of acquaintance was extremely wide and he was certain that he would be able to find her some form of employment if he couldn't persuade her to rejoin her family.

The thought of trying to convince her of anything made him smile. Despite her bedraggled state he'd sensed a core of steel that had impressed even his cynical cold heart. For the first time in a long while he was looking forward to meeting someone again.

"Mrs. Smith? Are you well?"

Elizabeth struggled to focus on the anxious face hovering over her. The struggle not to swoon in front of the obnoxiously handsome and silver-tongued Mr. Delornay had used up the last of her meager resources. He'd seemed far too golden and perfect to be real—until he'd revealed a dark sense of humor that she'd been unable to deflect in her present state. Now all she wanted to do was lie down in the nearest gutter and give up.

"I am quite well, Mr. Ambrose."

He guided her down onto a bench in the warm kitchen, where she'd accosted him earlier. The smell of baking bread and pastries curled around her, and she was suddenly nauseated.

There was no sign of any of the staff she'd seen before, and she was glad not to be observed.

"Call me Ambrose. I don't have another name. Now bide here while I fetch you something to eat."

That stirred her interest, but she didn't have the resources or the energy to question him now. She folded her hands on the solid pine table and stared down at them. Her nails were ragged, and despite her best efforts, her skin was never quite clean. She'd never considered water a luxury until she'd been forced to do without it.

"Here you are, ma'am."

Ambrose slid a bowl of porridge topped with brown sugar and milk in front of her. Elizabeth swallowed convulsively as he handed her a spoon.

"Take it slow, ma'am, and you'll be fine."

"I'm not sure if I can eat anything anymore."

Ambrose took the seat opposite her and smiled. "Yes, you can. Your stomach is probably the size of a walnut, but you can at least manage a few spoonfuls."

Her eyes filled with tears at his unexpected kindness. "How do you know that?"

"Because I've been starved myself." His smile died. "If it hadn't have been for Mr. Delornay, I would've died on the streets."

Elizabeth licked the rough brown sugar from the spoon and some of the porridge and wanted to moan at the influx of rich tastes against her tongue.

"Does Mr. Delornay make a habit of rescuing waifs and strays?"

"Despite what he might claim, he follows his mother in that respect. No one is ever turned away from the pleasure house without a crust or a coin."

"Or a bed for the night, in my case." Elizabeth ate two whole spoons of porridge and for the first time in weeks she felt warm inside. "I am very grateful for that." She glanced across at Ambrose. "I had no more coin to pay my rent, and my landlord took all my remaining possessions until I could come up with the money."

"We can probably get them back for you."

"I'm not sure how." Elizabeth sighed and ate another spoon of porridge. "I still have no money."

"I'm sure Mr. Delornay will have some ideas about that, too, when you talk to him."

Elizabeth put down her spoon as her appetite deserted her. "He said I was too weak to work here in a menial capacity and that he didn't employ whores."

"With all due respect, ma'am, he does have a point. You are indisputably a lady."

"And ladies whore in different ways, don't they?" she whispered. "They are sold into marriage and cannot deny their husbands sexual congress."

Ambrose stood and came around the table to her. "I think you should go to bed, ma'am. I will escort you."

She took his proffered hand and looked up into his face. She reckoned they were of a similar age. "If you are just Ambrose, will you call me Elizabeth?"

"If that is your wish, I would be honored." He kissed her hand. "And now let's get you somewhere safe and warm to sleep. If you leave your clothing outside the door, I will arrange for it to be laundered and returned to you tomorrow."

"Safe..." Elizabeth sighed as he walked ahead of her. Mr. Delornay was right: She'd been a fool to run away without taking the things she valued the most. Getting them back seemed impossible now. She swallowed another inconvenient wave of tears. It was impossible to think in her current state, but at least she didn't have to worry about anything until the morning.